Ami Reb

The Day the Flowers Died

FORWARD:

This novel holds a special place in my heart. Inspired by a dream while teaching in Thailand in the fall of 2009, I awoke with such a great emotional experience between the two main characters, that I had to tell the story. The feeling stayed with me long after I awoke. I could not rest until the story was told.

Following that day, I researched books, the internet, You Tube, and read historical accounts from survivors as well as quotes and popular music and poetry of that time. Listening to music of that period and watching Heindenburg in black and white walk on german streets into a building to vote for an election, as well as seeing first hand the actual footage of Hitler in Munich was astounding.

I wanted to stay true to the time period and so outlined the story according to history and survivor's accounts. I read a variety of points of view to gather a broader picture of events that actually did happen to people living during that time period in Munich. Sometimes what occurs in life is in the history books, but many times we learn about events from the mouths of individuals. I also read old Nazi propoganda from that time from magazines and on brouchures, dating back as early as 1930.

Each chapter begins with a day of the week and date. This is accurate according to the calendar from the 1930's in Germany. All feasts fall on the correct days. All days of the week are matched with the appropriate dates. I did this deliberatley to coincide with reality.

I prefer the old English grammatical usage of an before words that begin with H, as the article is softer than the hard a; therefore, I utilized that preference in my title page. This is not accidental or a result of carelessness.

The novel was edited once for grammar and content and then edited again for German Jewish accuracy and the one last time for German historical accuracy. This does not mean perfection, but the novel is pretty close.

If you find anything out of place, please fell free to write the author:

touch-of-grace@hotmail.com Subject: The Day the Flowers Died

Please read the activism page at the end of the novel. I include a page of activism at the end of all my fiction novels.

Ami Rebecca Blackwelder

Praise for The Day the Flowers Died:

'This is truly a love story. I love the way they meet and everything else. They are two people not from differing worlds but upbringing. This is a situation that is very close to my heart. Your descriptions are brilliant and in my opinion for a book of this genre perfect. This is a sensitive subject for some even now but you deal with it perfectly.' -Ron S

'I will say that I liked your use of color. Not only does it set the scene in the opening chapter, but you keep it as an on-going theme.' -B. J. Winters

'You have something very special here. You have created a world that you cannot have known personally, but which is completely believable, and that is what all writers aim to do, but only the really good ones achieve as well as you have.' -Philip Carlton

'This is simply so adorable and sweet at the moment, although I am sure it will not continue that way. The prologue shows the strength of their loving union and the first chapter deals well with their introduction. I love the minute character descriptions - the blue silk tie, missing button, the contrasts of manicured hands and slightly dirty fingernails, but overall, the almost awkward interaction between them as they so obviously are attracted to one another.' -Kendall Craig

'The gentle love story is told with realism for the time and with the caution of ethnic difference. That's not referred to very often and this shows where Germany was before the Nazi powers were in control. It feels well-researched. The flow of the story is very readable and the particulars and setting give it much atmosphere. You've captured the social ambiance preceding a wrenching time. This promises much more'. –Katherine

Book Taste Review:
Lovers in a turbulent Europe:
Ami Blackwelder paints with words. Her special talent is creating scene and atmosphere populated by credible characters. The Day the Flowers Died is a love story, gently narrated, that recreates prewar Germany during the 1930s, and the German government's menacing swing to the Nazis. The girl's sweetheart is Jewish, her parents point out the brutal dangers, but innocent ecstasy ignores the politics and the racial hatred that are sweeping the nation.

As fascist ideology becomes law, the lovers encounter the harsh reality of life and death. Released as an E-book, this novel has quickly gained an unusually large number of downloads. Can there be a trend (much welcomed) away from vampires and back to realistic human passion? This author's books vary in genre. Happy reading! Posted by Cathy, 9 December 2009.

The Day the Flowers Died

An historical fiction

Ami Rebecca Blackwelder

Ami Rebecca Blackwelder

The Day the Flowers Died
An Historical Fiction
© 2010 by Ami Rebecca Blackwelder

Ami Blackwelder's books may be ordered through local book venues and online retailers or by contacting the author:
http://amiblackwelder.blogspot.com

This is a work of fiction. All of the characters, names, incidents, organizations, and dialogue in this novel are either the products of the author's imagination or are used fictitiously.

ISBN: 1450571689
ISBN: 9781450571685 (eBook)

Published by Eloquent Enraptures Publishing

Content editor Magnolia Belle
German Jewish editor Ryan & Joanna B.
Historical editor Jennifer L.B.
Cover Art by Web Designs
Printed in the United States of America
by Lightning Source.

Eloquent Enraptures Publishing

The Day the Flowers Died

The Day the Flowers Died

By Ami Rebecca Blackwelder

Summary:

An historical fiction set in Munich, Germany in the early 1930's before the outbreak of War World II. Eli Levin and Rebecca Baum fall passionately in love and while their differences should have separated them, they instead forged a passionate bond that would change their lives forever.

While religious and social differences weigh heavily on their families in an increasingly tense Germany, the lovers remain unadulterated in spite of the prejudices. After overcoming family issues and social pressures, the two must sustain under a growing violent governmental regime. When the Nazi party heightens in popularity and the party's ideas influence law, they must face the harsh reality of life and death.

Poetry used in this novel by Heinrich Heine

For Mom and Dad

With Eyes of Prejudice

With eyes of prejudice upon us,
Shades of color to hide,
Ashamed of what they see,
Ashamed to look inside,

Encroaching around us,
Like coffins closed,
To describe the act of violation,
There could never be enough prose

–Ami R. Blackwelder

The Day the Flowers Died

Table of Contents

FRIDAY, SEPTEMBER 25, 1931

Autumn in Munich was always the most beautiful time to her. The leaves changed colors and fell beneath her feet. She loved to walk over orange, yellow, and brown irregular leaf shapes on the cobblestone sidewalk near her home and listen to the crunch. Chalky white clouds and streams of variant blues filled the sky. She skipped off the sidewalk and onto the wet grass, lowering to the rose bushes aligned around her apartment.

She snipped a few deep pink roses with the pruning scissors she kept in her side skirt pocket, a pocket stitched just below a 1920's German Dresden Wire Mesh purse dangling from her left shoulder. She chose the purse because of the lavender colors and flowery design. Her long brown skirt dangled over the grass and moistened around its hem. Her black blouse was missing its top button and it ruffled out of her skirt as she bent.

"Rebecca! Rebecca!" A man's voice yelled down to her from five stories above. She placed the flowers in her left hand and glanced up against the sunlight, raising her other hand to protect her eyes. Not recognizing his voice, she squinted to make out his face, his shape, anything, but no one she knew came to mind. The window above closed and then boots clogging against the hard cement steps raced down to greet her. She placed the roses into a brown paper bag nestled under her arm.

A man a foot taller than her, with eyes chocolate brown and wavy dark, short hair, stumbled out of the door. His beige wool trench coat caught the door's latch as he fumbled with his silk embroidered pale blue tie which swayed over a crisp white shirt. "Rebecca." His soft shaven face featured kind eyes under thick eyebrows. He reached his hands out to untangle his coat from the door and rolled his eyes at himself. "I always get stuck here. They ought to do something about this latch. It's a hazard."

Rebecca giggled, holding her hand over her mouth to keep from being impolite. He took a long moment to study her face and then, after a few moments of awkward silence, he pulled an envelope out of his trench coat pocket. "I meant to give this to you. It came to my mailbox by mistake."

Reaching towards the envelope, Rebecca noticed miniscule amounts of dirt underneath her fingernails when she brushed across his soft, manicured hands.

"Thank you," she said surprised, but then felt herself relaxed.

"I don't think we ever were formally introduced. My name is Eli Levin."

Her summer sky blue eyes widened, framed by her honey touched dark brown hair draping over her shoulders. He extended his hand to shake hers and she reciprocated, then stepped back, allowing him room to walk away from the door. Like children with lanky arms dangling and not knowing what to do with them, they walked together to the sidewalk.

"How did you know who I was?" she asked. The sounds of cars and buses from the street vibrated through the soles of her feet.

"I've seen you around. I live…" Eli pointed to the fifth floor, "…right above your room."

"I think I've seen you…" Rebecca thought back, "two nights ago. You were coming in, holding a leather briefcase."

"That was me." He raked his fingers through his hair. "I get home late from work. I remember seeing you heading out that night." He glanced sideways at her.

"I was meeting friends for dinner. It was an unpleasant day."

"What do you do?" Eli asked with curious wrinkles in his forehead.

"I'm a waitress at the local diner down the block." She pointed up the street with her out-stretched forefinger. "Do you know the place?"

"I've tried the food," he said with a stressed smile.

"Didn't like it?" She tilted her head.

He shrugged with a half gesture of uncertainty. "My friends enjoy the culinary experience there."

Rebecca straightened her back and wiped her nails with her fingers. "But you don't like the food there?" Rebecca caught him off guard with her blatant honesty.

He fidgeted with his umbrella. "I've eaten there once, maybe twice and it wasn't my favorite." His eyes widened. "Except now that you work there, perhaps I might have a change of heart." The corners of his mouth rose and he blushed in his audacity.

"It's not my life's ambition, but it pays the bills."

"What do you want to do?" Eli emphasized.

"I'm going to University for nursing. I want to help people."

"That's wonderful." He played with his tie. "Are you about finished?"

"Next summer." She glanced into the street and noticed cars rushing to get home from work. Then she returned her gaze to Eli and shifted her weight to her back foot. "What about you, what do you do?"

"I'm helping the family business." He kept his sentences short. "The only son." He rolled his eyes. "The eldest." His lips wiggled a bit and then he finished, "my father wants me to learn the business. I finished school at the University of Ludwig Maximilians a year ago, business school. Didn't have much choice in the matter." He wiped his chin.

"Don't you hate that, parents choosing our lives for us?" He chuckled at the way her nose wrinkled in frustration as her lashes batted toward the sky.

"How about your parents? Did they force you into nursing?"

Rebecca laughed at his question and, out of habitual high class expectation, covered her mouth with her hand again.

"No, no. I fought to convince my mutti I was not destined to be a house wife."

"At least you convinced them. I can't even get a word in edgewise with my father." The guffaw of both faded into a comfortable silence which they rested in before Eli cleared his throat. "So, I guess you were on your way upstairs before I interrupted you?"

"No intrusion. Thank you for the letter. I don't know what's wrong with the postman these days. This is the second letter I haven't received. At least this one found me."

"Let me walk you back to the door. It looks like it's about to rain." Eli opened his grey umbrella in his left hand. The rain began to pour and the beads dropped and slid off the grey cascading canopy. Eli kept most of the umbrella on Rebecca's side and walked her to the front metal door where the apartment ledge offered another canopy from the rain. Rebecca reached for the doorknob and then turned around.

"It was a real pleasure speaking with you. At least now we won't be strangers."

"True," Eli smiled, "and if I get any more of your mail, I'll drop by your room." Rebecca beamed at his suggestion with a certain flirtation familiar to Eli from other women while at University.

"Maybe I'll stop by later in the week," Eli said with a tone of propriety, "perhaps when we're both free?" He paused for her answer.

She grinned and her brows rose. "I'd like that." They each stepped toward the other, without realizing it, with peering, inquisitive eyes and felt each other's breath on their skin. As they each recognized their own indiscriminate and eager draw to the other, they both stepped backward and allowed the conservative city to intervene between them.

"I have to go." Eli blinked and retreated and Rebecca twirled to go inside, her long hair bouncing at her sudden movement. Eli took in a deep breath of her, the woman he had seen for months, wishing he had the courage to speak with her. He turned towards the street with a jaunty smile.

Rebecca ran up four flights of stairs to her apartment. The door squeaked opened to a musty room with a variety of room deodorizers. She pulled the roses from her paper bag and took out a clear crystal vase to fill with water. She arranged the roses in the vase and set it on her kitchen table.

"There, perfect." She moved the vase a bit to the left so it sat in the center. Picking up a washrag, she wiped down the table and dusted off her small vanity and dresser chest against the living room wall. In a brief moment, she studied a picture resting on the dresser, a picture she imagined through the black and white exterior of a blond, blue-eyed doting father and dark haired, blue-eyed mother holding their hairless blue-eyed baby wrapped in a thick quilt.

"I'll see you guys soon." After pressing a kissed fingertip to the photo, she strolled to her bedroom. Minimal furnishings scattered through the small one bedroom apartment, which Rebecca preferred; it allowed her more space to move about. After showering, she pulled out a plate of chicken with broccoli from the fridge and sat on her white sofa to eat it cold. For company, she watched her British 1928 Baird Model "C" television set, without sound. Her father, with adamant resistance from her mother, bought it for a birthday gift a couple years ago after his business trip to London. He always bought her expensive presents, even during the Depression, since his mind for business kept his family living an affluent lifestyle.

She sat with her legs curled underneath her, admiring the mahogany detail of the television's cabinetry. It was a wooden rectangle, styled with long legs and ornate glass circles at each high corner. It was the subject of much talk in the building and her friends were envious of her to receive such an expensive gift. The reception came in by electro-mechanisms and, though it carried no sound, the pictures kept her entertained. She sifted through many channels of white fuzz until finding a black and white silent program. After watching for several minutes, her eyelids drooped and she fell asleep.

Over next few days, Eli and Rebecca caught each other's glances in the hallway, while one was leaving and the other was coming in. Occasionally Eli said, "have a good day." Rebecca would smile and wave, motioning she had to depart. But minutes and stolen moments were all they had that week.

Upon the weekend, Rebecca nestled on her sofa to watch television that evening. Someone tapped on her door a few times. She pulled her hair to one side, letting it dangle over her left shoulder, and straightened her knee length skirt and silk white shirt before answering. The safety latch let the door open a few inches for her to peek outside. When she recognized Eli, she relaxed and released the lock.

"Are you available?" he asked.

"Yes." Rebecca tried to conceal her enthusiasm and opened the door wider to allow him entry. "No duties to attend to?" she joked.

"Freed myself up." Eli returned the humor while mimicking handcuffs falling off his wrists.

"Freed from your business plans or your parents?" Rebecca raised an inquisitive brow.

"From parental expectations. Besides it's almost evening and my father doesn't like me to finish up work on Shabbos." Eli walked through the opened door into her apartment. He set his briefcase by the door and headed to her living area. Glancing around, his eyes broadened at the television set.

"My home." Rebecca closed the door behind her. "It's miniscule, but its mine."

"You've made the space very accessible. It's quaint."

"Thank you." Rebecca went to the kitchen. "Would you like some milk, tea or coffee?"

"Tea, please."

Rebecca filled her teapot and set it on the stove, separated from the living area by the sofa.

"How long have you lived here?" Eli sat on the sofa.

"For three years, since college. I left when I was nineteen. My parents live outside the city and I didn't want to travel. It makes it easier for me this way."

"My mama would never allow something like this for my sisters, away from home to attend college."

"I'm an independent lady. I've always been. I fought my mutti on it, but my father was on my side." Rebecca snuggled between the sofa cushion and a pillow sitting next to Eli.

"Papa's girl?" Eli questioned.

"My mutti is now used to the idea of me being away, though it was difficult for her my first year. But I had my mind made up and I wasn't going to change it."

"You have a television." He gestured toward the wooden box, eager to ask about it. "I've only seen one other in another home." Eli stood a brief moment to brush his hands over the soft wood frame and then sat down next to Rebecca.

"My father." Rebecca grinned and lowered her chin.

"How are your parents doing since the Depression?"

"My father saves a lot and has been able to take care of tuition for me, but it has hit them too, even with their successful business. We can't buy the luxuries we once did." Rebecca's voice stressed the last sentence, "My mutti is still not used to that." She turned towards Eli with her lean legs moving closer.

"Why do you work then?" Eli laughed in his question.

"I told my parents I wasn't going to take their money for living expenses, only for tuition. My father didn't want me working. But I

14

wanted to make my own way, so I found a job." She spoke quickly, then emphasized her question, "What about you?"

"I went in '24. My parents do well and we haven't had to worry about money. As long as I followed my papa's plans for my life, he paid my way. So even after the Depression hit in '29, my last two years of law school were taken care of for me. I've been working for the last two years at my papa's firm."

"And you're a successful lawyer now?" Rebecca's right brow quirked upward.

"I handle business law at the firm."

Rebecca met Eli's eyes with her sensual gaze and Eli's long lashes flitted as he watched her in return. He reached out and caressed her hand, his thumb pressing into her palm while his fingers memorized the softness of her skin. She stayed motionless, mesmerized, until the kettle on the stove whistled – toooot. Leaping from the sofa, she took the kettle off the burner, feeling Eli's eyes on her. She poured Eli a cup of tea and then one for herself, placing them on wooden coasters on her coffee table. Eli sipped a few times and then stood in anxious propriety. "I should get to my room."

"I'll see you again?" Her eyes invited him back.

"Most certainly." Eli stepped out the door and Rebecca followed him, waving goodbye until he scurried upstairs and out of sight. In his room, Eli took out his file from his briefcase and laid it on his teak table. Big and rectangular, it filled the middle of the living room. Books and papers rested on top of its maroon placemats. He went to his fridge, took out his cup of juice and swallowed in one gulp. His phone rang and he raced over to pick it up.

"Eli?"

"Yes, Mama, it's me. Who else would it be?"

"Are you going to make it to the feast this year? You know it's just two days away. I don't like it when you're not there. It's not the same."

"Yes, Mama, I'll be there."

"It's going to be real nice with lots of food and all your relatives."

"Should I bring anything?"

"Don't worry about it, son."

"Your place again?"

"Yes, Eli, of course."

"What time?"

"Try to be here by six. I love you."

"Love you too, Mama." He hung up and walked to the shower.

Rebecca cleaned up the cups before snuggling into bed and wrapping up in expensive quilt bought by her mother. Hours later, the alarm sounded when the sun barely rose in the sky. Rebecca lifted herself in slow motion out of the bed and rushed her bath before dressing in two beige shirts layered over each other and a long white skirt. She wrapped her neck with a black scarf and then headed out the door to hail a cab.

The streets saturated with busy workmen, the homeless, and fathers struggling for their family's survival. Rebecca sympathized with the struggle, never flaunting her wealth and never fully understanding the sacrifices each man and woman made. Though her upbringing was rigid in polite mannerisms and social expectations, she remained as free as the flowers she picked blowing in careless winds. She carried a crisp white lace apron inside her school bag for the job she procured and would attend after nursing classes at University.

Eli tightened his button down blue shirt and fastened his dark blue tie around his neck before heading to his office. Last night's rain still dampened his dark blue car. He wiped his window off with a towel and opened his door, laying the damp towel in his glove compartment. The streets teemed with vehicles and people rushing to get to work in the very early morning. Anyone who had a job was happy for it and employers took no excuses for tardiness.

Everyone felt the tensions of Germany. Families fell apart; children went to bed hungry and more layoffs were on the way. The future of the country was uncertain, except for the promises made by eager politicians. Eli pulled up to his building a few streets away from his apartment. It felt like a second home to him, filled with family and friends. He walked in with a big grin and a beige brief case swinging in his hands.

"Eli! Just the man I wanted to see." A tall man with a short brown beard ambled up to him and handed him a few papers. "We need these checked this morning."

"I'll get on it." Eli walked through the hallway, passing a few doors until reaching the one with his name etched into a metal tag. He went

16

inside his office and sat down in his cushioned chair, ready to begin the workday.

Rebecca's cab drove her to University and she hopped out while handing the cab driver the fee. She scrambled to her first class and then attended her next two until her academic day finished and she took another cab to the local diner. She rushed inside for the afternoon shift, pulling her hair into a bun and fixing it in place with bobby pins. She walked to the counter, smiled courteously at the cook with his head bobbing behind the pots, and opened the cash register. Meticulously handling the cash, she counted it twice for accuracy. The diner's owner walked in through the front doors, his pinstriped shirt dangling over his black pants and loose belt.

"Good to see you, Rebecca. How is everything today?"

"Good, sir." She lowered her head and tended to her afternoon duties behind the cash register. The owner with a rounded stomach walked with a limp, caused by an accident some years ago. He passed the counter on his way into his small office where he disappeared behind the shut door.

The day passed in typical fashion for the both of them until they found their way back to their apartment building just before the sun set. The next day was almost as un-notable until Rebecca found an envelope underneath her door after work. Eli? She thought to herself, and with innocent and unbridled enthusiasm, she tore open the envelope to read the letter.

> Dear Rebecca,
>
> If you are not otherwise engaged tonight, I would be very happy if you would accompany me to dinner. I will be waiting for you outside our apartment building at five. Looking forward to seeing you,
>
> Eli

A sure smile spread across Rebecca's face as she read and then placed it on her coffee table. After showering, she changed into a long white and pink dress with a flower print. Raised in an affluent part of town, Rebecca had grown in the habit of washing regularly to appease her mother. Something the lower class did not. Gazing out the window, she saw Eli waiting below with his hands to his face, blowing in them to keep warm. She pulled on a marshmallow colored sweater and skipped down the steps to meet him.

"Eli!"

He turned around, not expecting her so soon.

"Rebecca!" He walked to her and wrapped his arm around her waist to usher her into his 1923 dark blue Audi parked against the curb. They drove to a radiant restaurant, a mix of French and German cusine, its elegance caused from high lighting and extended windows let Rebecca know this dinner would be expensive. Eli parked and escorted her, with his hand over hers, into the posh dining facility.

The hostess glared at them under the façade of an elegant smile and walked them to their table, careful not to linger too long. Wrapped up in each other's glances and emotions, neither Eli nor Rebecca noticed the discourtesy.

Eli brought his hands up to his chin as if in prayer. "I must confess something." He whispered loud enough for only her to hear.

Rebecca moved in closer, leaning over the table, stretching one hand out to his. "What?" The light from the high ceiling reflected in her eyes. Her pinky ran across her lips in an unconscious invitation to a kiss.

"I have had my eye on you for some time and have been trying desperately to find a way to talk with you." He couldn't look away from her playful little finger.

"I'm flattered." Her eyes squinted, "but what kept you away so long?"

"Humility? Fear? Work? Take your pick."

Rebecca laughed at his jest, picked up the menu and read over the items. "Eli coq au vin." The waiter noticed Rebecca across the room preparing to order and, before she could ask for him, he stood beside her. "I would like to order this," she pointed with her forefinger "and this to drink." She moved her finger to the water with lemon. The waiter jotted the order down and walked beside Eli. He cleared his throat while waiting for Eli to decide. Rebecca noticed the waiter's

impatience and flipped her menu open facing Eli. "How about this?"
She pointed to the German sausages with sauerkraut.

"No, I can't eat that," he said mostly to himself. The waiter
flinched at his remark. Rebecca looked at him, confused. "Pork," he
clarified. "I'll just take this." He pointed to the sautéed chicken with
vegetables and then moved his finger up to his favorite white wine. "A
bottle with two glasses, please." The waiter moved away to fulfill his
orders.

"You don't like pork?" Rebecca asked.

"I try to keep kosher. My father would kill me if I didn't."

Rebecca smiled in childlike form. "Do you mind if I eat my pork in
front of you?"

"Go ahead. Enjoy. This is your night." Eli touched her hands
resting close to him. An elderly couple at the next table stared at the
two of them in their unfettered mingling and then the look of disgust
appeared just before they turned away and whispered.

The sommelier set the wine in the center of the table with two
glasses beside the bottle. The chef served the food on expensive white
porcelain plates. Placing the chicken before Eli, the waiter winked at
Rebecca when he set her dinner before her with his back to Eli.

"Will there be anything else?" The waiter asked with folded hands,
his eyes focused on Rebecca.

"No, thank you. That will be all," Eli confirmed his departure and
the waiter left.

"This looks delectable." Rebecca began eating and Eli smiled,
watching her enjoy each bite.

"I'm glad you like it."

The room filled with sounds of muted chatter in French and
German, glasses clicking and soft music. Eyes circled around the room,
over at them and then away again: eyes curious, eyes confused, eyes of
distain.

Nearing the end of dinner, Eli looked at his watch and pursed his
eyebrows.

"Are you alright?" Rebecca asked.

"I'm sorry, but I'm heading to my mama's Sukkos feast tonight and
I can't miss it. She will be especially upset with me if I'm late, since I
missed last year's."

"Oh." Rebecca's blue eyes clouded and she shaped her plump lips into a pout.

"My mama makes a big deal of it every year and my relatives are expecting me to be there, too."

"Maybe we should get going then?" Rebecca recognized the gravity of distress on Eli's face. "We can finish up. I'm just about done and then you can drop me off and head to your parents for the evening."

"You don't mind? It's so rude of me to be departing early."

"I don't mind. I'm getting tired anyway. We can go out again when you have more time." Rebecca slid out of her chair, eager to encourage Eli to honor his parental expectations and he plodded dutifully with his arm slid around her waist, drawing her close. He smiled when she rested her head on his shoulder as they walked to his dark blue car.

SATURDAY, OCTOBER 17, 1931

The light of day radiated through Munich and, for Eli and Rebecca, in an inconspicuous way, it somehow shone brighter over their apartment building. Rebecca awoke to the daylight shining through the drawn curtains. She opened the framed glass and smelled the fresh air blowing into her room. "Munich in the fall." She smiled and loved how she felt at this moment.

After clipping the orange Marsh Marigolds she bought at the flower shop on the street corner, she arranged them in her crystal vase. Marsh Marigolds reminded her of Buttercups, another favorite flower. Expecting Eli early, she then hastened to clean the mess on the kitchen counter and coffee table,. Saturdays gave them more time to spend together than the busy weekdays.

She tossed the dirty plates into the sink and let them soak while she luxuriated in a bath scented with fresh orange soaps. The white satin dress she chose for the day unapologetically emphasized her womanly shape.

Eli skipped steps to his cheerful whistle on his way from his apartment to hers. He wore a blue shirt that buttoned to the top, but decided against a tie. A brown belt accessorized his brown slacks, and his dependable trench coat covered all. He knocked, calling her name.

Rebecca opened the door and, for a moment the sunlight from the kitchen window shone through the white satin dress, settling over her delicate female silhouette underneath which became visible to Eli for the first time. Eli blushed, the sunlight vanished, and his gaze jerked upward. Rebecca walked into the hall, clasping her arm around his, and turned to lock the door. Eli held his other arm behind his back and, before Rebecca could get her key in the lock, he revealed a single bright blue Cornflower.

Her eyes widened in surprise and, when he stroked the velvet petals once down her cheek, she closed them for a moment. "It's beautiful."

She made sure her hand touched his to take the flower. With an alluring smile, she stepped backwards into her apartment and, after adding it to her other flowers, Rebecca came back to Eli. "Thank you."

"I noticed you loved them."

"I do; my second favorite flower next to Gerber Daisies."

"I'll have to get you one of those next time."

Colder than previous Octobers, their breath fogged in front of them when they reached the sidewalk. Rebecca tightened the black scarf around her neck and Eli blew into his hands and rubbed them for warmth while they walked up the street.

"Where are we going?"

"It's a surprise," he told her, trying to keep a secret he desperately wanted to share. "How was your week?"

"Busy, but I'm almost done with school. I'll be able to concentrate on nursing full time soon." Eli noticed her shivering and took her hand into his.. "And you?"

"Always a long work week with clients." Eli shook his head.

"Have you ever worked on a big case, an important one?" Her blue eyes widened.

"Every client believes his case is the big, important one." Eli laughed, "So I guess I have." They strolled a few more blocks until reaching a park filled with kids. The youngsters, bundled in heavy winter coats and knit wool hats, played under their mothers' watchful eye.

"It's beautiful here. I've never been to this park." Rebecca scanned the greenery.

"I thought you'd like it. You said you never have enough time to smell the roses. So, I thought I'd take you to them."

Rebecca pulled her hand from his and lifted it to caress his shaven jaw. Watching his eyes focus on her lips, she recognized the longing on his face, certain hers mirrored it. Her mouth rose up to his ear and breathed a whisper,

"I love this dimple in your chin." She played in it with her pinky finger.

"Maybe we should conceal this moment for only us." His eyes searched the mothers' faces of the park, but the twinkle in his eye belied his frown.

22

"That would probably be wise." She slid her hands up his chest, pulled his coat lapels down and placed a tender kiss on his bottom lip. Before she could move to the top one, he wrapped his arms around her waist and pressed her close, returning her kiss, deepening it.

"Well, now I guess we broke our rules," he said when he finished the kiss.

"I guess so." She stood in his embrace, unable to concentrate on anything but the smell of his cologne, the strength of his arms, and the taste of his lips. Then, stepping away, she twirled like a pinwheel, arms outstretched, into the park. She reminded Eli of a dancer, until she settled on an empty wooden bench where he quickened to sit next to her.

He crossed his legs and she crossed her ankles, both turning to face the other. Their hands interlaced on top of their legs, making it difficult to tell which set of hands belonged to whom. Eli took one hand to brush his dark hair back and then placed his hand over Rebecca's delicate fingers. Gallivanting children's laughter permeated the park and nothing but their innocent sounds intruded the quiet morning.

"How did I get along in life before meeting you?" Eli asked half in jest and half seriously. They moved closer with each breath they took as if touch alone could make them warmer in this cold weather.

Eli lifted his pinky finger to Rebecca to brush a few hairs dangling over her mouth, and nestled them behind her ear.

Rebecca inspected his chin with her eyes and then her forefinger. "Ah…I think I've found a hair you've missed this morning." She left her finger on his chin.

"Really?"

"A stowaway," she said, convincing him.

He raised his hand to feel the hair when a knit hat flew across the grass, getting caught beneath the bench. One of the children without his bonnet ran up and bent to grab it. Eli picked it up for him, handing it with a childlike gesture.

"Here you go." The child nodded, grabbed it and ran off.

"No thank you?" Rebecca remarked with a grin.

"Never mind. He's just a kid."

"Who'll grow up to be an uncouth adult!"

"We'll hope for better," Eli said with a hint of humor. They watched the child of six or seven return to his friends. He tugged on his knit hat while his mother's eyes peered at the bench, then returned to her son. Eli drew away from Rebecca in the most minuscule of measurements, so much so that even he didn't know he'd done it.

"If my father knew I was here in the park on Shabbos instead of synagogue, I think he'd come here himself and drag me there."

"He doesn't attend Munich's Synagogue?"

"No, he lives nearly outside of Munich. He takes the family to a smaller synagogue closer to his home."

"He is traditional?"

"You could say that," Eli said, implying his strictness stemmed from more than mere tradition. Rebecca giggled. "Maybe he is not that bad, but he could give me a little more room to breathe, to spread my wings and live my own life."

"He is your father; fathers only want what's best for their sons. I'm sure he means well."

"He does. That's what makes it all the more awful." Eli smiled in his words and, unnoticed to himself, moved closer to Rebecca.

"Do you have to work later today?" Rebecca asked, hoping the answer to be no.

"My father closes the business every Shabbos, from Friday evening to Saturday evening."

"Then I get you all to myself." Rebecca reached to his chin and, with more bravery than usual, brushed her soft forefinger up his jaw line and over his lips.

Eli blinked, forgetting himself in public, and leaned in to kiss her. Catching himself, he lifted the side of his trench coat to cover them from the mothers in the distance, as if his coat somehow secluded them from the rest of the world. Rebecca laughed, forgetting to cover her mouth and Eli enjoyed seeing her sizable, white teeth.

The early morning approached noon and Eli accompanied Rebecca up the street for lunch. A panhandler squatted outside the diner, holding a small pan in his dirty hands, and wearing ripped black trousers, probably his only pair. Eli reached into his pockets and pulled out loose change, tossing it into his dish before opening the door for Rebecca.

"Thank you, kind sir," the panhandler said.

Eli smiled and turned to escort her inside. They jumped to the side when a waiter dashed out the door, motivated by yells of the owner to "move that bum away from my place of business!" The waiter dragged the panhandler up and asked him to leave the street, his eyes filled with a silent apology.

"Can't a man make a living anymore?" the beggar grunted, stuffing the money from the pan into his pockets, then waddled away with a limp in his left leg.

The owner behind the counter watched Eli and Rebecca select a table by the window. Dressed in common white pants and beige shirt, his tall frame made its way to their table.

"Eli, it's nice to see you today. How's business going for you?"

"I can't complain. So many have been hit hard by the crashing stock market."

"Yes, yes. It's a real shame." The owner didn't try to build any façade of real concern. "Here are your menus." He smiled into his mustache and headed behind the counter.

"A compassionate man," Rebecca remarked with sarcasm.

"Yes, the sincerity is overwhelming," Eli returned her humor.

Studying Eli's face, she admired his sculptured features in privacy, a jagged nose, bushy brows, and defined cheeks. When he glanced up, her gaze darted to her menu.

"How do you know him?" she asked.

"I used to eat here on occasion with my father." He stopped to give the waiter their orders.

When the waiter left, she asked, "How did things go for you when you arrived at your mama's party?"

"The eating had slowed and the drinking had intensified. Many of my relatives were there, so when I slid in, no one missed me. I didn't have such luck with my mama, though." He made a funny grimace. "She made it very clear I'd better be there for the entire celebration next year or she may disown her only son."

Rebecca's face grew alarmed.

"She doesn't really mean it. She says something like that at least once a year." His voice went up an octave into a motherly tone, "Eli, you'd better make it to Shabbos this morning or I'm going to have to disown my only son and you know what a heartache that will be for me."

Eli moved his hands in sway and wrinkled his forehead, imitating his concerned mother. "Eli, the Seder for Pesach is only a couple days away and you still haven't gotten the bitter herbs, the eggs, or the chicken I requested. Am I going to have to disown my only son? Don't do this to your mother." He finished with a pointing, wavering forefinger, making Rebecca laugh at his antics. He settled when the waiter set his pastrami on rye in front of him, and Rebecca enjoyed her chicken sandwich. She tore the sandwich into tiny pieces, then placed one into her mouth, savoring each taste.

When they finished with lunch, he waved away the waiter's offer for coffee.

"The meal was delicious. Thank you so much, Eli."

"It was my pleasure." Eli picked up the tab and they ambled towards their apartment building. Rebecca let go of Eli's hands just before he opened the door to the brown brick building.

"So, I'll see you later. I have to get going. My parents are expecting me to visit them this weekend," Rebecca reminded.

"Yes, of course. I almost forgot. I'll see you later then." Eli reached to her cheek and kissed her once. Rebecca turned away to hail a cab and, before she jumped into it, she glanced at Eli to find him still watching her.

"Thank you again for the tulip. It's lovely," she said, then the cab door shut and she disappeared. When the cab drove up to Rebecca's home just outside of Munich, she felt that familiar knot in her stomach, hoping to avoid another argument with her mother this time. The driver stopped in front of a large, lavish home on a street filled with other large, lavish homes. It had been several months since her last visit, before meeting Eli. A maid in black garb and a white apron rushed out the front doors, waving and calling out to Rebecca.

"It's good to have you back with us." She spoke with a light Austrian accent, her blond red hair twisted underneath her white bonnet and only strands of it escaped around her face.

"Mildred!" Rebecca's smile widened and she hugged her.

"No luggage, Ms. Baum?"

"Please call me Rebecca. Just because I've moved out, Mildred, it doesn't mean you have to go back to formalities." Mildred's rounded cheeks puffed pink from the cold weather.

"Yes, Rebecca," she said with a servitude tone. A tall man with a receding gray-blond hairline stumbled out of the front doors and embraced Rebecca.

"Papa!" Rebecca kissed him on the cheek and he took her hand as they walked together.

"The daughter whom I haven't seen in ages."

"It's only been a couple months."

"You're going to have to tell us all about your adventures in Munich and University. Your mama is excited to talk with you. She found someone you'll really like."

"Papa, I don't need setting up," she declared through gritted teeth, "Besides, I've already found someone." Her voice softened.

"Really? You're going to have to bring him home sometime and let us meet him." Father and daughter stopped inside the entryway, where she took off her coat.

A tall woman wrapped in a long, grey, silky dress walked through a swinging door and into the entryway, arms extended. "Rebecca." She glided over to her daughter and kissed her once on each cheek.

"Mutti." Rebecca tried to ease the tension inside as she hugged her.

"I've found someone for you," she whispered into her daughter's ears. "He comes from a long line of strong German ancestry. His family is well off and he is so polite and well mannered. You're going to love him."

"Mutti, slow down." Rebecca rushed her words, "As I was telling Papa…I've found someone in Munich."

"Ah!" Her mother shook Rebecca's arm in delight. "Courted by two men. Maybe there is hope for you yet, my darling. You're going to have to let us meet this stranger," she rushed her thoughts in excitement, "Perhaps this Christmas. It's coming up quickly."

"Perhaps, Mutti. I'll have to see what he's doing. He's a lawyer and they get busy." Rebecca offered the detail of Eli's profession early, hoping to soothe her mother's expectations and satiate her appetite for more details. But this information only teased her mother for more. She walked with Rebecca, holding onto her arm, into the dining area

27

for a proper discussion. Rebecca's father headed into his study to read, wanting to avoid his wife's gossip. After dinner, he could spend more time with Rebecca.

The two women wandered onto the balcony patio while sipping tea. Rebecca's mother kept her busy with questions of matrimony and University well into the early evening. Rebecca bit her lip when she told small white lies to keep her mother happy. Her mind fluttered back to moments she spent with Eli and somehow the time flew without agitation and with dinner almost served.

Dinner brought a welcomed interruption for Rebecca, and her father made it known he intended to dominate the conversation by a loud clearing of his throat.

"You are happy in Munich?" He filled his plate with the assortment of foods brought by the chef and servants.

"Yes, very much, Papa. It's so busy, I'm rarely ever bored."

"Your studies are going well?"

"I've almost completed my courses. By summer next year I should graduate."

"That's very good." He paused for a sip of wine. "So, what is this I hear about a new man in your life?" Her father, always predictably direct, arched an eyebrow.

Rebecca knew she'd have to answer the plethora of questions from her parents. She came prepared with the easiest and most accurate answers, though not necessarily completely truthful.

"He's a lawyer, working for his father. He graduated from Ludwig Maximilians two years ago." She emphasized his university. "He's smart and funny, too." She laughed in thought of some of their conversations.

"So when will we meet him?"

"Soon, I hope. Mutti wants me to bring him down for Christmas, but I have to see what his plans are then."

"Well, don't keep him away too long or your mama might just make arrangements for your wedding with…what is his name…?" Her father looked to her mother.

"Carl," her mother said through her teeth, disappointed that no one could remember the name of the young man she chose for Rebecca.

Rebecca laughed at her father's remark, hiding her large teeth behind her hands.

"Dear, you know it's impolite to laugh at the table while we are trying to have a serious conversation," her mother fussed, quick to point out Rebecca's fault.

"Yes, Mutti."

Her father glanced at Rebecca and the two shared a secret smile.

Rebecca headed to her room after dinner, which had remained the same since the day she left. Many of her old clothes still hung in the closet and many of her favorite toiletries still lingered on the vanity and in the bathroom. She prepared for bed and let her head fall to her thick feather pillows while pulling up the Egyptian silk comforter over her body. Recounting the evening, she felt happy that she avoided all the anxiety ridden questions.

Sunday morning, her mother made her dress in her Sunday's best to attend mass at the Lugwigskirche Catholic church. The dress buttoned to the very top of Rebecca's neck and draped in length, covering her ankles.

They sat in the second row near the front; her parents sat on either side of her. She felt squeezed by proper society while sitting tightly between them. Peering ahead at the tall brown worn wooden pulpit, she waited for the priest to give his sermon. Mass was long, even longer then Rebecca's work day at the diner. After mass, her parents drove her back to their home up a long high hill and parked their black Daimler-Benz. "Mildred!" Her mother called out to the maid who still remained only the help since her hiring twenty years ago. Mildred raced to the Benz, dusting off her apron with her hands.

"Yes, Mrs. Baum, may I do something for you?"

"I need help getting inside. My feet are swelling underneath me." Rebecca's mother clung onto her like a patient to a doctor stepping in her high heels over the grains of pebble and sand until she reached the door. "Thank you, Mildred." She let go of the maid's arm and plodded into the large house. Rebecca and her father walked arm in arm over the bumpy walkway. At the door, Rebecca kissed her father on his cheek and announced her departure.

"I've got to get going. I don't want to get back into Munich too late."

"Certainly, dear." Her father smiled cordially and her mother scampered back to the front door and asked in motherly disappointment, "Leaving so quickly?"

"I'm sorry, but with the traffic I would like to make it to my apartment before dark."

"I'll see you at Christmas then. Don't forget to bring your special someone. We're looking forward to meeting him." Rebecca hugged her mother, who kissed her again on both cheeks, then headed to the front gate for the waiting taxi. In the cab, Rebecca stared out the window, watching the scenery of lush living fade the closer she got to Munich. In the city, she drove past a struggling mix of the homeless, now abundant on the streets, and knew the employed lived inside the warm buildings.

Once home, she rushed upstairs to get her bag of laundry to wash by hand in her bathroom. Normally, Rebecca would have more time to finish up her menial tasks, but since she kept a promise to see her parents and go with them to service, the day offered less time then she hoped and her legs couldn't move her fast enough.

She laid her apron out in the bathroom, knowing it wouldn't be dry in time if she didn't wash it first when she returned with groceries. She heard a few steps in the apartment above her and wondered if Eli was home yet from his day. Without hesitation in her step, she smiled at the ceiling and then headed outside for fresh air before the evening caught up with her.

SUNDAY, NOVEMBER 8, 1931

Rebecca and Eli ambled down the chilly sidewalk hand in hand, their bodies close enough to keep each other warmer than if they walked alone. Rebecca fiddled with her rose colored knit hat her mother gave her. Benches lined the sidewalk outside the park and they cozily sat side by side on one in the middle. Eli wrapped his arm around Rebecca and saw her nose turning a fast red. He rubbed it with his hands, a task Rebecca was becoming familiar with. Laughing at her easy vulnerability to the cold, he took off his long strapped, leather brown bag carrying a few books and laid it across his legs. He took out a book, laid his head on her lap and gazed up at her. Though certainly taboo, being around her made him feel free. Caressing his face, her fingers touched his cheeks and forehead and then circled around to his chin.

"Feels like you've missed a shave again," Rebecca remarked without feeling she would offend him.

"You are a very perceptive young woman." He raised an index finger in emphasis. "I'll have to remedy my error later."

"No error," she smiled wide. "I kind of like it, all rough and manly."

She lowered her head to his and Eli planned to give her a peck on the lips. Yet, after their lips touched, he lingered there and then laid his head back on the warmth of her lap garbed in a thick dark wool skirt. Eli opened the book.

"Who are we reading today?" Rebecca asked.

"Heinrich Heine, a German poet of Jewish origin."

"Oh." Rebecca teased with catty intonation.

"Are you mocking me?" Eli asked halfheartedly with the look of sensuality in his dark brown eyes.

"I really do love poetry," she insisted. Eli flipped through a few pages and read aloud, loud enough for her to hear and soft enough for the words to travel through the ears of the strangers passing by.

The Day the Flowers Died

E'EN as A LOVELY FLOWER
   by: Heinrich Heine (1799-1856)
E'en as a lovely flower, so fair, so pure thou art;
I gaze on thee, and sadness comes stealing o'er my heart.
My hands I fain had folded upon thy soft brown hair,
Praying that God may keep thee so lovely, pure and fair

"There is something about his words. The poetry...the words...are captivating," Rebecca whispered, elating Eli by her enthusiastic approval.

"He is one of my favorites. He blends French modernism with German sentiment." Eli turned the page to Heine's bibliography and read the line quoted at the top without so much as a waver in his voice.

"Where one burns books, one will, in the end, burn people." Eli opened his mouth about to say something political, but before he could, Rebecca interrupted his thought.

"Read me some more of his poetry," she asked like a child with a bedtime story. Gazing at her blue eyes that matched the sky, he turned the page to find another poem. "I really like this poet," she said in her naïve age, never hearing of him before today and not fully comprehending the significance he had for Eli.

"He's more than a mere poet. He's a writer and political-religious thinker of Paris. Have you read him?"

Eli educated Rebecca as she shook her head no and then he spoke in audible softness.

MY DARLING, WE SAT TOGETHER
     by: Heinrich Heine (1799-1856)
MY darling, we sat together, we two, in our frail boat;
The night was calm o'er the wide sea whereon we were afloat.
The Specter-Island, the lovely, lay dim in the moon's mild glance;
There sounded sweetest music, there waved the shadowy dance.
It sounded sweeter and sweeter; it waved there to and fro;
But we slid past forlornly upon the great sea-flow

Rebecca rested easily with Eli on her lap. He wrestled to keep his eyes from shutting with sleep. Their intimacy from an embrace on this almost secluded bench in the middle of a cold winter etched into their bodies, the way his head fell onto her legs and the way she kept his head afloat. She was like the frail boat and he the passenger, amidst a dim day with the sweetest symphony surrounding them, sliding upon a great sea flow.

"Do you think it could stay like this forever," Rebecca whispered to him, "with us in each other's arms, laying here in the quiet breeze of winter." She knew it could never be true, and yet hoped it all the same.

"Nothing lasts forever," he said.

"Then at least for a few hours," Rebecca sighed, crumbling into his chest with her head against his stomach. Eli lifted his hands up to her snuggled head and stroked her hair in the few moments left of pleasant retreat. Then he pulled himself off the bench, lifting Rebecca with him.

They returned to their apartments, knowing they each had obligations to fulfill before the day disappeared. Standing outside the building, Eli continued with some of the thoughts heavy on his mind.

"Prejudice and political unrest," Eli thought aloud, wanting Rebecca to join in.

"What do you mean?"

"Do you think they go hand in hand? When a country is falling apart, it inevitably divides within itself. People cling to what they know, and fear foreign ideas and differences."

"I think it takes a unique kind of a person to think or do something differently from the majority of society," Rebecca said, and Eli curled his body into hers, holding her gaze.

"In these times, it's important to think about these things."

"But it's more important to laugh." Rebecca tickled Eli and he yanked away, holding his side.

"Rebecca." He laughed, hoping she wouldn't dare do it again. "I'm very sensitive." Rebecca reached out anyway, testing him with her fingers. He grabbed hold of her and tried to stop laughing. Before they parted, Eli to his office and Rebecca upstairs, he stopped her by gripping her arm.

" Would you like to go swing dancing next weekend?"

"That sounds fun." She nodded and Eli let go of her arm.

"Have you ever been before?"

"No, my mutti would never let me. But I've always wanted to." She almost begged in her words.

33

The Day the Flowers Died

"Then, I'll pick you up just after the sun goes down Saturday night."

* * *

The crowds brought in by the music and dance of swing epitomized what the youth wanted the country to be — soulful and free. It defined a counter sub-culture opposing the repression and work-bent society of their time, longing for everything not German, but English. The bright lights circled around on the high ceilings. Young boys wore checkered jackets, showy scarves, loud hats and swung their umbrellas as they passed the doors. Young ladies wore excessive makeup coupled with hair sprawled over their shoulders, knowing this bright, boisterous room offered the only place they could truly be free.

A high school crowd packed the room and a group of college youths on occasion stood on their tables, shouting, laughing and then sat back down. Colorful dresses worn by the young ladies swayed side to side on the wood floor and then, when their partners lifted them up, for the briefest moment, their exposed womanhood reminded everyone in the room this place was like no other in Germany.

The women cavorted high over the heads of the men bracing them and then swung back to the floor. Feet moved quickly, sliding from one side of the floor to the other and the sound of heels and toes smacking the wood echoed with each thud. The band on stage comprised of an anchoring rhythm section, loosely tied wind and brass players, and a soloist who took center stage.

Rebecca couldn't take her eyes off of the room, loud, bright and free. She had never seen anything like it before and wasn't sure if it was proper. Eli grabbed hold of Rebecca, swinging her about in his arms and then carried her onto the dance floor. Rebecca tried to escape at first, pulling herself toward the wall, unsure of her ability to dance. But Eli held her tightly, lifting her into the air and rotating her around and around high above the floor. He placed his hands under her shoulders and then on her stomach, raising her over his head as she gazed down at the swirling world below her. The dark red dress, cut too low at the neckline, swung as Eli held her with strong, sturdy hands.

Rebecca caught her breath when Eli placed her back on the wooden dance floor. Though swing wouldn't become widely accepted for several more years, the lack of popularity of the dance didn't matter to Eli. He only ever followed his passions, and he was passionate about two things for sure. Rebecca and swing.

"That was wild!" She shouted to him over the sounds of reckless rhythms, keeping a four beat jive. Feet slid and jumped while toes tapped across the floor. A short robust young man with dark hair, a flashy thick scarf, long black and white checkered jacket and umbrella still in his hands slid over to Eli.

"Eli! You made it!" he shouted.

"I did." Eli pulled her close to him, proudly displaying his affections, "And this is Rebecca."

"Nice to meet you." The short man took her hand and kissed it twice. "I'm Jacob." He held her hand and pulled her towards him, twirling her. Her eyes widened in surprise and Jacob grabbed hold of her other hand before she collided into him. He tapped his feet and then, with a swing of Rebecca's arms, he danced with her for a moment before returning her to Eli.

He nodded when he let her go, grasping his short black hat to pull it down in old fashioned politeness before tapping his feet across the floor to the other side of the room where his other friends awaited him.

Rebecca whispered to Eli in intimate closeness while Eli held her waist. "What a character," she giggled. Eli guffawed at his friend's antics and then mimicked Jacob's audacity by pulling Rebecca back onto the dance floor. He grabbed her hands, swinging them back and forth and moved his feet like everyone else in the room, slowly at first to show Rebecca how and then quickly, like he had done this many times.

Rebecca tried to keep up with him, laughing at herself and then at Eli. The band slowed down the music, out of a Gene Kardos and his orchestra into a jazz-blues rhythm. The music beat like a heart slowing until the floor became saturated with couples arm in arm. The lights dimmed and Eli held Rebecca close.

Rebecca draped her arms around Eli's neck and rested her head on his shoulders. They swayed in a naïve bliss forgotten by society outside the doors. When the slow jazz-blues music ended, the band revived the quick stepping swing and the room filled up with throbbing musical improvisations, causing everyone to get up and dance. The long night of dancing tired their feet and they sat down at a table near the wall.

Rebecca watched Eli laugh and smiled as he watched the youth of his generation free and jovial inside this room.

"When am I going to meet more of your friends or your family?" Rebecca asked him with inquisitive eyes.

"New Year's Eve, I'm having a party at my house and I want you to come. Many of my friends will be there. They're looking forward to meeting you."

"You've told them about me?"

"Well, not everything," he smirked. "What about your family? When will I get to meet them?" Eli turned away from the spontaneity of the swing around him and focused on Rebecca.

"I'm not sure. I mean if you have time, you could come up for Christmas. My parents were asking about meeting you."

"You've told your parents about me already. I must admit, I'm impressed."

"You haven't spoken to your parents yet about me?" Rebecca asked with a hint of hurt in her voice.

"It's complicated with my parents. I will, but I have to find the right time. After the New Year, I promise."

"I'm not waiting any longer than that."

"I would never make you."

They left shortly after that, and Eli drove Rebecca, checking to make sure she was warm. The weather had progressively cooled from autumn into winter and snow already lumped up in corners of streets and trees. When they arrived home, Eli strolled with Rebecca to the front door, bent down in her favorite spot of grass and broke off a single rose dressed with a light snow lace dripping off its petals.

"I think we ought to keep this a secret," Eli smirked while handing the purloined rose to Rebecca.

"You could get thrown in jail or something," she teased, knowing the offense would only ever escalate to paying a fine to the landlord. "Then they'd throw me in there after seeing all the evidence laid out in vases in my apartment." She chuckled into Eli's coat shoulder.

"How are you going to keep all your flowers alive in this cold climate?" Eli asked.

"I keep them close to the window for the morning sun and give them lots of tepid water and nutrients." She darted her head upward with an idea. "You know, you could help me next weekend. I'm going to change them into new pots and refill their vases."

"Next weekend?"

"The twenty-first." She clarified the date, knowing Eli kept a tight schedule.

"Alright," Eli hesitated, thinking of his former obligation to attend synagogue. "I'll see you in the afternoon."

"About two?"

"Let's make it three."

"Alright, it's a date, a garden date," Rebecca smiled. Eli strolled with her up to her room, kissing her on the lips, and then headed to his room.

The week progressed like all other weeks in Rebecca and Eli's life, going to work, coming home, and repeating the cycle all over again until the weekend arrived, when they could spend time with one another.

On the twenty-first, true to his promise, Eli knocked on Rebecca's door while he juggled a few pots, bags of soil, and vases in a brown box. He purchased the items during the week in between his hectic schedule at work and stored them in the box for this day.

The knock on the door ripped Rebecca from her work and to her feet. Eli walked in, lowering the box next to the wall, then scanned the untidy room with pots and bags of nutrients sprawled all over the floor and dining table. A small gardening shovel with an orange handle sat next to one of the pots on the coffee table and many flowers lay in the sink, soaking with water.

"Wow, what a mess," Eli chuckled realizing the grand project he'd just entered. "When you said repotting some flowers, I envisioned a small venture." Rebecca laughed at how little he knew of her love for gardening.

"It won't take too long," she reassured.

"It's no problem, really. I didn't have any other plans for the rest of the day...or for the week, if it takes that long," Eli joked, walking to the sink to examine the flowers. "You have an assortment here."

"Though winter, a few of the flower shops still hold a variety and I collect them from wherever I can. They bring life to the room, you know?"

Eli's fingers tarried over a tulip in the sink and he pulled it out to show her. "I see the Cornflower I brought you is still alive. That must be a good sign."

"Yes, it is." Rebecca handed Eli a pot and pointed to the bag of soil on the floor. "You can start with refilling this one. The potted flowers are in this corner of the kitchen." She went to the box of flowers sitting in soil on top of the kitchen counter. "And the ones in the sink will be put in vases with new water and nutrients."

Eli scurried to the box on the counter and peeked inside in awe. "Where do you find all of these?"

"At a few of the local shops, but many I find outside the city where my parents live."

Eli lifted a few Gerber Daises out of the sink, delicately washing between the petals and refilling their vases with water. He then took a handful of nutrients from her bag and sprinkled it inside the vase. Next, he arranged the assortment of white Edelweiss, bright blue Cornflowers, and purple Spindles, and placed the vase on top of her cabinet next to a picture of a mother cuddling a baby.

"Who is this?" He tried to contain his joyful surprise upon discovering something new about her. "Is this you?"

Rebecca sped across the room to defend her turf. "Well, if you must know, this is Mutti holding me when I was a baby."

"Your mama, the woman I'll meet at the Christmas Eve dinner?"

"And my papa's picture is here." Rebecca lifted the photo of her father standing under a tree with a book in his hands.

"Where was this taken?"

"Switzerland. Just after my high school graduation. It is the last photo I have of all of us. Perhaps at Christmas we can take another with you?" she asked.

"I'd be honored, and I'll drive us up so that you don't have to worry about it."

"That would be nice and you can also show off your car to my parents." She quirked her brows.

"It's not anything notable. I'm still saving up for a more reliable car."

"Still, at least you have a car and in a time when many don't even have work."

"I'm glad you're so easy to please." He tickled her on her ribs. She grabbed her side and, when she tried to tug Eli's hands away, his fingers intertwined with her own. Eli pulled her hands up to his face and then her fingers wiped over his lips holding a touch of soil in the corner. Her gaze caught his, her long lashes touched his, and their noses brushed as their lips found comfort in one long, delicious moment.

The Day the Flowers Died

Thursday, December 24, 1931

Christmas Eve: The Baum house was decorated in keeping with their Christmas tradition with lush fake flowers and vines winding up and through the metal gates. Ornate lights hung high on the house roof eaves and around the doors. Shoveled snow lined the street and the walkway leading to the front door. The two story house reached far from one side of the property to the other as if two homes had been fused to make this one magnificent spectacle. Evergreens wrapped in snowy ermine shawls marched up the driveway in majestic elegance.

When Eli stopped his beat-up Audi at the front gate, he knew he should have bought a BMW, even though he couldn't afford it at the time. First impressions went a long way in this German town, making up for any preconceived failures Rebecca's parents might bestow upon him. He thought arriving in a BMW would have made all the difference but, as he doubted his choice in cars, Rebecca grabbed his hand and squeezed it, content in whatever car they pulled up in.

The gate buzzed open, the lock was released by Mildred, the servant of the home, who raised Rebecca almost entirely by herself. Eli gawked at the mansion-like home and his face flushed red when he parked his aged car behind their pristine Daimler-Benz.

With the car doors still shut, in this quiet, private moment, Eli allowed her to see a frail side of him. "I will be an embarrassment. Just look at what I drive!" His palms hit, then gripped the steering wheel.

"Don't worry about the car," she soothed. "And you are never an embarrassment."

He paused a moment, then nodded. "Ready?"

"Yes."

His confidence returned and he pushed the door open with his shoulder. Moving to her side of the car, he helped her out, both of them taking deep, calming breaths before making their way over the pebbled walkway leading to the two oak white front doors.

Mildred opened the door before they reached it, her face alight with joy. "It's so good to see you this time of year. You bring festivity and felicity with your youthful city charms." Mildred spoke proud like a parent to the girl who was like a daughter to her. "Your parents are waiting for you in the dining room. Chef Ruben has prepared the Christmas feast and will take it to the table once the two of you have settled and seated."

Rebecca smiled at the name Ruben, her favorite chef of the four they'd had over the years. He always had a way of adding flavors she could never quite name, but never forget. Eli went back to the car while Rebecca and Mildred paused in conversation, and returned with Rebecca's small suitcase. She'd insinuated before they left that she might stay a few nights before returning to Munich.

Eli planned to leave at the end of the night, hoping to impress her parents well enough to be invited back again. But, since Rebecca's father was German and her mother Dutch American, raised to honor German values, Eli worried about his reception and acceptance. Social pressures and financial morass plagued 1931 Munich. A Jewish man was not the typical choice for an classy German born daughter. For this reason, he bolstered a hard confidence, like a stone wall, to keep his innermost weaknesses hidden.

It drove him to always work twice as hard as his colleagues, proving himself to be of service to this German world, proving himself to be of value to his German peers. Most important of all, he knew he would have to be twice the man a German would have to be to win the hearts of Rebecca's parents.

Stepping inside behind Mildred and Rebecca, who were busy rekindling their fondest memories, Eli saw a butler holding the door. He greeted Eli with a nod, took Rebecca's suitcase, and motioned him to proceed.

"This way. This way." Rebecca grabbed Eli's wrist and pulled him through a long corridor of marble floors and stone white walls adorned with original art. In her excitement of Eli meeting her parents, she forgot herself momentarily until she reached the dining hall. Her mother sat at the teak engraved table, peering from behind a large vase filled with vibrant Marsh Marigolds.

Her mother's hands rearranged the flowers Mildred had arranged in the morning and Rebecca remembered why she felt reluctant months ago to tell her parents of her relationship. Her mother never approved of anything she did, not moving to Munich, not going to college. And now, instead of accepting her mother's choice in Carl, a man she wanted Rebecca to date and eventually marry, Rebecca invited Eli home.

When Rebecca entered the dining hall, her confident demeanor dropped to one sheepish grin and she knew her mother still had power over her. After all this time, she still yearned for her mother's approval, despite the impossibility of ever obtaining it. Eli walked in behind Rebecca, his hand on her shoulder to soothe the tensions he felt boiling inside of her.

Gliding to her mother sitting on the left side of the long table, Rebecca kissed her mother's cheeks, signifying her gratefulness at the reception. Rebecca's golden brown silk gown, which wrapped around her waist and draped over her ankles, contrasted her mother's beige white lace gown. Her mother had called to tell her what she would be wearing so Rebecca could find something suitable.

Rebecca couldn't bear to have her mother's disapproving glare aimed at her throughout Christmas dinner because of any untamed manners. Her greeting, garb, dining, cordial conversation and salutation for the night would all be without reproach. Rebecca had escaped the clutches of her mother's cultural refinement when she immigrated to Munich. However, her strict upbringing, enforced primarily by her mother, remained with her.

The freedom Munich gave her allowed her to fill her apartment with too many flowers, to leave her laundry sometimes unattended for a few days, and to charcoal dinners in her attempts to learn how to cook. This achieved freedom remained concealed to keep it from seeping out of her and spoiling the night, a night she hoped would belong to Eli and his impressive accomplishments.

Eli unwrapped his beige trench coat from his body and draped it over his left arm while waiting for instruction on where to leave it. The butler, appareled in black and white and who had held the door for them upon arriving, scurried to Eli's side, took the coat and carried it away.

Rebecca's father sat on the right end of the elongated table positioned horizontally to the dining hall entrance; her mother sat at the opposite end. Eli addressed Rebecca's father with an outstretched hand. Her father shook it, his sharp blue eyes reminding Eli of Rebecca's, and he unconsciously smiled.

"I'm Ralph Baum, Rebecca's father."

"Eli Levin."

With the last name, Deseire swallowed hard on her appetizer of ham.

"And this," he pointed across the table, "is my dear wife, Rebecca's mother, Deseire. We call her Dessie. Please, have a seat."

Eli sat closest to the door where he first entered. Rebecca kept her eyes locked on his to give him support and herself comfort as she took the seat across from him. Genuine silverware bordered each placemat and crystal stemware sparkled at the top. Eli straightened his dark beige slacks which matched his jacket. Rebecca especially picked out his tie because of the hint of gold infused into its fabric which she knew would compliment her gown and the garb of her parents.

Her father wrestled with his brown suit jacket, and then waved with his fingers to the butler for help while he struggled to take it off his arms. Over the years, Ralph had gained a few extra pounds which harbored in his upper body, stomach and arms. The butler helped wrestle the brown jacket off of him and carried it away in a quickened pace.

Deseire glanced at Eli with a polite smile and sharp hazel eyes, reminding him of someone at the meat market picking out steaks. Servants carried the food out on silver platters with Ralph's company name engraved along the sides.

Three servants, also in black and white, held the plates high in their hands. Two males and one female with brown hair tied into a bun set the platters and plates around the table without much sound and then became invisible again, disappearing through the door behind Deseire.

Roasted duck sat at Rebecca's end and honey roasted ham at Eli's. Boiled potatoes and peas decorated Ralph's side of the table and cranberry sauce, sauerkraut and corn sat near Deseire. Rebecca lifted her fingers to snitch a piece of duck, but pulled away at her mother's glare burning into her hand.

43

Ralph filled the delay in waiting for the servants to serve the main entrée with opportune inquiry.

"So, Eli, Rebecca tells us you are a lawyer. That profession must keep you very busy."

"It does." Eli smiled lightheartedly.

"She tells me you graduated from Ludwig Maximilians University."

"Yes, two years ago, and I've been working ever since." Eli answered with an ease learned from working cases in the court room.

"You found work after graduation; that is serendipitous," Ralph commented, while his wife's gaze flickered between the two men.

"Ralph owns factories throughout Germany," Deseire remarked with a curt smile. The servants prepared each of their plates with a slice of ham and duck and a few spoonfuls of corn and peas and lastly a dip of sauerkraut.

"Looks delicious," Eli remarked and dug his fork into the corn.

"It really does. I can't wait to taste Rueben's duck," Rebecca agreed.

When Rebecca picked the duck up with her silver fork, the red brown sauce dripped and the green herbs aromatically filled the space between the plate and her nose and she closed her eyes, whiffing in the seasoned flavor. Ralph dug his fork into the duck and then the ham, savoring both meats at the same time. Only his love of food surpassed his love of business.

"Where did the two of you meet?" Deseire intruded on the moment of succulence. Eli's wide eyes widened further and his lips stretched with pleasure in memory.

"I live above Rebecca and noticed her in the building."

Rebecca cut in. "He kept receiving some of my mail by mistake and kindly brought the letters to me."

"Did any of our letters make their way somewhere else?" Deseire snipped.

"I don't think so, Mutti. I'm sure I received every one of your verbose letters." And out it popped, the civility Rebecca tried so desperately to hold onto throughout the night.

"Verbose?" Deseire cleared her throat and the wrinkles around her eyes intensified as if preparing for war. "Darling, we never hear from you and some-one in the family has to keep communication. We don't know if you're alright or what kind of strange people may be involved in your life."

Eli's shoulders jolted back into his chair, creating a gap between him and the dining table, hoping to become invisible and avoid the bickering about to take place.

"Mother," Rebecca used the elongated form instead of mutti whenever she was frazzled by her. "I only mean that your letters are very long and I am busy between work and University."

"Rebecca's right. She is a very busy young college woman these days and we can't expect her to contact us with every free moment." Ralph interrupted the growing feud before the embers had time to burn and explode.

"But a phone call a night is not asking too much, Rebecca. How else are we to know you're safe? If you don't have time to read my letters and respond, then at least phone us."

"I do, Mutti. I called you just…" Rebecca replayed the past couple months in her mind and couldn't recall a night when she had phoned her mother recently.

Deseire took advantage of her daughter's delayed response. "You see, you cannot even remember a time, because it was so long ago. All I'm asking for is a little more communication so that I know my only child is still alive."

With her mother's last words, Rebecca crumbled in her seat, resenting the correction, especially in front of Eli.

"Alright, Mutti, I will try to make more time to talk with you by phone, but I can't promise you anything with writing. I just don't have the time."

"That's all I ask," Deseire concluded.

As the discord between Rebecca and her mother settled, Eli found it comfortable to lean towards the dining table and eat again. Ralph took a spoonful of peas to his mouth and soon the plates around the table sat empty.

"Dinner was absolutely delectable," Eli said and pushed himself out of his seat. The butler handed him his trench coat. "Thank you." Eli brushed his hair back and took the coat from the butler's hands. Rebecca finished licking red brown sauce still on her plate with her fingers and then glided over to Eli with her arm squeezing under his.

"Eli has to get going. He has a big day tomorrow with his family," Rebecca said. Ralph stood, walking to Eli to shake his hand. Eli reciprocated.

"It was nice meeting all of you."

"It was a pleasure finally meeting you," Deseire said. "I have been waiting awhile to meet the secret man Rebecca has been hiding."

"I'll see him to the door," Rebecca said. The two of them strolled out of the dining hall and Rebecca nestled her mouth to Eli's ear. "You ate your ham."

"Yes, well, I was trying to be polite. I didn't want to offend your parents," he thought for a moment with a childish grin, "or the cook."

Rebecca nudged his shoulder and they walked out to his car.

"I guess I'll see you after Christmas."

"Do come to my New Year's Eve party. It will be at my place and everyone will start arriving around eight. You will meet my friends, or at least some of them."

"I'll be there."

Eli's lips moved towards hers and, after a brief moment of passion, Eli slipped into his car and Rebecca watched him drive away, back to Munich, back to her home.

Retracing her steps to the lavishly decorated house, she saw the curtain in the side window wrinkle back over the glass and the silhouette of her mother disappear. Rebecca's muscles tightened and her lips pressed hard, knowing her mother's hidden disapproval and peering eyes always kept watch on her, even after all these years. She did not want to walk through those doors, back into the house, knowing the discourse she would have, defending the man she was with, defending the university she attended, defending her choices in life. Rebecca sighed and opened the large oak doors, entering to the living room where her parents waited with Mildred's strong smile telling her she would be fine.

A large Christmas tree sat in the corner of the room with a red silk rug engulfing its base. Five presents packaged in silver, gold, green, white, and red wrapping paper waited underneath the tree's boughs. Rebecca passed her mother and sped to the tree, as if she were twelve again, to examine the gifts, then tried to sneak out of the room.

Deseire watched Rebecca ignore her and followed Rebecca into the corridor before she escaped to her room upstairs.

"We have to talk about this," Deseire insisted.

"I don't want to have this conversation with you, Mutti. It's Christmas Eve and I don't want our arguing to spoil anything. Can't you just wait until after Christmas?" Rebecca implored and, with that reasonable suggestion, Deseire's tightened jaws loosened and Rebecca's tightened muscles relaxed.

"After Christmas morning, but we will have this discussion," Deseire insisted. Rebecca turned from her mother, rolled her eyes and pouted her lips, then pranced up the stairwell to her private room with a tub.

Rebecca knew the conversation her mother wanted to have, both of them pulling a string in opposite directions, each insisting they knew what was best for Rebecca's life. Only Rebecca did know best without the doubt that plagued her in previous times when they argued.

Doubt questioned, when she insisted on leaving for college, if Munich would work out for her. Doubt made her choice of Nursing uncertain. But Eli — she knew in the deepest parts of her heart Eli was right for her and no amount of whining or arguing from her mother could change that. Rebecca took a bath and Mildred helped her get into bed. Before turning out the lights, Mildred sat beside Rebecca's pillow and kissed her forehead.

"You've always had a strong will just like your father, your own mind to do things. But your mutti is just trying to do what she thinks is best for you. You might not think about such things, but these are worrisome times and she doesn't want to see you get hurt. She does love you, dear."

Mildred rubbed her calloused hands over Rebecca's thick hair and then left the room. Rebecca fell asleep with those words on her mind, worrisome times.

The morning whistled into Rebecca's room with the curtains drawn by Mildred and the birds singing songs for the new day. "It's time to get up dear. You don't want to miss opening the presents," Mildred urged. Rebecca yawned, lifting her arms above her, and nestling her head in her warm silk sheets once more before pulling herself off her bed and into her bathroom where Mildred had drawn the bath.

"I'll see you downstairs for breakfast." Mildred's words muffled behind the closed bath door. Rebecca heard her bedroom door shut and Mildred's heavy walk down the steps.

When Rebecca made it into the dining room for breakfast, she found her parents already there, eager to start their day.

Ralph walked over to his daughter and placed a small pink box in front of her after she sat down.

"Daddy," Rebecca's stern face, kept that way from a night of anticipating her mother's conversation the next morning, soothed. "You didn't have to do this." Rebecca caressed the package with her fingers, investigating with tactile concentration.

"Well, go ahead, open it," her father said. Rebecca loosened the thread of pink ribbon to undo the bow and then lifted the box lid. She peeked inside, noticed a metallic key and then closed the box to keep the gift safe.

"You didn't, Papa!" Rebecca leapt off her chair and rushed to hug her father. Ralph let out a guffaw at being squeezed.

"You need a new car. You have no way of getting around in that big city and we worry about you. Besides, now you have a way to visit us more often and we won't need to hear anymore of your mother's bickering to come see us." Ralph glanced at Deseire at his last words and winked. Deseire smiled.

"Thank you so much, Papa!"

"Well, let's go see it."

Rebecca sprinted out of the dining hall, past the butler holding open the front door, and to her new car. The blue Audi tickled Rebecca to uncontrolled elation as Ralph and Deseire caught up to Rebecca. Even Deseire smiled at her daughter's enthusiasm.

"Adorable!" Rebecca became giddy, swinging the door open. "Can I drive it?"

"Of course. Take it for a spin and then head back for breakfast," Ralph said in a fatherly tone. Rebecca jumped into her new car and heard her mother say, "You shouldn't spoil her like that. It was her decision to go off to University." But the wind from the rolled down windows brushed over Rebecca's hair and face and her mother's words, like the wind rolling off of her, blew away."

Rebecca returned to the dining hall with breakfast already served on the large burgundy breakfast plates. They ate breakfast without the daunting conversation Rebecca had been waiting for, but her mother's eyes had peered at her more than once during the morning meal. Rebecca knew she would not return to Munich without speaking to her. The three of them left the dining hall to enter the living room where the tree and gifts waited. Rebecca's cheerful demeanor from receiving a most unexpected gift in the morning spread to her father and the servants, leaving everyone, except her mother, in a jovial mood.

Four presents sat under the tree for Deseire and Ralph. Her parents opened them, revealing a pearl necklace and a broach for her mutti and a silk neck tie and a leather wallet for her papa. One last gift remained for Rebecca from Deseire. Rebecca opened the silver wrapped present to find a small white box much like the box her father had hidden the Audi key in. She opened the lid and found a small silver band ring that matched the one her mother wore on her index finger.

"I hope you like it, Rebecca. Is it modern enough for you?"

"Of course, Mama, I love it." Rebecca slid the silver ring over her left index finger and gave her mother a hug, who held her tight and then let go while still holding onto her arm.

"Rebecca, we need to talk about your future."

Rebecca pulled free and sat in the chair across from the sofa where her mother made herself comfortable.

Ralph lifted his cigar to his mouth and escaped to the porch adjacent to the living room. Rebecca scrutinized her mother's eyes, her fake smile and her raised brows and waited for the words. "In these fragile times, who you date is important; the reputation you build for yourself is important. You don't want to have doors shut for you because of the mistakes of your youth."

"What mistakes, Mother?" Rebecca remarked in a contrived innocence.

"He is a Jew. I can't have my only daughter, my only child dating a Jew." She said the word Jew almost in a whisper, like she'd catch an illness from saying it too loudly.

Rebecca fell back into her chair at the words her mother actually said aloud, words she knew formed in the corners of her mother's mind during dinner and tried to ignore. But her mother sat in front of her and would not let her hide in the fanciful dreams of her unbridled youth in Munich.

"I...I..." Rebecca stuttered at what she wanted to say. "I'm not going to do this with you, Mama. You always try to control every decision I make and it's not going to work with him. It's my decision, not yours." Rebecca pulled herself out of the chair with both hands and stormed out of the living area while Ralph blew cigar smoke out the open glass door.

Fifteen minutes later, Rebecca returned to the living room with her luggage in hand and placed it between the living room and the corridor.

"I have to get going. I have a lot to do, and don't want to be late arriving in Munich." She scurried past her mother to her father and gave him a hug and thanked him for the car. Then she plodded to her mother and offered a worn smile. Her mother stood and they politely hugged out of aristocratic expectations. Rebecca turned with her long dark brown hair swaying about her and lifted her luggage to walk out the front door. Mildred hurried to her side with a square treat wrapped in foil and handed it to her.

"Don't forget to take this. I made it myself for you, your favorite banana bread." Rebecca's tense cheeks and stretched eyes lightened and she hugged Mildred before exiting to her new blue Audi.

Ami Rebecca Blackwelder

THURSDAY, DECEMBER 31, 1931

The New Year's Eve party was one of a many in this apartment building and they reminded everyone a new year was born. Perhaps the jazz music and gaudy decorations or perhaps the idea of the past ending and a future beginning allowed everyone the freedom of the untamed. The last night of 1931 gave people an excuse to be rowdy and wild, despite the growing conservative German culture toward a more civil society. On this night, those rules did not apply anymore. On each floor of the apartment, music permeated the walls and the sounds of chatter and laughter filled the halls.

Rebecca walked through Eli's open door into a room filled with guests, music, dancing, food and drinks. Her maroon dress swayed over her slim ankles and her sleeves cuddled her elbows. A white ribbon adorned her waist and her hair, holding her long brown hair up into a looped braid. The dim lights lit enough for everyone to make out shadows of who everyone was with. Eli noticed Rebecca from across the room and darted to her side to escort her through the crowd and help her untangle the long, thick, white scarf around her neck. They stood near the kitchen, the light from the moon shining through the window and over their faces.

"How are you? It's so good to see you." Eli held her shoulders, stroking his hands down her arms to her hands and then took one into his.

"I'm...good. I'm good." Rebecca strained to keep the argument at her house between just her and her mother.

"Did everything go well with your parents at Christmas? Did you have a good time?" Rebecca tried to resist remembering the tense scene and her drive back to Munich, desperate to see Eli again.

"My papa bought me a new car." She gleamed, tilting her head to one side, hoping conversation would revolve around that singular topic. A tall blond haired man, whose hair reminded Eli of the military, and a

51

woman with long blond hair and taut lips, held hands as they half danced next to Rebecca. She introduced them to Eli.

"These are my friends from University, Louise and Barnard." She gestured as she said their names. "Louise is also studying to be a nurse and Barnard wants to be a lawyer, like you." Her eyes glinted of pride, glancing at Eli.

"It's so nice to meet some of Rebecca's friends." Eli shook Barnard's hand and Bernard politely reciprocated, recoiling his hand just before Eli let it go. Eli smiled and nodded to Louise, whose fluffy dress matched the fluffiness of her hair, and then turned to Rebecca.

"Would you like to dance?" Eli scooped Rebecca's hand into his and whisked her onto the dance floor which was his living room with all its furniture rearranged against the walls. Eli's grey vest over a crisp white button down shirt looked sharp over his grey tie tucked into his grey slacks. His black loafer shoes slid across the wood floors with Rebecca in his arms. One hand pressed her straightened back while his other lay in her hand, guiding her along the floor like two ballroom professionals.

The floor filled with more couples eager to escape the clutches of civil culture. Twirling and swirling became a ruse to disregard propriety.

Laughter and music drowned out minds throbbing with the changing face of Germany. Food and drink offered splendor to savor what might not be there tomorrow. After a few times around the mock dance floor, frolicking to a jazzy beat, Eli cuddled with Rebecca in a corner of the room, standing next to a bookcase with his hands clasped over hers. The two lovers whispered in each other's ears with intermittent bursts of laughter, whispers and laughter seen throughout the room.

"Could you get me something to drink?" Rebecca asked. Eli scattered to the other side of the room to the table covered with plates of food and drink. A dark, curly haired young man, taller than Eli and more plump, surprised him from behind, pinching his shoulders. Eli spun around, spilling a bit of Rebecca's drink.

"Aaron."

"Eli."

"Glad you could make it. I wasn't sure if you were coming."

"Well, I managed to get out of my prior engagements."

"Good. It's been too long since I've seen you."

"Is that her?" Aaron pointed toward the secluded spot near Eli's bookcase. He'd seen Eli whisk Rebecca away there after the dance. Eli's face lit up, gazing at her, and nodded.

"Yes."

"She is beautiful." Aaron admired her for a moment and then returned to Eli, "…and not Jewish." Eli's eyes retreated away from Rebecca and looked at Aaron with harsh sharpening around the edges at the words not Jewish. "Have you told your family yet? No, you couldn't have; they would have killed you. Specifically, your father would have killed you."

Aaron asked, "Do they even know you're dating someone?" Eli relaxed with the worried words from his friend who only meant well, a good friend he had known since University and saw regularly at Synagogue.

"I will tell them. It's complicated. I've been waiting for the right time." Eli bit his lip. "Besides, it doesn't matter what my family wants, what my father wants. I'm the one dating her, not my family."

"Are you sure about that?" he asked, knowing that solid friendship between them protected him from any hard truths. Rebecca looked Eli's way, smiling, washing away all the nuances of unspoken prejudice, shades of differences that seemed to only disappear in this room on this night in this very moment between the two of them, and then she looked away and they all returned. The harshness of reality always returned to him like cancer, knowing it could only be ignored for so long before rupturing. Eli watched Rebecca's gaze over his face and her smile under the moonlight. He knew in this moment with absolute certainty that they were meant to be together and he would let nothing tear them apart.

"Yes, I'm sure," Eli said, patting his good friend on the shoulder, then he walked away to return to his Rebecca. Her arms opened wide to wrap around him and with their embrace, Eli's left foot moved up into the air and their lips pressed together. He handed her a glass of pineapple juice mixed with a touch of rum. When the music slowed down, the table with food and drink became a center for political conversation, everyone taking views and offering their advice. Aaron stood by the table, speaking with his hands.

" The Nazi party is growing at alarming rates. Something has to be done to stop them," Aaron protested. A taller young man in a white sweater and beige slacks joined the topic.

"You're right. Berlin was sterilized of its wild ways. In the twenties, it was one of the most free cities in Europe, and look at it now. It's only a matter of time until they sterilize us all from our indecencies." A blonde with long hair pulled back into a pony tail wrapped her arm around the young man in the white sweater and used her political wits gained from reading the newspaper.

"The papers say they are the largest political party in Germany now." Her voice carried a refined sophistication to it. "They say it as if it's favorable," she ended in dismay.

Rebecca overheard the dialogue and pulled Eli with her towards the table on the other side. She interjected as she poured another glass of juice, "This time next year, Hitler and his party won't be here. It can't be. Everything he stands for, everything he is pushing for is wrong. His ideas strangle the very fabric of what it means to be free, until there is nothing left to breathe," Rebecca said and sipped her juice from its crystal glass.

Eli smiled at her dedicated persuasions.

"I must admit, Rebecca, I hope you're right, for all our sakes," Aaron said, staring at Eli, and his forehead wrinkled with thought.

"What is it?" Eli asked.

"Nothing. It's just there is so much going on with Japan and China and now with our Nazi Germany, the future is starting to look bleak…" Aaron looked at Rebecca, "but don't let me digress down that train of thought and spoil everyone's New Year's Eve. Besides, I haven't met the new lady in Eli's life." Aaron smiled at Rebecca and took her hand to his lips. "I'm Aaron, one of Eli's closest friends." Aaron played with his hands like boxing fists at Eli's chest and then dropped the playful fists to his side.

"I'm Rebecca," she said and slid her fingers through her loosening braid to pull it tight.

"And I see you are on the side of throwing Hitler and his Nazi regime out of Germany. That is a good sign." Aaron smirked in Eli's direction.

"How can anyone be on his side?" Rebecca intensified her expression and in the corners of her mind, she wandered back to her mother.

The young man with the white sweater interjected, "With the stress from the Great Depression and the war that has left Germany in economic ruin, it's no wonder everyone is gripping towards extreme nationalism." He rolled his eyes. "People need something to hold onto in times like these, someone to tell them everything will be alright." Bernard listened and directed his views at the table with Louise standing behind him, "But we can't prejudge the party's abilities. They may make good on their promises and bring Germany to its once splendor."

Aaron darted his eyes at the man. "At what cost?" Aaron didn't ask to receive an answer, but to leave a trace of question in his mind.

The young man with the white sweater kissed the blonde with the ponytail. "Let's not spoil our evening with political talks," he replied and they spun off toward the mock dance floor.

"He's right. We shouldn't weigh down our last night of 1931 with heavy discussion. We should be weighing it down with lots of alcohol," Eli joked and lifted up two more glasses of rum juice for Rebecca and himself to enjoy. Then the two of them twirled off under the dim lights with refined feet bouncing against the wood floors to the sweet sounds of swing music.

Everyone wore sophisticated garb with a hint of frivolity in it. Even the young man with the white sweater brought a tall black hat with him in case the feeling emerged. Big gold butterflies in metallic design embossed Rebecca's shoes, her felicity for the year's end on her feet. Eli's grey tie when swaying and overturning in dance was clearly decorated on the opposite side with silver glitter.

The night filled with more gaiety and delight than deep political discussion, but the mix represented a small paradigm of Germany's existence. It was the last night of an upcoming new year that would hold such pleasure and merriment combined with civil discourse before Hitler's regime changed the face of Germany.

Rebecca grew tired and Eli walked her to her floor. They said goodbye at her front door with a kiss and a hug that told them both they wanted more. Eli's hands caressed Rebecca's back, leaving his tender touch over her shoulders, they both knew then that the moment would be soon. Eli let Rebecca move into her room without following her as he was mannered and didn't want to take advantage; therefore, he found himself wandering the apartment halls inebriated and alone.

Eli swung his feet up the steps, clicking his heels and singing the jazz music he had just left in his room, elated at the relationship blossoming between himself and Rebecca. Losing his way, he walked up two flights of stairs and knocked on a stranger's door. She answered with long red hair and light green eyes and a pale white face, appareled in a white night robe. She looked as if she had missed all the festivities of the New Year's Eve night.

"Yes?" Her tiny voice asked like a baby bird just waking.

"Sorry. I'm looking for my room." Eli stumbled and hit his head on her door.

The redhead held his wobbly form up and asked, either because of politeness or because of earnestness to return to her bed, "What is your room number?"

"104…no, no." Eli thought for a moment, his mind wandering to Rebecca and then back to the question, "room 404."

"You're one floor too high," she said and directed him to the stairs. "You have to go down one floor."

"Thank you." Eli struggled with her name and then realized he didn't know it.

"Betsy."

"Betsy, thank you." The redhead smiled shortly and returned to her room, hiding from the night. Eli pranced down the steps and fiddled with the doors, following the sounds of boisterous noise until he made his way back into his room. The party was half as crowded as when it began and Eli fell to his sofa against the wall with his head on the armrest. Aaron walked over and sat next to him.

"What a night." Eli slurred his words.

"Sounds like all the alcohol is hitting you. Did you get Rebecca safely back to her room?"

"Yes." Eli stared at Aaron with stark concentration like a boy to his father. "Yes, I did."

"She seems like a nice lady."

"She is. She is the most wonderful woman I have ever met in my whole life." Eli exaggerated his words from the unrestraint provided by the rum.

"And your family has no idea about her, the reason you've been missing so many Shabbos at synagogue."

"And you are not going to tell them," Eli defended her, "not until I have spoken with them."

"I promise. This is your dilemma." Aaron patted Eli's leg with his last words.

"And I gladly take it." Eli pounded his chest with one fist over his heart like a gorilla in war and then fell on top of Aaron's lap.

"Why don't you get to bed? I'll take care of the party." Aaron helped Eli to his feet and wobbled with him into his closed bedroom in a familiar wobble the two had participated in at a previous New Year's Eve party.

* * *

When Eli awoke, his room door was closed. Stumbling over his exhausted feet from a long night of showing Rebecca a good time, he made it to the door. He gazed around the living room and saw cleaned tables, the leftover food and drink refrigerated, and his good friend Aaron sprawled out on the sofa. Eli thanked his friend in a whisper, though he still slept, then unrolled the quilt in the corner of the sofa and laid it over Aaron. Aaron shifted his body, rolling his face towards the cushions and hugging the pillow.

Eli remembered today was the first day of the new year and his eyes lit up. He gazed at his floor, knowing Rebecca was just below him, the woman he had his eyes on for several months, the woman he had been enamored with before even speaking with her. Eli walked to his kitchen, planning to make scrambled eggs for himself and Aaron, shuffling pans and pots around to create enough room to cook.

The smell of the eggs flowed into the living room, over the sofa and into Aaron's nostrils. His head lifted from the couch with his eyes still closed and, like a carrot leading a rabbit, he sniffed a few times before opening his eyes and asked, "Are you cooking something up for me? I'm starved."

"It's the least I can do after all the help you gave me last night."

"It wasn't all me. I have to admit, I had help. The political squad swept while I wiped." With the words political squad from Aaron's lips, Eli knew exactly who he meant, the tall blonde in a ponytail and the man with the white sweater. Eli hadn't learned their names, but he knew they were friends of Aaron.

Aaron often referred to the three of them as the political squad because at his office every discussion inevitably led back to the state of the country. His two friends, who dated each other, would huddle around his workroom, impassioned by all the latest news. The three of them enjoyed thinking of themselves as the rebels of the office, the rebels against the growing Nazi party, though in truth, the only rebellion manifested in whispered words and private conversations among them.

Everyone knew the power of the country was shifting like a wave from a storm in the ocean heading towards shore — forceful and sure.

The President of Germany, Paul Von Hindenburg, had a failing mind, and political intrigue plagued the previous year, destroying the young republic Germany tried to develop. Political parties squabbled over issues, never directing a certain course. Disrupted proceedings by the hundred Nazi elected officials in Reichstag left a crippled government. Coupled with the economic crises of the Great Depression and the desperately needed reparations caused by War World I, the country yearned for leadership.

Many people began to believe the Nazi party was this leadership. The party's power grew and tensions increased in Munich. Facing reality, Eli and Aaron both knew a rebellion to the Nazi party would cause problems for them in the city and at their work. So political discord became a whisper, a nuance left in the shadows where few could see its disturbance. Adolf Hitler offered decision and a better future to the six million unemployed and, like a stranger tempting a child with candy if he would get into his car, few could taste its poison while savoring its delectable flavors.

Aaron could taste the flavors of the eggs which sent him walking half asleep to the kitchen, where he took in a giant whiff over the stove. Eli scraped a few eggs onto a plate and handed it to Aaron. The two ate standing up, clad in pajamas in the kitchen. Friday morning grew late, but neither had to report to work because of the New Year holidays.

The Day the Flowers Died

Friday, January 8, 1932

Eli remembered this day well. The detailed flower print of the pale blue dress Rebecca wore stained his mind as she swung around the banister on her porch. Her dress lifted with the currents of the cold wind still trying to separate from winter and grow to spring. The spring flowers on the lawn began to bloom again, reminding them both a new year was born. He remembered this moment more passionately than others because, on this banister under the changing skies of Munich, he realized he loved her.

He walked like a heavenly string lifted him high off the ground. Her baby blue eyes complimented the blue in her dress and the sky. Her hands clutched the metal bars as she played ballerina on her tiptoes and swirled across the porch in her beige thick snow socks. Eli enjoyed watching her spin like a child on her birthday.

She often played like this, but in this moment, a primal hunger saturated him, and only Rebecca could quench it. He grasped her hands mid-spin and spun her such that her face and his touched nose to nose. Rebecca giggled, lifting her hand to cover her laugh and then Eli took her hand and held her cold fingers inside of his warm hands.

"Rebecca?"

Her eyes glistened at her name on his lips. "Yes?"

"I love you," he said succinctly and sure. Nothing now could be more certain than he loved her. In this city and country where finances were failing, culture was crumbling, and government was grappling for decision, his love for her would not waver. He wasn't sure how it happened, how he had fallen in love. He had never loved anyone this deeply. Perhaps it was the way she accepted everything about him, or the way they felt as ease with each other, or perhaps it was the uncommon manner in which she carried herself, courteous, and yet free.

Now his gaze searched her face while his heart waited.

"I love you, too." Her words filled him with a new sensation. He lifted her into his arms and swung her around the porch for all peering eyes below to see. Rebecca tilted her head back, letting her hair catch the wind and then moved her lips to Eli's soft mouth.

The passion from their kiss erupted inside both of them with an instant flutter of their bodies from the public porch into the privacy of Rebecca's apartment. She brushed her cheek over his chin, clad with a hint of stubble. Eli glided her into her room with his hands moving up her legs and under her dress, eyes intense on one another as they fell to the bed like currents on the ocean, crashing into each other.

Into each other's hair, into each other's necks, into each other's lips, into each other's legs, intertwined and lost so that no one could make out where one body ended and the other began until they journeyed like seamen into each other's seas and the sounds of sweetest rapture left their bodies sweating on the sheets. Rebecca, in swoon like fashion, leaned her limp body against Eli's on top of the sheets, legs still interlaced with a sheet tangled between them. They laid there until the sun fell behind the horizon and the Shabbos began. Then in thought, Rebecca rolled on top of Eli and propped her body up with her elbows against his stomach.

"When will I meet your family?" Rebecca implored with more intensity in her eyes than in her voice. "You've met mine." She concluded with a fact as any good lawyer would do. Eli couldn't help but smile at her persistence, enjoying the affection.

"You will, soon. I've told my mama I'm seeing someone and she wants me to invite you to the Pesach, Passover this April at her house. You'll meet everyone there and even have a taste of some good old-fashioned Jewish cooking."

Rebecca bounced up, elated at Eli's words, then leaned over to nibble on his naked naval. He giggled and instinctively pulled back at the tickle before drawing to her.

"Is your family upset you've missed synagogue recently because of me?"

"My father's friends told him I've been neglecting Shabbos and he asked me about it. I was honest with him. I told him I was dating

61

someone and sometimes Friday and Saturday are the only times we have together."

"And he understood?" Rebecca asked. Eli scrunched his face and uttered something slurred between yes and no.

"My mama doesn't understand why the both of us can't just go to synagogue together. I told her it is not something you're accustomed to doing."

"And she understood?"

"And then my father insisted on asking me a rhetorical question involving something to the effect of what kind of Jew works on Shabbos and then I told him."

"You told him?" Rebecca's body tensed, knowing what prisons her own mother had built around her life and knowing Eli's father did much the same.

"I told him, she isn't Jewish, and he just stared at me for a few moments with his mouth ajar and then my mama interrupted and told me to invite you to Passover dinner, that way we all could meet you."

"And then they understood?" Rebecca's hopes lingered with the words repeated.

"And then they all wanted to meet you," Eli said with a higher pitch in his tone and tickled her sides. "My oldest sister seemed most excited about the idea." Rebecca giggled and then the stern expression returned to her face.

"Sounds like an intense conversation."

"It was, but not to fear. Everything will be fine."

"What are their names?" Rebecca asked, "Your sisters names, your mother and father's names?"

"Ah," Eli's eyes grew wide, "Sarah is my oldest sister. Miriam is my youngest sister and Leah is in the middle. My mother's name is Deborah and my father's name is Ezekiel." Rebecca's body shifted off Eli's chest to his side, plopping comfortably onto the thick sheets. Her face lost its pink shade from the friction they shared and her gaze fixed itself on the ceiling. "Are you alright?" Eli tended to her with his fingers raking through her long hair stretched over the sheets such that it gave the illusion of waves on the ocean.

"I'm fine. I'm just trying to digest it all."

"It's really nothing to worry about. They will love you. I know they will. I love you, how could they not?" Eli squished himself close to her and she smiled halfheartedly until he tickled her stomach again and she bellowed out a scream-laugh that could be heard upstairs. The early evening became late evening and the night belonged to only the two of them lying like branches twisted on her bed under the stars of Munich, innocent of the country choking around them.

* * *

Saturday morning newspapers piled up around the city block, waiting to be read by the many still asleep. Eli walked downstairs early in the morning to collect his paper from his mailbox. The news was never something he wanted to read anymore, but he knew ignoring it didn't make it go away and he had to be prepared for whatever came. Eli skimmed the front page, reading the recent politics which make him throw the paper to the bedroom floor.

Adolf Hitler received a telegram from Chancellor Bruening, inviting him to come to Berlin to discuss the possibility of extending Hindenburg's present term. The invitation delighted Hitler.

"What is it, my darling Eli?" She said darling with a smile, trying to console his sudden disturbance of serenity.

"The President of Germany welcomes Hitler's visit; he welcomes the wolf to the flock of sheep."

"What are you talking about?" Rebecca lifted the paper off the floor and read the news. "I heard from my friend at the paper that Hitler told Rudolph Hess he has them in his pocket, because they recognize him as a partner in their negotiations."

"And yet you won't find the press printing that." Eli raised his hands. "They're cowards, all of them. They won't print what's really going on, who the man really is."

"The Nazi's stormtroopers can hurt the press too, people with families. Everyone has to be careful. No one is going to put their head on the chopping block." She rose off the bed and rubbed her hands over his shoulder. "You know how violent the Nazis can get."

"And if no one is willing or strong enough to control them, what will become of the country? Hindenburg invites him into the political arena, the Chancellor sent as messenger." Eli's tone became sharp, serious like she had never seen him.

"Hindenburg is a fair-minded man." Rebecca cuddled Eli in her arms and then turned his face to her own. "Look at me. Hindenburg is not letting Hitler run the show, but he also knows Hitler has many people on his side. Hindenburg has to consider the influence Hitler has. They're just political games. It doesn't mean Hitler wins. We can trust Hindenburg in the presidency. He will protect this country from radical madness."

"But for how much longer?" Eli stood next to Rebecca with his eyes intensifying and his words more certain. "There is already talk of Hitler wanting to run for the Presidency. What if he wins?"

"He won't. He can't. He doesn't have enough support."

"Not yet, but his support grows every day," Eli said. Rebecca saw the weight of the country falling on Eli's shoulders and she threw her hands around his face; her eyes lightened and widened.

"We should go see a movie." Her head nodded and her lips became perky. The color in her skin flushed pink with her enthusiasm.

Eli half smirked and half frowned, "You ought to be a lawyer. You're good with distraction."

"So, that's a yes?"

"What's showing?"

"Two Kinds of Women," she said with a high pitched tone like she wanted to see it. "Scarface," she looked at Eli and shook her head no, "and the Jan Kiepura movie, Das Lied Einer Nacht." With the last movie listed, Rebecca sauntered to the bathtub until Eli chased her and she raced the rest of the way to the tub. Rebecca leapt in first, pulling off her nightgown, and snapping her hands together as if she had won a race. Eli poured in the water, watching it slowly drizzle over her hair, her breasts, her legs and then hopped in with her, sitting with his legs wrapped around her waist. His legs were a fortress around her, keeping their love strong and holding it sturdy against the brutality of the city.

Afterward, they took Eli's car after he insisted on driving and pulled into the parking lot behind the theatre. The short line indicated not many were spending money on movie tickets. Standing in line, down the block they watched a fight break out between two men, one dressed in ripped brown slacks and a dirty white shirt and the other in a business suit. The poor man threw a fist into the other's face, and the business man stumbled back for a moment until repositioning himself and then returned a fist, knocking the poor man in the nose and to the ground.

"What's going on?" Rebecca asked.

"He probably lost his job," Eli said matter-of-factly, and walked to the ticket window.

"That's so sad. He appears so desperate."

"Desperate times." Eli glanced over the movie titles, trying to distract her and himself from the reality around them, "What do you want to see? Scarface?" He raised his brows up and down with the title.

"I'm more of a Two Kinds of Women girl." Rebecca replied and Eli winced.

"How about the Jan Kiepura movie, Das Lied Einer Nacht?" He nudged her shoulder and she smiled at the idea.

"I do love Joseph Schmidt's tenor."

"Settled then." Eli grabbed the tickets at the counter and followed the worn burgundy carpet to the theatre room. A chill ran through the dark room since the heater had been turned off to save money. Eli took off his long, brown coat and wrapped it around Rebecca before they sat. She snuggled with his coat pulled over her long, beige skirt, white blouse and sweater, burrowing her head into his shoulder and neck.

As Joseph Schmidt sung Heute Nact oder nie, Tonight or Never, Rebecca's eyes filled with teardrops rolling down her cheeks and she rubbed her nose. The sounds of his high pitched voice, soft and melodious, saturated the theatre and touched her soul, making her feel like he was in the room with them. Eli forgot the stresses of politics and all the backhanded maneuvering Hitler and his party were guilty of while he sat in his seat, listening to Joseph Schmidt's sweet words to tonight or never.

Heute Nacht oder nie sollst du mir sagen nur das Eine: Ob du mich liebst.

Heute Nacht oder nie will ich dich fragen, ob du deine Liebe mir gibst.

Heute Nacht oder nie will ich für dich allein nur singen bis morgen früh nur die Melodie: Heute Nacht oder nie.

Tonight or never you are to say to me only one: Whether you love me.

Tonight or never I want to ask you whether you give me your love.

Tonight or never I want to sing for you alone to tomorrow morning only the melody:

Tonight or never.

* * *

Next weekend, dark rain clouds filled the Munich weather with gloom and Eli went into work Sunday to review documents for an upcoming court trial. He shuffled papers on his desk, filing them into neat piles, lost in his thoughts until his father walked in.

Ezekiel Levin, tall and muscular, carried himself like a king with a black briefcase in his left hand. The case involved a claim made by a customer directed at a dry cleaning shop around the corner. The customer insisted the shop owner deceived him in how much he was owed for cleaning the suit. The client claimed the shop owner charged him twice the amount of his other customers.

The client was also a friend of the family and, justly, his father took the case, though he knew the difficulty in proving it in court, especially now that Hitler had gained so much fervor behind his ideas and party. No one wanted to see a Jew getting more money, but his father insisted on doing what he knew was right and he believed the dry cleaner swindled his client.

"Eli, do you have the receipts ready?"

Eli bundled the files into his folder and handed them to Ezekiel. "Do you think we have enough to get his money back?"

"Even if we do, will it be enough?" Ezekiel said, always with realism in his words. "We will put up a good fight." He took the folder out of his son's hands and placed it into his briefcase. Eli followed his father through the halls of his office, halls his father helped to build himself in renovations. They went to Ezekiel's office where he retrieved a file from his desk and then the two of them walked to an exit to the parking lot.

"Let me run this to the court office for you. I'll hand it to Ekkehard and then we can argue the case Monday morning," Eli offered. His father nodded, pensive in thought.

"I'll wait here for you and then we'll head home." Home to Ezekiel meant the outskirts of Munich, a large house built for a large family, now empty of their son. Home to Eli meant the apartment building in central Munich where he and Rebecca shared many Friday and Saturday nights.

Eli drove with cautious speed through the intersections and roads until approaching the courthouse, then parked behind the building. He raced up the steps and handed the file to Ekkehard, the clerk who worked for Ezekiel Levin, responsible for organizing all the paperwork for each case of the Levin Law Offices. The clerk ensured all parties had received their disclosed information before proceedings.

But Monday morning found the office in shambles, with everyone running to and fro and a few shouting, trying to find Eli's father. Eli grabbed the arm of Kevin, a tall, light haired older fellow who wore glasses.

"What's going on?"

"The papers you gave to the clerk yesterday never found their way into the hands of the defendants, and now the papers are missing. We've been searching everywhere trying to find them."

"But I gave them to Ekkehard yesterday evening before seven," Eli said in defense.

"He claims to have never gotten them," Kevin insisted and, for a moment, Eli doubted himself until his father surprised him from behind and patted him on the shoulder.

"I saw my son drive off to the courthouse myself. The son of a bitch Ekkehard lost them!" His father's stern words took Eli aback, since most of his life he never heard his father swear. The sturdy and strong man never lost his temper. "I'd venture to bet he lost them deliberately," Ezekiel demanded, but the halls were silent of supporters, never uttering the subtle ways the injustices of the Nazi party seeped into their lives. "Bought off at a minuscule price, no doubt!"

Eli saw no way to win the court case now, not without the receipts. They had a slim chance with the information, because of so few fair judges left from political and social pressures. But now, without the evidence, there was no ounce of hope at winning and Eli knew that itched inside every vein of his father.

The Day the Flowers Died

"We'll get them next time, Papa," Eli said, knowing that was unlikely, too.

SUNDAY, FEBRUARY 14, 1932

Valentine's Day was a big day for Eli. He wanted to do something special for Rebecca and met her early Sunday morning to tell her she would have to let him blindfold her. She did of course, and Eli guided her down the steps to his car and then drove her to an unknown location. He walked with her over soft grass until pausing and sliding off the blindfold. A wood picnic table under a large cascading tree sat next to a blue green lake. Two lit candles sat in the middle of the worn wood table with two plates of delicacies.

Rebecca leapt into the air, eager to enjoy the Valentine meal with the man she loved. Two long elegant glasses stood next to each plate, filled to the brim with white champagne. Rebecca in gaiety scuttled to the decorated table and smelled the plate of food as she sat. She laid her Dresden Wire Mesh handbag on the chair beside her. The soft painted pink petals and pale green leaves decorating the bag were a perfect compliment to the nature encompassing them. The late winter chills in the wind pervaded the park and tossed Rebecca's long hair.

"This looks lovely." She smiled subtly and Eli returned her gaze.

"A plate of your assorted favorite foods," Eli pointed showing her each one. "Smoked duck, a pocket of caviar, baked carrots, and sautéed pears." With each named food, Rebecca's smile grew wider, realizing Eli knew her so well. Rebecca savored the duck and then picked up a spoonful of carrots. She nibbled a pinch of caviar and then sipped her white champagne.

"Did you cook all of this?"

"I spent all Friday night a slave in the kitchen." Eli smirked.

"You told me you had to work late."

"And I did," he joked. After the meal, Eli pulled up two paper bags and handed one to Rebecca.

"Another surprise?" Rebecca's warm gaze fell over Eli's face like shadows on the sidewalk.

"Open it," he said and Rebecca didn't resist. She pulled out a pair of pink ice skates with matching laces. Holding the skates beside her foot, she danced on the grass in spins. "Looks like they will fit." Eli stared at her. "Thank you Eli. The color is beautiful."

"We have a lovely frozen lake." Eli grinned, "a picnic, and a wonderful day to ourselves. What more could two people want for?" Eli persuaded. Rebecca's loud guffaw was coupled by her tousled hair. Staring at her, she felt Eli wanting something."

"What?"

"Please, try on the skates." Eli encouraged.

"Now?"

"Just a moment. We can test them out on the ice near the shoreline. I will hold you hand."

"But..."

"Don't worry. I will hold you." Eli winked.

"Alright." After Rebecca pulled her two skates over her feet, they walked, hand in hand, with Eli doing most of the balancing, to the frozen lake.

Her honey touched brown hair glistened under the late winter sun and the dew from the grass also hung in the sky on her nose. Eli brushed the loose strands off her cheeks and collar before lowering his lips to her supple neck. Her lake blue eyes radiated under the blue sky and Eli's contrasting deep brown eyes sat like steady stones.

Holding her hand steady, Rebecca pushed off the shoreline onto the hard ice. The two separate bodies twined so close became like one, at least to a distant observer.

"Stay near the edge. We don't want any accidents." Eli stated.

"Are you sure this is safe?" Rebecca questioned with furrowing brows as she stared at her feet over the ice.

"I used to come here with Papa as a boy. The ice is hard. Just don't leave my hands."

"I won't." Rebecca giggled in a smile, thinking she would be a silly girl indeed if she broke hands with the one man holding her up securely.

"I love the weather this time of year," Eli whispered and she could only smile, closing her eyes against the soft breeze. Rebecca pushed with Eli at her side and she almost slipped when she tried to turn around, but Eli caught her. Stumbling in his grip, he grinned and she gritted her teeth, but soon she stood and smiled.

Stepping off the ice and onto the grass, Eli pulled her up spun her into his arms, even the weight of skates could not keep him from her. Carrying her to the picnic table, she sat to pull off her skates. Then, they lay on a quilt Eli straightened out over the grass near the picnic table. Letting the cool sky fall over them like a blanket, they rested in each other's arms, their toes touching.

In this quiet moment, the only disturbance between them was of past words of politics reminding them that the country and the world were changing.

"Do you really think Hindenburg won't remain president for much longer?" Rebecca inquired.

"Elections are coming up. Anything is possible." Eli glanced away at the sun before returning his gaze. "Hindenburg is the favorite, but he's getting old and his mind is not what it used to be. If Hitler runs this year, who knows what will happen. He makes promises the people want to hear and, despite his party's violence and radical ideas, the people want bread on their tables." Eli kissed her lips. "But we can hope." The morning trickled into late afternoon and they headed back to their apartment building.

* * *

Monday morning, Eli read over briefs and statements that needed to be reviewed for court in the afternoon. Aaron burst into the office with a newspaper swaying in his hands.

"Did you read the morning paper yet?" Aaron's voice sounded frustrated and his movements agitated. He sprawled the paper over the mahogany desk in front of Eli. "President Hindenburg reluctantly agrees to run again, announcing his candidacy for re-election."

"That is a good thing."

"I'm not finished." Aaron ran his finger across the next line in the paper, "Hitler decided to oppose him and run for the presidency himself." Eli sunk in his chair, remembering Rebecca's words, "do you really think Hindenburg won't be president much longer?" It wasn't set and Hindenburg had a stronger following than Hitler, but it was one more step forward for the Nazi party.

"Why aren't you in your office next door?" Eli asked.

"Not very busy for me these days." Aaron's lip curled. "My colleagues, Cynthia and Robert from the party, have no trouble finding new clients. I, on the other hand, am having a hard time holding on to my old ones."

"Sorry," Eli said in a soft voice, both of them knowing the reason wasn't that he was a bad lawyer, but that he looked too Jewish.

Aaron ruffled his fingers through his dark curly hair. "You're lucky. You get to work with your father. He makes sure you acquire clients."

"Even our business has lessened this year. The Nazis are first-rate at spreading propaganda." Eli glanced over the newspaper again, reading the quotes enclosed: "Freedom and Bread," was printed underneath Hitler's picture as his personal slogan to perpetuate his campaign.

"Freedom and bread! How memorable!" Aaron reacted in disgust.

"Hitler has a monster of a campaign and Hindenburg is essentially resting on his reputation as former president."

"Hitler won't win," Robert said, squeezing through the opened crack in the door. Aaron and Eli both jerked their heads up at Robert. "He won't have enough supporters and he knows it. This is just a ploy to gain more Nazi sympathy and followers." Robert closed the door behind him.

Aaron's eyes sharpened in the corners, "And it's working. His influence has already reached into our law offices. What's next, synagogues?"

"I don't know," Robert said with sincerity, "but he has another speech scheduled in Berlin today and there's a Nazi rally downtown."

Robert handed a Nazi pamphlet to Eli, who stood to take it. "This was handed to me this morning on my way to work." The pamphlet read: The Sensationalist Newspapers Lie! Biased and racial slurs filled the pages, propitiating a Nazi world view. Eli clutched it in his hands, then crumbled it, thudding heavily onto his seat.

The work day was long as all days were without Rebecca at his side, but this day was worse, because Eli could see the grip of the Nazi party tightening like a rope around the neck of the country he grew up in, of the country he once loved. Eli walked to his old Audi and drove home for the day, seeing plastered over the city walls posters of Hitler and his Nazi campaign.

Some announced sixteen simultaneous mass meetings in Berlin on the problem of unemployment, 5,600,000 demand work, and some stated:

"Germans! Give your answer to the System! Elect Hitler! Everyone knew this system meant a pejorative Nazi term for the Weimar Republic, blamed for the problems the country faced.

Other posters came more to the point of the problem, to the very core of Germany's economic collapse, stating, "The Jews are our misfortune," after the meeting by Julius Streicher, a leading Nazi who stood by the displayed words during his speech. Posters plastered with Jewish and African derogatory comments became more frequent and more widely accepted. Eli slid behind the wheel of his car, tugging on his pale grey tie with sparkle on its opposite side which reminded him of Rebecca on New Year's Eve.

He drove over the roads he grew up on as a child, riding his bicycle and falling from it for the first time, over the roads he walked to school on, over the roads he had his first kiss. When he parked his Audi and plodded to his apartment building, he grabbed his chest at pains burning inside, though no such physical sensation was there, before opening the front metallic door with its broken latch.

* * *

Rebecca spent the first half of her day at University, preparing to end her courses in March and pick up her Bachelor's of Science diploma. She could taste the thrill of completion in her mouth. It took her longer than four years, but she was proud of her accomplishment.

The second half of the day, she cleaned up spills and served food at the local diner, offering everyone a smile, even those who annoyed her. She needed the money to spend on food, clothes, and things she liked to do. Her mother pulled the strings of her father, like a jockey pulls a horse, when he offered to pay for college to make sure the extras were not in the deal. Her mother used this tight fist on the money to try to get her daughter back, to live home with her again, as all high class daughters did. But Rebecca would not have it that way. She wanted to pave her own way out of her mother's grip. Yet she never thought about how much her mother tried to control her life as she served at the diner. She thought about how much freedom she had because of that job, that university, and that life with Eli in Munich.

She placed food onto tables throughout the afternoon rush, picking up tips and putting all the coins inside her small apron pocket unraveling around the seams. Toward the end of the rush, she plodded over to one of the two tables left. A blonde older woman with wide blue eyes had her hair pinned up tightly like a honeycomb. Her companion, a thirty-something man, also had structured blond hair, blue eyes and a square frame from his shoulders to his feet. She overheard their conversation and leaned in to listen.

"This place is crawling with Jews. I've seen German girls walk hand in hand with them. Disgusting. This is what's wrong with our youth today. They're being corrupted," the blonde woman said as sure as day that she was right and sat haughtily in her seat.

Her companion didn't disagree and even encouraged her thinking, a thinking he also shared. His stiff movements and rigid posture reminded Rebecca of the Nazi men. Her ear had pulled itself in their direction and, before they noticed, she yanked herself back to her job, but not before overhearing his comments.

"Soon, we won't have to worry about them anymore. We've got plans."

Rebecca slipped away, wondering about his statement and if it had anything to do with the stormtroopers terrorizing the cities. In this moment, she felt fear for Eli and herself for the first time. She slid her hands into her apron pockets and felt the coins she had earned for the day.

"Everyone needs to be served, Rebecca, even those you don't like."

He knew Rebecca was an open minded girl, a girl whose sentiments swayed as freely in the wind as the flowers in spring, and he knew she was a principled young lady brought up by strict parents. He'd never seen the young man she dated, but knew of her mother's disapproval. But none of this mattered as he shoved Rebecca forward. It didn't matter if the customers' values vehemently differed from her own or if she desperately didn't want to do this, because they were only customers and Rebecca only a waitress.

Rebecca bit her lip and almost curtsied out of habitual nervous politeness at the customers at the table, the customers who repulsed every bone in her body. She took their order and served their food without so much as forgetting her smile, an outstretched smile which she learned from her mother and reserved for them.

At home in her quiet room, the thoughts of the unpleasant, overheard conversation weighed heavily on her and then her phone rang. She pranced over to it, happy for the interruption, believing it to be Eli.

She answered the phone with an enthusiastic hello until the speaker at the other end asked, "Is this my daughter, Rebecca?"

The roughness in the voice jolted her back to the earlier unpleasant conversation. "Yes, of course, Mutti. This is Rebecca. Who else would it be?"

"You sound different." Her mother paused and then continued, "I was calling to see how you were doing."

"I'm fine. I'm doing well. I just got back from work."

"Work." Rebecca could feel her mother's glinting eyes. "You know you wouldn't have to work if you just stayed home to study at University."

"Mutti, we've been through this too many times. I'm not going to do this with you again." Rebecca's voice was worn with arguments between them and then her voice soothed, "Besides, I've almost completed my diploma so you won't be able to complain about it much longer."

"Your diploma? That's fabulous, dear. Has it been four years already? It feels like just yesterday you were packing up your luggage and leaving your mutti in tears."

"You are so dramatic, Mama." Rebecca rolled her eyes.

"So when am I going to see you?"

"I was just up for Christmas."

"Over a month ago and besides, you didn't stay long."

"Can you blame me?"

"Yes, I can. We bought you a new car and you show us your appreciation by leaving on Christmas day."

"Dad bought me the car, and you kept pushing the issue with Eli. I told you I didn't want to talk about it on Christmas of all days."

"But I am your mutti and I worry about you. You see everything that's going on with the posters and pamphlets. Hindenburg can only do so much to keep this country under control, and there are many supporters of the Nazi party. I don't want you getting hurt."

"Just admit this is about you. This is about you not wanting me to date Eli because of your own prejudices." Rebecca's nostrils flared.

"This doesn't have to do with me, Rebecca. There is so much you don't understand because you're so young." She paused and then continued, "He could change your life forever, your reputation, your hopes for settling down with a fine German gentleman."

"These aren't my hopes, Mutti; they're yours."

"And they should be yours, too. I forbid you to see him." Deseire held her tongue after her strong statement and Rebecca hesitated to answer at first, surprised her mother had actually said, "forbid."

"You can't forbid me, Mama. I'm not a little girl anymore. I make my own choices."

"Just promise me you won't do anything rash with him." Deseire's voice softened, soothed and Rebecca knew what rash meant to her mother: intimate, pregnant, married, anything that couldn't be undone.

Rebecca knew her mother was too late with the first forbiddance and she was exhausted at what else to say to her.

"Goodbye, Mutti." Rebecca clicked the phone down as the white cord tangled. She plopped onto her soft sofa with a weary sigh from a long day and closed her eyes to sleep.

SATURDAY, MARCH 19, 1932

Missing her the past few weekends because of a stressful office atmosphere, Eli took it upon himself to invite Rebecca for tea at his place Saturday morning,. He'd tried to make up for the loss in the office since Ekkehard's betrayal concerning the dry cleaning receipts. It didn't sting Eli personally for he didn't know Ekkehard very well, but it was a betrayal to an office he had worked at for more than five years, a betrayal to his father.

Ezekiel and Eli vowed to never allow something like that to ever happen again. Over the past few weeks, Eli had to do twice the amount of his usual work, his own and the clerk's duties, since Ekkehard had been asked to leave and they didn't trust hiring another man.

Since Valentines was the last day Rebecca had seen Eli, it took very little encouraging on Eli's part to arouse her interest. Rebecca yearned to see Eli: touch his skin, hold him, lay her hands in his, caress his soft lips with hers. She found the more she didn't see him, the more she dreamt of him while she walked to her classes at University and while she served food at the diner and while she slept.

She had grown accustomed to his dark hair brushing up against hers on the sofa or in the bed. She had missed his tender voice calling her name. So, when Eli had phoned Saturday morning to invite her to tea at his room, she skipped from her sofa and dashed up the stairs.

When Eli opened the door at her soft knocking, their eyes met and all the feelings emerged that they felt on the porch the day they first made love, intensified from a lack of satisfying it. Rebecca's body burned, longing for his touch and Eli's eyes glazed over her as his fingers played with her hair and neck. Before Rebecca could address her sensual desires, Eli reached out for her hand and escorted her to his small table with two teacups on top of it.

He had a lot on his mind, yet somehow from his eyes falling on her, all the thoughts that preoccupied him disappeared. Social anxieties or political nuances no longer filled the space between them. This space filled with her smell, an expensive perfume, and the air she breathed, the same air that filled his lungs. In this space with her, the betrayal of Ekkehard and the loss of the case, the woes of a growing Nazi party and the propaganda plastered on the walls vanished. This space held only him and her and their love, pulling them like magnets unable to resist its dangerous polarity.

As Eli watched her sip her orange flavored tea, he reached across the minuscule wood table which pressed against his chest and pulled her free hand to his lips. Rebecca put the teacup down, wrapped her other hand around his and then touched his lips. He held her hand there for moments. Fingers interlocked, she tickled his leg from underneath with her lifted toes like feathers brushing against bare skin. Control diminished and Eli leapt, tossing himself around the table and sweeping her into his arms.

His hands glided up her arms covered in white lace and then held her face. Impassioned, her body fell into his and both of them fell onto the hard wood, pushing and pulling the spaces between them. Clothes ripped, hair pulled, chests became bare, sweat fell from their bodies. With heavy breathing and legs sturdy, he lifted her up over himself and she wrapped her legs around his waist. He carried her into his bedroom, into the quiet space that held them. All the insecurities which Eli buried deep within a hardened confidence lifted and all the words spoken from Rebecca's mother fell from her ears unattended and onto the wood floor.

Rebecca awoke with Eli next to her, lying on his large sized bed and beige white sheets. Pillows cushioned Eli's face and his body sprawled out with his arm over her. She slipped out from under him, tiptoeing into the next room and grabbed her lace blouse and skirt on the small wood table to cover herself. The sun had not yet risen, leaving the sky still dark with heavy blues and grays. Rebecca poured water into his kettle and boiled tea. While the kettle warmed, she tiptoed back into his room and washed in the bath. While she relaxed in the orange scented water, she closed her eyes and let the flavored water soak and soften her skin. The kettle sung toooot and Rebecca opened her eyes. Eli leapt up from the bed, alarmed.

"It's just the kettle. I'm boiling tea." Rebecca meandered out of the bathroom with a towel wrapped around her, her wet feet leaving prints on the wooden floors. Pulling the kettle off the stove, she poured them both a cup and dropped a piece of lemon into Eli's, knowing that was how he liked it. Eli kissed her shoulders, then lifted his tea from the counter and sipped it with his navy blue robe hanging over his bare body.

Rebecca returned to her bath, leaving her tea to cool. She closed her eyes again as she soaked in the tub with the water tingling her feet. Eli sipped a few times from his cup before going to the bath to join her. He hung his robe on the door and slid in softly, not wanting to disturb her serenity. They laid twine for several minutes until the knock at the door startled Eli for a second time this morning and with a disgruntled groan, he slid out of the tub and put on a crisp white button shirt with an ironed collar, pulled up his black slacks with two black straps over his shoulders, and hobbled to the door. He swung it open and saw Aaron on the other side with puffy, blue lips and his nose scraped and bloody.

"What happened?" Eli's stunned reaction left him staring at Aaron.

Aaron's short build stammered in with a limp.

"I threw a punch at a bully in a Nazi uniform. He was pinning up posters over the walls of our building, declaring how the Jews are our misfortune." He wiped his nose with a checkered napkin folded in his pocket. "We got into a scuffle."

"What were you doing at the office Sunday morning? I thought your offices closed Sunday?" Eli walked to the kitchen, searching for a towel and ice.

"They are." He rubbed his lip. "But then they decided I should be doing more work for them. They told me I wasn't pulling my own weight, all the clients preferred other lawyers." He waved his hands. "They said if I wanted to stay on the payroll, I would have to come in Sundays and make up for hours I wasn't working during the week."

Eli ran the white towel under the sink's water and then enclosed ice inside of it. "Here, put this on your lips and nose to help with swelling."

"As if I don't do enough during the week; I have my hands filled with files and papers other lawyers want me to handle."

Rebecca heard bits of the irritable conversation from inside the tub and slipped on her white lace blouse and beige skirt that swayed just below the knees. She towel dried her hair and ambled into the living area.

"Aaron, what a surprise to see you so early."

"Sorry for the intrusion." Aaron's eyes glanced at Rebecca and then back at Eli, comprehending what exactly he has just intruded upon.

"It's good to see you," Rebecca said, sympathetic to his puffy lip and blood stained nose. She placed her hand over the towel filled with ice and helped Aaron tend to his wounds like a mother.

"Are you heading back to work?" Eli asked, sitting down on the wooden stool near the kitchen table. Aaron plopped down on the sofa across from Eli. Rebecca returned to her tea, cold now, sipping it in the kitchen area.

"I don't know if I'm invited back to work, frankly," Aaron said and Eli's brows wrinkled.

"What exactly happened?"

Aaron lowered the towel of ice to his leg. "I was walking to the office and saw the Nazi, no older than twenty, putting derogatory posters on the walls of the office and so I told him he would have to take them down." Aaron scratched his head. "He glared up at me and said, "Don't tell me what to do Jew boy," smirked and finished posting it." Rebecca walked into the living area and sat at the other wooden stool on the other side of the table.

"And you hit him?" Eli interjected.

"No. I took a deep breath and then ask him again to stop or I would have to take them down myself." Rebecca tightened her hands around her teacup. "He stood up, taller than me, mind you I'm not that tall, and he pushed me backward with both arms."

Aaron lifted the towel of ice back up to his nose. His words muffled under the towel as he finished, "I stumbled back and threw a punch, missing, and then he hit my nose." Aaron laid the towel on his leg and used his hands to exaggerate the action. "I threw another punch, hitting his cheek and then he hit me on my mouth before my boss came out, pulling me away. He told me to go home."

"He didn't fire you?"

"He told me to not come in Monday. He said I've been causing too many problems."

Rebecca's teacup cracked when she dropped it on the table.

"He can't fire you for fighting outside the office," Eli insisted.

"He did."

"We can take it to court," Eli persisted.

"And what? You know I'm not going to win and even if I do, then what? Do I spend the rest of my time at the office handling the jobs no one wants to take?" Eli looked down and then back up at Aaron who was nursing his wounds with the ice filled towel. He knew his friend was right.

A chill migrated up Rebecca's spine as she thought about Eli and his work. The thought that Eli worked for his own father gave her reassurance that he would have a stable income, but then nothing was really certain anymore and worry began to consume her.

"I'm going to get the morning paper for you." Aaron put his towel down and headed toward the door. "It's the least I can do, barging in unannounced." He raced down the steps and on the first floor grabbed the folded newspaper from Eli's mailbox. He swung open the front door of the apartment building, catching his grey spring coat on the broken latch, spending a few minutes trying to untangle himself.

The morning sky, cloudless and lucid, was one of the clearest days that spring. He took in a deep breath and then returned upstairs. He didn't look at the paper, but out of the exposed corner he could make out the words, Nazis wave of the future? Eli left the door open for Aaron. The race up the stairs left Aaron's fuller figure panting. He dropped the paper on the wood table next to Eli.

"Read the headline," Aaron suggested with cynicism.

"I try to avoid the papers as much as I can nowadays, unless I feel like beginning my day depressed," Eli joked.

"That explains why the paper is dated March 13th." Aaron rolled his eyes at Eli and opened the paper himself.

"Well, what does it say?" Rebecca inquired with her hair tied up over her head and her clothes neatly tightened around her frame.

Aaron read audibly, but with melancholy in his tone.

"In the presidential election held on March 13, 1932, Hitler received over eleven million votes (11,339,446) or 30% of the total. Hindenburg received 18,651,497 votes or 49%."

"So Hitler lost," Rebecca said with gaiety, "Why do you look so somber?" Her eyes fluttered in Aaron's direction, who shook his head and Eli responded for him.

"This isn't a loss for the Nazi party. They gained millions of supporters. He's just twenty percent away from Hindenburg."

"Can you blame the public?" Aaron spoke with his hands again, agitated, "With six million unemployed, chaos in Berlin, starvation, ruin, and threat of Marxism, this country has a very uncertain future and Hitler makes the future sound possible." Rebecca bit her lip.

* * *

Graduation for Rebecca fell on the last Friday of the month. Eli took off work and drove her to the university in his Audi so that Rebecca would not have to worry about driving. The lawn extended from the parking lot to every main building. Sidewalks paved in red brick wound throughout the campus. The university filled with the graduating class and their families. Eli walked with Rebecca hand in hand up to the main hall where the ceremony would be held and where she would meet her parents.

Upon opening the door, in the distance Eli could see Ralph in a navy colored suit and a white button shirt tucked in under a navy suit jacket. His stomach pushed outward, stretching the shirt and the jacket. He held a bouquet of flowers and sat down and then Eli lost sight of him.

"Do you see them? Are they here yet?" Rebecca asked.

"Your father is ahead. I just saw him sit down." Benches outlined the hall in a square fashion where the majority of parents and waiting graduates sat. Eli pointed with his forefinger, directing Rebecca to her family. Deseire saw the two of them approach and cordially stood with her lean, tall figure in a lengthy beige gown. A gold plastic flower hung on her left shoulder clipped onto the dress.

"Eli." Deseire's smile was a farce, warm, wide and manipulated. She shook his hand and then walked to her daughter. Ralph stood, tightening the loose button on his jacket, attempting to fit into a size smaller than he needed, and shook Eli's hand with a firm grip.

"Have a seat, Eli." Ralph patted the seat next to him and Eli sat down, feeling welcomed. Rebecca noticed in the corner of her eyes Eli sitting next to her father. She didn't want to sit next to her mother, so while Deseire asked how her week had been, Rebecca answered, rotating her body so that the closest seat to her was no longer next to her mother, but next to Eli.

"It's been a good week, very busy with work and preparing for graduation, but the day is finally here." Rebecca blushed a peach color of excitement and looked behind her casually, sitting next to Eli as if she had not planned her seating at all.

"These are for you." Ralph showed the bouquet of flowers to his daughter. "Do you wait here or do you have to sit in the middle?" Ralph set the flowers in Eli's lap and pointed to the center of the hall where chairs lined up row after row. Eli held the flowers, though they were laid upon his lap like one would hand a coat to a servant.

"I have to wait for my department to be called. There are many graduates today."

"We'll be looking out for you," Ralph said, smiling at his daughter and Rebecca smiled wide, hiding her mouth with her hand. They called each department one by one: Mathematics, English, Sciences, Nursing, etc and upon the announcement, the graduates belonging to the department moved to sit in the center of the hall. Rebecca wore a long black robe signifying she was graduating.

Eli adjusted her graduation cap on her head and played with the tassel. Rebecca swatted his fingers and straightened her posture. Eli rested his hands in his lap, unsure of how much humor to display upon graduating and in front of her parents. The family waited patiently until Rebecca's department was announced and then Rebecca stood along with her family and made her way to the center chairs.

She glanced backward and locked eyes with Eli, then she darted her head around with a childlike grin as if she had just stolen a cookie from the jar. It felt like forever to Rebecca, waiting for her name to be called, for the last years to be summed up into one single document. But to Eli the moment was abrupt.

While Rebecca sat in silence, Eli sat in whispers and questioning eyes of young and old that peered his way, wondering why he was sitting with the Baum family. Even Deseire at times, though accustomed to social decorum, appeared uneasy. Eli noticed all of this and began to feel uncomfortable, lost in his thoughts of the shades of prejudice.

When the announcer said Ms. Rebecca Baum, the sound drew him out of the world swallowing him and back into Rebecca's graduation. To him, it seemed to have happened suddenly.

He watched with an unspoken pride only noticed by the keenest of observers as Rebecca marched up to take her diploma like a winning horse paraded around the track. This paper granted sure freedom from the grips of her mother and she took it from the professor with eagerness and stillness. Rebecca was not anxious about the future like many of her graduating class.

She knew what she wanted and she was now free to do it, because she no longer had to rely on the money her parents provided with strings attached to accomplish her goals. She now had the right to procure a nursing position and earn her own wages, wages that would guarantee she could stand on her own feet.

Returning to her family, she could see Mr. Schwartvitz approaching Deseire. He had been a long time family friend of the Baum's and Deseire had thought at one time that Rebecca and his eldest son would make a lovely couple. Deseire noticed Mr. Schwartvitz waving in the distance, and her refined demeanor grew self conscious, her hands not as steady, her feet not as firm. But her rehearsed smile spread easily up to her flushed cheeks.

"Mrs. Deseire Baum." The gentleman took her wedded hand into his, kissing it once and returning it. "It's a pleasure seeing you here."

Ralph stood, nodding to Mr. Schwartvitz and Eli stood next to Ralph, ready to give his timely greeting, but Mr. Schwartvitz asked a few more questions of Deseire. "Is your daughter graduating today?"

"Yes, she is coming now." Deseire gestured in the direction of her daughter. Mr. Schwartvitz looked up and smiled at the sight of her.

"And your son," Deseire's intonation flared, "he is here today also?"

"Yes, graduating with the business department. He was chatting with his peers somewhere." He looked away, searching with his eyes.

Rebecca stepped close to her mother with her diploma in her hands. "Hello, Mr. Schwartvitz." Rebecca reached her hand out to his and held it. "I guess Sean is graduating today?" She used her other hand to pat the top of his and then released both, returning them to her side.

"Yes, yes." He looked around the room again. "He is somewhere," he said with a deep chuckle. Rebecca glared at her mother. Deseire returned the glare, an expression she had gotten to know well, one that meant don't embarrass me.

"I've forgotten my manners," Deseire uttered and gestured to Eli. "This is Rebecca's friend from Munich." She said it as if nothing more could be possible. Mr. Schwartvitz shook Eli's hand. "They live in the same apartment building." Her last sentence hinted of an apology, an explanation of how they could possibly be acquainted. At that moment Eli, being a lawyer trained to recognize every detail, realized Rebecca's mother was ashamed of him.

Sensing Eli's insecurity, Rebecca left her mother's side and joined him, holding his hand and admiring his eyes in an overt fashion. Mr. Schwartvitz cleared his throat, noticing the embraced hands, and pardoned himself to look for his son. When Rebecca, Eli and her parents headed toward the exit, Deseire pulled her aside in a quiet corner. Deseire's upper lip curled and her grip on Rebecca's arm became firm.

"How could you embarrass me like that in front of Mr. Schwartvitz?" she asked, saying his name with great weight, the kind of weight that comes from doing business with a long time friend in the neighborhood, the kind of weight that worries about reputation.

"Embarrass you. You blatantly disregard Eli's feelings, my feelings. You couldn't even muster the courage to admit to our friend that Eli and I are involved. Did you even for once think about how you made Eli feel?" Rebecca's whisper sounded gritty and her arms pushed Deseire away, creating a clear space between them.

"Everything is about you, always you." Deseire kept her whisper balanced between quietness and firmness, a whisper she had had much practice with in high society. "You are a part of this family and what you do reflects on us. It isn't just your life which is affected by your actions." Deseire gripped her daughter's wrist again, moving in close to her, close enough to hide the grip. "I won't have it! I won't let you prance around with that…boy of yours. You are breaking it off."

Rebecca tore her arm away from her mother and stomped out of the hall with her mother following closely behind. Ralph and Eli stood together, waiting for them to return. Rebecca abruptly kissed her father on the cheek, whispering goodbye. With her mother's intense glare, she grabbed Eli's hand in rebellious frustration. Eli saw Rebecca's haste to depart and waved, saying, "It was nice to see you both again." Rebecca whisked Eli away from her parents and towards his blue car.

WEDNESDAY, APRIL 20, 1932

Normally Rebecca had classes to ready for in the early morning, but after graduation, she found herself sleeping in since her diner shift began in the afternoon. Today, though, she set her alarm for the first sign of the sun and woke up feeling nervous, knowing Eli and his family had a big day planned. She had never been to a Seder or Pesach, Passover and she threw her clothes one item at a time over her bed, weeding through everything to find the right first impression. Eli had told her it was a feast his mama prepared for every year weeks in advance, and his entire direct family would most certainly attend. Other family members would be there, too, which added to the anxiety.

Rebecca asked for this day off of work after Eli told her the date, the twentieth of April. Eli warned her they had already begun some of the rituals on the nineteenth, two days before the official Passover on the twenty first, but she would only be dining for the Seder. Eli, knowing the Hebrew celebrations were new to her, and after much deliberating with his father, decided that would be best. Eli did not go into the discussed details, but his enthusiasm about her arriving to dine with them made Rebecca elated as well.

She pulled a lengthy blue flowery dress up to her and fixed a stare into the bathroom mirror. The minuscule mirror, not large enough to capture her full figure, forced her to look at her shape in pieces, the upper neck line and shoulders and then, standing on her tub, the dress covering her legs and ankles. Dissatisfied with the blue color, she tossed it over the rising pile on her bed.

Eli told her to wear something conservative and Rebecca knew exactly what he meant. Years of practice, living with her socially conscious, conventional mother taught her that. Rebecca had not even learned of a flapper dress until well into her twenties. While other young ladies freed themselves from the constraints of the older generation in the twenties with dazzling, sexy dresses celebrating cleavage and makeup that used to be considered a sure sign of prostitution, Rebecca's parents coddled her with cultural courtesies and propriety. She had mixed feelings about that; on the one hand, she considered it a luxury to have been brought up with money, servants, cooks, and a large home and, on the other hand, she missed out on many of the reckless teenage experiences of her less fortunate friends in Munich and University.

Rebecca knew reds and yellows were too loud and short dresses were not conservative enough. She wanted to be a part of Eli's life and this meant dressing the part for his family. A flustered emotion arose as she chose between two dresses still in her closet. A long sleeved, dark forest green outfit covered the ankles, and white flower embroidery decorated the collar and sleeves.

The other, a light bark brown dress whose sleeves broke right after the elbow in a white lace, also hid the ankles. A crisp white belt accompanied the garment. Rebecca pulled out the bark brown dress, a pair of gold earrings and her brown heels.

Eli wouldn't pick her up until late afternoon, giving them time to arrive at his parents' house before sundown, but Rebecca did not want to rush her appearance and desired to make sure of every detail before he arrived.

An hour before sundown, Eli rushed down to her room and knocked. Rebecca opened the heavy door with a delighted, nervous smile.

Eli had grown to know her smiles. She had a wide eyed smile that meant surprise. Her short stretched lip meant she was trying hard to be courteous. She had a hand covered smile when she felt elated, but remembered her cordial upbringing, and she had this smile where her lips were crooked in their corners. He knew she was anxious about meeting his family and, despite all his reassurances, he knew she still felt anxious. But deep inside, he also harbored doubts that everything would be fine.

Eli escorted her to his Audi and drove out of the heart of the city to the outskirts. Rebecca could see many low trees full of dark green leaves bundled up like a quilt about them, and elongated trees whose light evergreen feathers blew over the ground below them. It reminded her of the drive up to her own house while departing the busyness of Munich.

The Levin home was quaint, but one of the larger homes in the area. Unlike the Baum house with its luxury statues and daily tended gardens, this held a small garden in the front next to the windows. When Eli pulled his car into the driveway behind an expensive white 1931 BMW 3/15 DA 4, Rebecca saw a young girl peek out the window, giggle, and then drop the curtains. The car was unique in its appearance with a strong box shape, white and black contrasting colors, and thick tires. Seeing the car, Rebecca understood why Eli talked about wanting to buy one earlier.

"Your father's?" she asked, knowing already the answer.

"Yes, he just bought it a few months ago. Beautiful, isn't it?" Eli said beautiful with pride, eager to finally show Rebecca his family's wealth, in complete contrast to Eli's apartment and old car. Eli held Rebecca around the shoulders as they walked up to his parents' home. The wide, tall white house with columns at the entrance looked simple and comfortable. Eli opened the door and the festivities from inside permeated into the corridor. A short woman in her late thirties with blond hair, brown eyes, a blue uniform and white apron hobbled over to them with a warm smile squished into her soft pale white cheeks.

"Ada!" Eli gave her a hug replete with missing someone he hadn't seen in awhile and the maid kissed him on the cheek. "So good to see you again. Your surgery went well?"

"Yes, yes." She answered in a strong Austrian accent, too heavy for Rebecca to make out all her words clearly. "The hospital stay was long, about one week and terribly boring. Not much to do and not much good food. Your parents were so kind to bring me plates of home cooked meals."

"Did you fall ill?" Rebecca's curiosity brought her to the forefront of the conversation.

"Heavy heart palpitations. I have been feeling faint and fatigued and went to have myself checked."

"What did the doctors say?" Rebecca's study of nursing left her head spinning with questions, thoughts and she felt quite comfortable with this conversation, one most people would prefer not knowing the details of.

"After a week of rest, he told me I'd be fine, but Mr. and Mrs. Levin insist I rest and refuse I lift a finger during the feast. This will be different for me, being waited on instead of the one doing the serving." Ada grinned into her wide chin and wobbled back into the living room area where she tended to low stress knitting, and sewing sweaters for all the Levin kids, including Eli. Rebecca heard the three sisters Eli told her about in the next room with Ada giggling, and she looked at Eli and smiled her nervous smile.

"Let's introduce you, shall we?" Eli's eyes silently asked if she was ready to move forward. Rebecca nodded and Eli ambled hand in hand with her into the living room. Sarah, Eli's oldest sister, sat the farthest away in the room, gazing over Rebecca, watching her carefully with occasional intermittent smiles. Her long brown wavy hair draped, braided, over her shoulder. The tallest of the three, with her love of dancing, she maintained a lean strong form.

Leah, Eli's middle sister, sat next to Sarah on a closer side of the sofa. Her short, straight, brown hair was fashioned in a bob and her cheeks were puffy like her dress, or perhaps it was her figure. Her rounded eyes matched her personality. Miriam, Eli's youngest sister, sat on Ada's lap on the sofa to the left as they entered the room. Her kind big brown eyes hid behind curly long brown hair, the lightest of the three, which dangled to her waist. Eli guided Rebecca to the empty sofa to the right. Rebecca sat next to Eli while he held her hand.

"So, how was your drive up?" Ada inquired, easing the sisters into welcoming the new guest.

"It was a short trip, pleasant. Not any difficulties," Eli responded.

Ada directed her eyes at Rebecca. "And you, dear, did you enjoy the drive?"

"Yes, it reminded me of trips to my parents' house, roads bordered with trees and bush. It's always nice getting out of the city and into the country."

"The city can be so daunting, so much noise and crowds. The worst of Germany in one spot," Ada confessed. Rebecca had only heard the words: daunting, noise, crowd and nodded her head in agreement, knowing from Ada's expression she did not much care for the city of Munich.

Rebecca's lips pressed tightly when they pulled upward and Eli recognized her "polite" smile.

90

Eli also knew this because he was privy to her esteem of Munich, the freedom it provided her, the boisterous life, and the many hospitals in need of help. Rebecca had told him about the hospital close to the courthouse and the interview she had for a position there. She hoped to secure a job come May, but she was still waiting on hearing back from them.

Ada smiled at the sisters, encouraging their polite conversation.

"How did you enjoy your studies at University?" Sarah asked, not only out of courtesy, but out of sincere interest. She planned to attend a university for dancing.

"I enjoyed my classes very much," Rebecca answered and Eli interrupted.

"She received her diploma in Nursing."

"A nurse," Sarah remarked, her eyes softening, "That's a kind profession, dedicating your life to helping others."

"It's all I ever wanted to do since I was a child." Rebecca recollected old memories she had not thought about for some time, "I remember watching the doctors and nurses closely whenever I had to go to the hospital with Mutti, and admired their delicate skill and patient hands."

Sarah smiled at Rebecca's response and then Leah gained the courage to entertain the new guest. She played with her short hair when she spoke.

"Eli told us you worked at a local diner," Leah offered information Eli mentioned in passing.

"Yes, I do."

"Is it good work?"

"It can be stressful at times, but work is work." Rebecca shrugged and Leah played with her fingers before looking away from Rebecca.

"What grade are you in at school?" Rebecca inquired.

"I'm in the seventh grade," Leah said, like she had accomplished a great feat.

"Very good!" Rebecca reciprocated her feelings. Rebecca glanced away from the far sofa and focused on the sofa across from where she and Eli sat. She gleamed looking at the little girl. "This must be Miriam?" she asked, knowing the answer.

Ada cuddled Miriam in her arms, kissing her on the forehead. "She is the youngest in the family." Ada raked her fingers through Miriam's long, light brown hair.

"How old are you?"

Miriam raised her right hand and showed five short fingers, then pulled her hand down to cover her giggling mouth.

"Miriam doesn't like to talk to people she doesn't know very well," Eli confided to Rebecca.

Sarah leapt from her seat like she leapt in her ballet shoes and pranced to the other side of the room. All eyes followed her. "I think Mama needs me in the kitchen," Sarah said and disappeared.

Eli turned to Rebecca. "Mama is preparing the rest of the feast. Sarah is helping her today since Ada is resting from her visit to the hospital. Sarah enjoys helping Ada cook too when she's not busy with her schoolwork."

"Is there anything I can do?" Rebecca asked.

"No, no, it's real busy in there. I'm sure you'd get lost in the hustle of the preparations." Eli pinched her nose. Rebecca squinted at his dark brown eyes and sent him a private smile.

At the feast, Eli walked with Rebecca to the table and covered his head with a white fabric he called a kippah. A white lace cloth that could have been sewn by Ada covered the long table. Eight white ceramic plates sat on the table, three settings on each long side, with one setting at each end. A large round platter reigned in the center, with a roasted egg on a small plate, horseradish in small dish, a mixture of apples, nuts, cinnamon and wine in another dish, parsley in yet another dish, and a few chicken on a small plate.

Two plates of matzos sat at each end of the table and a glass of wine accompanied each plate.

Rebecca's eyes widened in awe at the procedural arrangement of the feast. Eli showed her to her seat next to him at a corner of the table. Eli strategically planned it this way so that she would be between himself and his mother, the two people he knew would be easiest for her to converse with during the lengthy Jewish remembrance. Sarah sat on the other side of Eli, filling up the last seat. Ada sat across from Rebecca, followed by Leah and finally Miriam who sat next to her father. Ezekiel entered the room, a tall man with a strong lean figure and a short grey beard and mustache. He also wore a white kippah covering his head. He walked to Eli, patted him on the shoulders with a hopeful smile, then greeted the lady Eli had brought to meet the family.

"Shalom. My name is Ezekiel. It's a pleasure to meet one of Eli's friends." Warm and inviting, Ezekiel put Rebecca at ease.

"It's a pleasure to meet you. Eli has told me so much about you, about all of you."

"He's told us much about you as well. Finally we get to meet you." Ezekiel felt like her own father when he finished his sentence and sauntered to his chair to wait with everyone else for Deborah to find her seat. Finished with the meal to be served after Seder, she pulled off her apron and rushed out of the kitchen adjacent to the dining room, both rooms smaller than at the Baum's house.

Her hair was a mix of grays and browns pinned up on her head. Her eyes were wide and her figure plump, but healthy. She looked more motherly than elegant, a stark contrast for Rebecca at her own house. She sat down and the Seder began. Eli had told Rebecca in advance to simply follow him and that no one expected her to grasp the entire feast tonight. The eldest daughter dimmed the lights and Ada set two candles on each end of the table.

Miriam opened her mouth for the first time for Rebecca to hear. "Why is this night different from all other nights?"

Ezekiel began with the Kadeish prayer over the wine. Then they each stood, one by one, and made their way to the washing bowl set on a cabinet near the table, washing and drying their hands. Eli told her normally there would be a prayer after this, but Pesach was a special holiday that omitted it in the hopes of exciting the child's inquiry to ask why. They sipped their wine and then dipped parsley into salty water while Ezekiel said a blessing, followed by another cup of wine and, a peculiar event to Rebecca, the taking of matzo, the breaking of it and hiding half of it under a napkin while returning the rest to the main plate.

After this strange display, Miriam spoke again in her soft, but audible voice and Rebecca smiled at the young child's patience and dedication which, at this point, surpassed her own. Miriam asked, "Why do we eat matzo instead of bread, why do we eat bitter vegetables, why do we dip our vegetables twice, and why do we recline instead of sitting up straight?"

Rebecca gazed around the room and noticed she was the only one with a straight posture out of habit from constant reminder by her mother. Ezekiel then began the retelling of a story she remembered from Catholic school, the story of the Exodus from Egypt.

Rebecca smelled the array of food hidden in the kitchen which was prepared by Deborah and Sarah while Ezekiel told the story. She found herself eager for the Seder to conclude so that she might eat, but knew the Seder would be long and she tried to hold onto her patience. After the story finished, everyone stood again and washed their hands and then Ezekiel gave a blessing. Rebecca followed behind Eli. Two more blessings were given over the matzo which, at this time, was broken and taken. Eli noticed Rebecca's fascination with each detail. Then a blessing was given, followed by the horseradish and mixture of fruit spread over the matzo.

Rebecca watched everyone and waited for the family to eat the matzo before taking any herself.

Deborah stood, followed by Ada and Sarah and they each brought in a plate of food to the table. Homemade matzo balls, baked potato pancakes, braised chicken, beets, briskets, and grilled duck filled the plates. But before anyone ate, they enjoyed eating the egg and then finally filled their plates with food. Rebecca's appetite was well worn at this time and Eli turned to her, whispering in jest.

"I told you it would be awhile before we eat." Rebecca could only smile and hold her tongue. After dinner, they enjoyed the dessert and chocolate-covered matzo, followed by two more cups of wine.

Miriam made it a point at this time to share her contribution to the dinner. "I made the dessert myself," she said with a high smile that pinched her pinkish cheeks.

"With Mama's help," Deborah added.

"The feast was amazing." Rebecca complimented Deborah and then Ezekiel. Deborah smiled with warmth like Ezekiel, but to Rebecca her warmth seemed more heartfelt, much like Eli's own smiles.

Eli escorted Rebecca to the living room and, on their way, Sarah brushed past Eli. Rebecca continued onto the living area and sat where she had previously, giving the two of them a chance to talk in private.

"She's very pleasant and sweet," Sarah said and Eli could hear the but in her voice, "but she is so very goy." Sarah tried to say the word with the utmost politeness, but tact came second to honesty for her. They whispered in the corner before the entrance to the living room and Rebecca overheard the word and, though not knowing what it fully meant, gathered it implied something about her in a negative light. Before Eli broke away from his sister, she concluded, "Father will never approve."

When Eli walked into the living room, an outsider wouldn't have known any discord had occurred between him and his sibling from his gay disposition and relaxed smile. But Rebecca knew something was wrong. Eli built a wall of confidence every time his insecurities festered, and she could see the wall now, a façade of ease when she could feel him crumbling.

He was crumbling, not only because he knew his father would disapprove of her despite his warm welcome, and not only because of Deseire's shame of him; he was crumbling because he also felt Rebecca pulling away. He could feel it inside of him ever since the argument she had with her mother at graduation. For the past few weeks she had been growing more distant. He didn't want her to know his family had oppositions too, or for her to sense any more uncertainty in the relationship.

Eli watched Rebecca watching Miriam and Leah play games on the floor. She watched the kids play for some time, whispering to Eli and stealing unseen kisses until Ezekiel called Eli to the den.

Ezekiel stood over a desk of papers and files when Eli arrived and he waved his son into talk with him.

"Yes, Father?"

"I need to speak with you before you go. You know I don't like to handle these personal matters over the phone or in the office."

"Yes." Eli's body became fixed, tense like it had when he was scolded as a boy.

"Close the door."

Eli followed his father's instruction and then returned to him.

"You know I don't have to tell you this, but I'm going to anyhow. I and your mama realize you have strong feelings for Rebecca, but the two of you come from different worlds and these worlds can't mix. It's dangerous for the both of you."

"I know, Papa, but I want to be with her."

"What you want and what is good for you are two different matters."

Eli relaxed at his father's soft tone. "She is good for me."

"I'm sorry, but your mama and I have talked about this extensively," Ezekiel rubbed his brows, "and we have overlooked your propensity to see her intimately. But you must find a Jewish woman." His rough words came from a place of softness and though Ezekiel had said we decided, Eli knew it meant he decided and Eli's face flushed, knowing the obstinacy of his father.

"This is my life, my decision." Eli's sturdy words were yet like a whimper, begging the world to understand.

"We cannot allow this under our roof. I am sorry, Eli." Ezekiel's face wrinkled with fret. "The Nazi party has only recently been ordered to ban the activities of the SA and SS. The violence is out of hand and you know as well as I do this ban will not last long. People are not sympathetic to the desires of your heart."

Eli's hand became a fixed fist of tension holding the anger of a world not ready to understand, and he slammed it on the desk.

"I love her!"

The anger his father knew was not directed at him, or at the desk of papers, but at the country falling apart, at the unfair treatment, at the tensions growing in the city he once loved and at his desperate grip, trying to hold onto a relationship with the woman he loved, loved more than any other woman. Eli swung the door open and walked out to the living room where Rebecca's ears perked and she pretended to have not heard anything. He reached his hand out to her and she gripped it with her own, then they walked out of the house and to his car.

SATURDAY, MAY 7, 1932

Eli had not seen Rebecca since Pesach and expected to see her this weekend since the whole of last week kept them both too busy to find time with each other. Eli worried the argument between his father and himself would cause one more reason for Rebecca to pull away from him.

He could already feel the awkwardness in the car on the drive home that night, an awkwardness Rebecca did not know what to do with, fidgeting with her fingers and then the car door and then her own door as she said goodnight to Eli with a simple kiss on the cheek. Her kiss felt different that night, still with passion, but sad, a subtle sadness, but there nonetheless. Eli never missed any of the little things when it came to her.

Knocking on her door Saturday midmorning, Rebecca answered with a warm cup of tea in her hands. Another teacup waited on the table. She knew Eli would come over that morning because he called her Friday night. She made his tea just the way he liked it with a slice of lemon. The steam from his teacup was still intense and Eli could see it rising from across the room. He shut the door and walked over to her wood table designed in a similar fashion to his. It always reminded him of the night they made love on his table.

He rested his feet from the race down to her room, sipping his lemon flavored tea. Rebecca's lace robe covered her silk nightgown, a gown she still wore from sleeping in that morning. She wandered from her bedroom back to the wood table and then hung there like moss dangling from the trees. It was hard for Eli to distinguish her emotions and this worried him. He was always good at reading her, but today she seemed aloof and a bit despondent. He nudged her and she used an unknown smile, one Eli had not yet seen.

"What's wrong, Rebecca?"

"Nothing," she insisted, but her avoidance only hinted her need of Eli to pry into her feelings.

"Something is wrong. Would you please tell me?" Eli's concerned tone wavered in uneasiness. Rebecca sat in the wood chair across from him. Her eyes appeared cloudy and she drew her hand to her other hand as if comforting and consoling herself.

"It's us…me. I don't think we can be together anymore." Rebecca said this statement with weak intonation and a flustered sadness. Eli was taken aback by her proclamation, feeling her pulling away the past few weeks, but never realizing the full weight until her round lips spoke those words.

"Why?" His response was sharp.

"My family, your family, this country, no one desires us to be together. Where is the hope in a future?" Her words were true, but painful to Eli, to her, all the same, "I heard you arguing with your father. I don't want to do that to you. I am tearing you away from them."

"No, Rebecca. My father will come to understand. My mother will grow to embrace you like a daughter." Eli insisted on solving this problem Rebecca had formed in her mind, but he wasn't accustomed to resolving feelings and the unseen emotions of the heart. Even a lawyer had his limitations. He enjoyed deliberating concrete evidence, figures and facts.

"It's not just your family, its mine too. It's everyone." Rebecca wiped her face, her tears from her reddening eyes. "You can't tell me the prejudice is not there when it is. I don't want to admit it, but it's there all the time. We can't even get away from it with the people who raised us, the people who are supposed to love us, no matter what."

"Don't do this." Eli's calm demeanor, which formed habitually out of practice at his law offices, crumbled and his emotions intensified. "Please, don't do this. I love you." His words pressed hard into her ears as he drew her close to him. The emotions she tried to hide, to forget, leapt to the foremost of her mind.

"I love you." Rebecca reached for his hand and her forefinger glided across his knuckles and wrist and back again, "but we have to be apart." With a heavy breath, she took her hands away and wiped more tears from the corners of her eyes.

Eli pressed her to his chest. "I don't want to let you go," he said and Rebecca struggled with her arms to push him back, wanting with every instinct to pull him toward her and make love once more.

"You have to," she said with a brief exhalation of air, her sigh caught between pleasure and retreat. They pushed and pulled in each other's arms, not in a dance of passion, but in a dance of sadness and pain.

Rebecca's robe became entangled in Eli's embrace, clinging to his fingers and then she pushed him with frail hands and red eyes, with a spirit that wanted to pull him back. Eli turned away, released the silk robe, and walked to the door with his head down and without looking back to say goodbye.

For Eli, goodbye would not come easily, not with someone he loved more than himself. He knew in this moment he loved her more than anything else, because when she asked him to go, he left not for himself as everything in him drew him to her, but for her, because she asked him to. The last request that he could honor between them and he did because he loved her.

The next day was terribly upsetting for Rebecca and she could barely get out of bed, regretting what she had done and second guessing her decision, but the phone rang and she did not have time to dwell in her thoughts. The man on the other end spoke and requested that she come back to the hospital to fill out paperwork if she still wanted the job.

Rebecca hung up with a new hope inside of her, a hope that the course of her life had not ended with Eli, but perhaps had another beginning, a beginning that would be spent in healing the sick and nursing the wounds of patients. She told herself this was best between them. He could live in peace with his family and marry the kind of woman they expected and she could fulfill her familial obligations. She, half despondent and half with earnest diligence, clad herself in a long black silk dress with a gold colored belt and made her way to the hospital across town.

She found the steps of the hospital to be wide and long and had to walk a bit before hitting each next step. The gentleman on the other end of the phone waited for her in the front office and escorted her to a back room where the man who interviewed her sat.

Her long brown hair with hints of warm honey was pinned up into a bun. A black silk scarf wrapped around her neck and her black long heels helped her decadent dress wear easy on the eyes. The man asked her to sit and she obliged with a tightened smile that curled downward in the corners. A bundled mix of nervousness and politeness, she fidgeted with her hands before placing them on her lap.

"Miss. Baum, it is Miss, correct?"

"Yes, I'm not married."

"Fine young lady like yourself should find a husband in no time at all." Rebecca tried not to linger in the thought of marriage and puffed her smile a bit to show she heard him, then waited for his instructions. "I guess I should get to the point."

He surveyed a pile of papers and then returned his gaze to Rebecca. "We recently lost a nurse who was with us for some time, a Ms. Eppes." He said her name slowly as if he had to read it off a chart, "and we need a replacement. She was mostly in charge of handling paperwork up front, but we also needed her to occasionally assist the doctors in the back with their patients. Does this sound like something suitable for you?"

Rebecca nodded before the words came out of her mouth, "Yes, yes," she said, excited yet uncertain of the way the job had become available to her. "You say a Ms. Eppes left the hospital?"

"Yes."

"May I inquire the circumstances of her departure?"

"It's really a private matter, but we received too many complaints from patients who didn't want to be treated by her."

With those words, those familiar words reminding her of Aaron, Eli's friend, who had lost his job because of too many client complaints, Rebecca knew exactly how the job had found its way into her fortunate lap. She nodded, knowing she would be given the job, knowing she would take it, and knowing guilt would bother her because of it.

* * *

Eli awoke Sunday morning early. He desired to divert himself from the breakup with Rebecca and focused on his job with his father. He didn't know how long he would be able to keep his mind occupied, pushing thoughts of her eyes, smile and body away, but he would attempt it. Rebecca asked him to leave. He had to respect her request.

Neither her family nor his demanded this breakup, though he knew their pressures influenced her decision. Nor was it a social requirement she had no choice but to follow. Rebecca made this decision with her own free will. He couldn't hold it against her, but it left him with no choice but to dive into the life of law.

He walked into work with his lips pressed tightly, holding in the recent unsettling events of his life, discouraging talk about it, keeping it from his father. He did not want to invoke drama around the breakup, a decision he had not fully accepted himself. He shuffled the papers on his desk and organized the files for the upcoming cases. He ensured the papers his father needed were classified correctly, ready to be picked up by Ezekiel when he dropped by Eli's office before the ending of the day.

Eli and his father developed this new routine, a system used where they did not need to rely on a clerk at the courthouse. Eli would handle the organization and his father or himself would handle the disclosure for the opposing council, receiving the files again before the day of the case. The system worked.

Eli used every minute, every second fighting his urge to invite the thoughts of Rebecca back into his life. Everything was a distraction from keeping those thoughts seeping too far inside where he would not be able to flee from them. Work was the only place they had not shared together. But the files, papers, and busy work only kept Rebecca at bay until late morning when Eli picked up the newspaper and read a critique on the tenor sounds of Joseph Schmidt.

The memories broke the dam he tried to build and she flooded his mind. Events of the day they spent in the theatre, sitting side by side, invaded his space, her gentle touch to his hand on the theatre seat, her coy laughter, her long brunette locks brushing against his face as he handed her the popcorn. Everything about her on that day infused with his current day and then all the other safely contained memories broke free, refusing to be ignored. Everywhere he went, everyone he saw in one way or another reminded him of her. She could leave him, but she would never leave his mind, his heart, his soul — pieces of her would always remain in him.

The Day the Flowers Died

***

One morning in the middle of the following week, Rebecca slept in her bed and swung her arm up over the pillow in an unconscious attempt to grab a hold of Eli. To her, he lay next to her where he should be. Her arm grasped for his body, needing him close to her, but it hit the hard mattress instead. She awoke and her fingers lingered in the emptiness beside her. A slow tear fell from her eyes and to her bed and then the alarm sounded.

She hurried to bathe and clothe herself in the white uniform provided by the hospital. She rushed down to catch her taxi and scurried through the front doors of the hospital. From the moment she walked into the building her day filled with patients needing care. Some needed her assistance with walking. Some needed her help with paperwork. Some needed a shoulder to cry on and, in the midst of all the healing she provided, her own soul felt as if it was breaking.

"Rebecca, we need you in the back room. A patient is convulsing." A doctor from the back yelled out to her through the swinging doors leading to the front office.

She hastened to the back room where they put difficult patients. The bald old man was coughing. A nurse had him pinned down with her hand to his arm at one end and a doctor holding him at the other.

Rebecca darted to the patient's side and the doctor smiled at her with just the left side of his mouth as he released his hand and brushed past her. The old man's body violently pushed up and down on the bed and Rebecca compared his pain to the way she felt the past week, though hers was not a convulsing of the physical body, but of the heart. The doctor gave the man a shot which settled his body and the nurses freed their hands from their stringent grip.

***

Saturday morning, Eli stood outside their building, behind a wall on the other side of the street that fronted another apartment. He wore his grey trench coat hanging over grey slacks and a white buttoned shirt whose collar had not been ironed down well. He watched Rebecca's room, her lights flickering on and her shadow behind the curtain until she drew it back and her soft face came into view.

He missed seeing her so much, he could barely breathe upon seeing her now, though in secret, though uninvited. He felt partly like a thief stealing something that did not belong to him, except she was a part of him and her physical separation didn't change that fact for him. He watched her prance down the steps leading to the sidewalk where they had their first conversation and his eyes glazed over her as she sprinted across a side street to catch a cab. In his mind he stood next to her, holding the door open for her and slipping into the cab beside her. He wanted to be there and only there.

Rebecca took the cab downtown to meet two new friends from the hospital. They all had this weekend off and decided to enjoy the day with coffee and shopping. The first friend was short with a full figure, and because she was older, the relationship developed into something akin to a daughter and mother. The second friend to greet her was lean, and young with blonde curly hair that swept past her shoulders and, like Rebecca, had attended University against her parents' wishes. Rebecca enjoyed her company because they both had to overcome social pressures of staying home and marrying in order to follow their careers.

The three of them sipped their coffees and then continued to shop. Window shopping had always been a pleasure for Rebecca, but every time she passed a clothing shop, she saw a tie and thought of Eli and his assorted collection. Then her mind wandered to the New Year's Eve party when Eli wore a grey tie with silver sparkles in support of the free spirit that night and she found herself in a regrettable demeanor. But Rebecca decided to enjoy this time out with her friends all the same despite her heavy heart.

Sunday morning, Rebecca awoke to the sounds of her own short scream, an ache resonating Eli's name on her lips. Her bones physically shook for him. His touch. His jokes. His whisper in her ear. She could almost see him next to her and feel her fingers playing with his hair. He would be there now if she had not asked him to go. A mirage of the man she knew, the man she loved stole her breath and she knew in that moment she could not be without him.

She threw on her cotton pale pink skirt that fell past the knees and her white blouse with a lace collar before running out of her room, pinching up her hair with bobby pins while she hurried. She raced up the steps leading to his room and knocked, hoping it wasn't too late, and hoping she hadn't severed the bonds. She found herself waiting at the door with no answer and tapped on it again.

But Eli was not at home.

Rebecca hurried down the steps and swung the front door of the apartment building open, searching with her eyes, with her mind at where Eli could be this early Sunday morning. Her heels clicked hard against the cobblestone sidewalk, running up to the city's busy street. When she reached its end, her heel snapped at the same time she saw Eli walking back from the park.

Her eyes made contact with his and her body tipped further. Her arms pushed forward, ready to brace herself for the fall but, before she hit the ground, Eli grabbed hold of her. She toppled over, unable to balance on only one heel and he giggled.

"Have you got it?"

Rebecca smiled a wide, long smile. "I think so." One leg stood higher than the other. Eli released his grip, but she didn't want him to let go. She grasped for his arms, no longer a mirage of her mind, and pulled him toward her, soaking him in.

"I don't want to have to miss you." She nestled her head in his chest covered in a warm beige coat.

"I don't want you to." He brushed his fingers over her hair bun and down her neck. "I'm right here." From all the hours, minutes, seconds they spent apart, a longing ached inside of each of them, leading them back to Rebecca's room. In the darkness of the lights turned off, Eli swirled with her in his arms and lifted her to her bed.

"I love you," he confessed a third time, but to her the words were still as fresh as if they had just been said. "Even when I am away from you, you are all I see." With his words, Rebecca bit her lip and carried them to his, as he wrestled with her beauty, and she became lost in his touch. Every minuscule motion of his fingers over her skin felt like a wave of water rushing over her, a saturation of sensation. Every brush of their bodies collided as if particles from their separate bodies mixed and pieces of themselves became one another's, drifting in and out and it was as if there was never any separation between them.

The Day the Flowers Died

THURSDAY, JUNE 2, 1932

Eli and Rebecca had spent the last two weekends together since their makeup, never parting, waking up in each other's arms. But Rebecca had to work both Saturday and Sunday this weekend. Her shift gave her Thursday and Friday off and Eli stopped by her place Thursday evening to spend time with her, calling his father to let him know he wouldn't be at work on Friday. His father, not asking him why, had a hint of the reason and, though displeased, finally agreed and found someone to cover Eli's work for the day.

With President Hindenburg calling Chancellor Bruening to resign in the end of May, one of the few men who had stood up to Hitler, this new month carried in its air a sense of loss for democracy. Eli knew Hindenburg was not to blame, but that the pressures from Schleicher and Hitler had resulted in this. Schleicher, a man for the conservative nationalist government, was now in control. His devious nature and backhanded maneuvers with Hitler only heightened Hindenburg's concern for the future of Germany, but Eli imagined that, to Hindenburg, Schleicher seemed the lesser of two evils.

Eli and Rebecca planned to spend the evening together and Friday morning to attend the Anti-Fascist demonstration in Berlin organized by the Communist and Social Democrat parties. Though neither of them favored communist politics to democratic politics and neither encouraged the often violent and agitated efforts to stop the Nazi party, this effort took a stand against Hitler. A few of Eli's friends would attend, too. Aaron and Jacob, like Eli, felt it was their civic duty to break the hold Fascism had on the country and Robert and Rosalyn wanted to show their support of the Communist party.

Thursday evening, when Eli arrived at Rebecca's place, he brought with him a new camera he bought at the shop in downtown Munich. He took it out of his carry bag and Rebecca's face lit up. On the side was engraved Leica II and it was small enough to carry in one hand. It had a silver metal rim on the top and bottom and a metal button on the right hand top side. The lens popped out of the center of the camera also with metal rims and Rebecca played with it, admiring its ingenuity.

Rebecca also had a camera, a 1922 Conley Kewpie, her mother had bought her ten years ago when she was just thirteen, stored away in her closet. It was more like a box and she usually had to stroll it around with her using both hands, taking postcard size images.

Eli slipped his new camera out from her grasping hands and took an impromptu photo of her. He caught her just as she leaned in toward him, trying to grab the camera, while her hair needed brushing, and cascaded over her shoulders. Her smile revealed her white teeth. The flash made her close her eyes and she called out to him in disgruntled amusement.

"Eli," she said with disapproval and Eli broke into laughter at the surprised expression on her face. Rebecca darted toward him but he scurried out of the way and ran into the bedroom. He leapt on top of the mattress with the camera still in his hands and pointed the lens at her as she jumped into the air, landing next to him to steal the coveted item.

He snapped another photo of her and then released the camera into her hands. She rubbed her fingers over it like she had confiscated a hidden, valuable treasure. "This is so clever," she said. Eli pranced off the bed like a child at Christmas and raced out to the porch.

Rebecca followed him, ready to take his photo. "Stay there. This is a good shot." She waved her hand, motioning him to lean backward into the banister.

"Like this?" He leaned his head and body into the railing, his face still focused in her direction. The soft summer sun dropped behind the horizon and over his face, lighting up his dark chocolate eyes with orange and yellow sun light.

"Not so far back," she exclaimed while her summer dress swayed in the breeze. Eli leaned into the metallic banister. He pulled himself forward a bit and Rebecca snapped the camera button. "It's stuck," she declared. Eli grinned and ambled toward her.

"You have to pull this latch back before the next frame." He laid his fingers over hers as he directed her. She played with the latch and then focused the lens over Eli as he returned to the banister and she took the photo just when a breeze blew his long brown scarf into the air and he smiled.

"Got it!" Rebecca swayed over to Eli and dangled the camera in front of him. Her sky blue eyes intensified in his stare and he took the camera out of her hands as they returned to the bedroom.

* * *

Friday morning, June third, hundreds of demonstrators from the Communist party crowded Berlin. People shouted and waved their angry fists in the air. The country was torn between opposing parties of Communism, Socialism, the Nazi's National Socialist German Worker's Party, and Democracy. The country was failing and so was the parliament of Reichstag. People wanted leadership that could provide jobs, security, and change. The angst for this change, mingled with the vehement resistance to the growing Nazi party, led many of the communist demonstrators to violence.

Eli and Rebecca arrived in the midst of these streets. He pulled his Audi into a back road and walked with Rebecca, exercising their disagreement with the changing politics. Eli felt it was their civic duty, their obligation to his country to fight against the threats that strangled it. Roslyn, Robert, Jacob, and Aaron met them in the back street and the six of them joined the crowds and threw their fists while walking through the streets of Berlin, though Rebecca's fists were not as tight as the many around her.

The crowds grew loud. Their clamorous cries demanded to be heard, demanding justice. Aaron and Jacob ambled side by side like brothers, though they had not known each other very long, introduced through their mutual friend Eli. Their common Jewish heritage and struggles through the web of German Nazi propaganda bound them. Eli tightened his fists with his friends, chanting alongside the protestors. Rebecca watched this new side of Eli, a side that walked in the face of danger and welcomed the fight.

She had seen Eli argumentative before, with his lawyer's instinct for debate and diplomacy often seeping into their lives, but in this rally he was different. This time, he added actions to his words, not behind a courtroom desk, but on the open vulnerable streets, opposing the politics of the country. This side of Eli she did not want to see again. She admired his courage, but in these streets in this crowd, a rush of chills ran through her body and she grabbed Eli from behind.

"Eli, I want to go home. I don't like this. Can we go?" She implored, her eyes begged. Rosalyn gestured to Rebecca with a shrug and without words, asking, what's wrong?

"Rebecca, nothing is going to happen. It's just a demonstration." Eli reassured her with almost a chuckle, but she couldn't believe it would end peacefully. Marching on the streets, the sounds pounded and permeated throughout the city, alerting everyone not marching that something paramount was occurring in Berlin.

Many who opposed the two marching parties shouted along the sides of the streets, throwing fruits, bottles, cans. Demonstrators retaliated, throwing items in return to the discord of the disapproving observers. Groups of Nazis hidden in common German clothing took offense to this protest and threw punches at some of the people who passed.

One Nazi, no older than twenty, with perfect teeth and short blond hair like that seen in the military, lunged at Eli when the six turned a corner and continued up the street. He wrestled Eli to the ground, smacked him across the face with a locked fist, and knocked Eli's face against the hard ground.

Rebecca gasped. "Eli!"

Aaron pounced on the Nazi and pulled him off with the help of Robert. Aaron held him while Robert threw two fists at the young man, busting his nose and splitting his strawberry lip.

Two more Nazis sprinted out from behind a corner and leapt on top of Aaron and Robert. Soon the streets flowing with peaceful marches erupted into brawls. This violence incited more angry spectators and protestors to fight and retaliate, and soon much of the street became disordered. Eli, Aaron, and Robert rolled over the ground with three young men who, from a disconnected society and a city of turmoil, had turned to a party that offered hope.

Jacob joined in the disturbance, pulling a stronger attacker off of Aaron.

The four of them, after bloodied faces and ripped clothes, finally thwarted the three young men and they ran off behind the corner from where they came. Jacob wanted to retaliate, but Eli yanked him back, almost in a wrestle like fashion.

"Let it go. This has gotten way out of hand," Eli shouted over the loud noises from the crowds. "I should have listened to Rebecca. We need to get back to Munich."

Aaron, a logical mind like Eli, could see there was not much advancement to be made since violence had broken out, and he stepped behind Eli to follow him away from the street. Eli tried to coax Jacob into coming with them, but Jacob shook his head and pulled away.

"We're staying to fight!" Jacob shouted to Rosalyn and Robert.

Robert and Rosalyn, though appearing delicate to the eyes, pushed forward as if fire burned behind them, shouldering through the crowds and shouting out for their freedom and for the politics of the Communist party. Eli grabbed Rebecca's hand and, with Aaron behind him, retreated off the streets onto the sidewalk, staying close to the buildings until they found Eli's car.

"What about our friends?" Rebecca inquired to Eli, "Aren't they coming?" Her voice shook from the violence in front of her.

"They'll come in Robert's car when they're finished." Eli turned his motor on and as he backed up, a wild, blond young man sure to be another Nazi jumped over the hood of his car with a glass bottle in his hands. He threw it through the windshield and Eli accelerated, thrusting the boy off the car. Eli whisked through the back streets back to Munich. He drove up to his apartment building and shook the bottle out of his car window before he, Rebecca and Aaron escaped into his room.

No one tended to the broken windshield, frantic from the recent events and both Eli and Aaron wanted to wash the blood off their faces and change their spoiled clothes. Rebecca tended to Eli's wounds with a wet towel from the kitchen sink and Aaron washed in the bathroom. Her gentle hand caressed the rough wounds left on Eli's face that marked his political resistance.

"Those bastards," Rebecca almost lost her temper. Her face burned red. "I told you we needed to get out of there. You can't protest like that without getting involved with the Nazis."

"I'm sorry. I didn't mean to scare you. If I had known, I never would have taken you there." He whimpered with hard honesty as Rebecca calmed the bleeding.

"None of us could have known," she whispered, wiping the blood under his nose, patting it like she had been taught in nursing school.

The next day brought more deplorable news when Hindenburg dissolved the Reichstag and called for new elections by the end of July.

However, the next week passed quietly for Eli and Rebecca and they were glad for it. With pressures mounting and tensions escalating in politics, they didn't want any more discord in their lives.

But in the middle of the following week, on Wednesday, June 15, the country altered for the worst. As a result of Hitler's backhanded maneuvers with Schleicher — promises of sympathy to his conservative national party — Schleicher awarded Hitler the ban to be lifted on the SA and SS, essentially allowing Nazi violence to prevail on the streets. Murder and violence soon erupted on a scale never seen in Germany. Patrolling groups of Nazi Brownshirts walked the streets, singing Nazi songs, searching for brawls.

In an attempt to sooth Rebecca's worries, Eli found himself hiding away in their rooms most of the month. Even Eli's father closed down the office for the last few weeks in an effort to prevent violence befalling any of his Jewish employees. Rebecca spent most of her time between Eli and the hospital, bandaging up victims from the venomous attacks.

As she walked up to the hospital from the curb she would often hear the rumble of song from the Nazi storm troopers and cringe: Blut muss fliessen, Blut muss fliessen! Blut muss fliessen Knuppelhageldick! Haut'se doch zusammen, haut'se doch zusammen! Diese gotverdammte Juden Republik! Blood must flow, blood must flow! Blood must flow as cudgel thick as hail! Let's smash it up, let's smash it up! That goddamned Jewish republic!

The month of Eli's sequestering left him feeling out of place in a country where he once always felt a part. The sting, like a scorpion striking his pride, kept him in the most dismal of dispositions and, apart from Rebecca's returning home from work and sharing time with him, he began to feel disconnected from the world outside. Germany grew more and more into a country he did not recognize, leaving him unsure if he even wanted to belong to it anymore.

The Day the Flowers Died

He occupied his idle time with phone calls to his parents and quiet readings from some of his favorite poets and writers, curled in the bed or sitting on the porch. Rebecca offered solace and she found herself wishing she could take away all his pain, but her small hands and thin arms could never be strong enough to hold up a crumbling country. They both knew they would have to somehow endure while the country fell apart around them.

SUNDAY, JULY 17, 1932

Rebecca readied herself for work. Eli, unwillingly put on room arrest by Rebecca until the violence stopped, stayed in bed. She had seen Jewish store windows smashed and shattered glass all over the streets. She heard the Nazis yell out slurs, "Germany awake!" and "Kill the Jews! Heil Hitler!"

The words stung her young ears. Rebecca requested Eli to not go outside until the intensity settled, because of Eli's descript Middle Eastern Jewish features. Rebecca was sure he would become the target of a Nazi stampede and she could not bear it to see him bloodied and bruised again.

Eli obliged while she held his face in her palms and admired his jagged nose, heavy brows, and hint of color in his complexion. To her, everything that the country was being taught to hate she adored. He lay in bed, watching her roll up her nylons over her long, lean legs. "C'mere," he called out to her with passion in his eyes.

"No, I have to get ready for work." Rebecca tugged the nylons and straightened out her white hospital skirt.

"Please," he used sympathy as a childish ploy.

"I can't. I'll be late."

"Call in and let them know you're running late." He used all his lawyer tactics. He slipped off the bed and, in his socks, made his way to her and rubbed her shoulders from behind. Her body collapsed at his touch and she felt herself giving into him with each impassioned kiss. She called into the hospital and Eli waited for her on the bed.

She arrived at the hospital an hour late, but the front desk expected it and the secretary smiled when she walked in. Patients flooded the hospital. Several young boys sat in the waiting room with scrapes and bruises over their faces and arms. An elderly man walked around the room with a limp needing usual care. Two older men had been escorted to the back room for stitches from gunshots.

Strolling from the lockers to the front office, she noticed the patient rooms were all taken and Rebecca soon found her hands full, assisting doctors, filling out paper work, and ushering the wounded. Her white hospital skirt and top blended with all the other nurse uniforms which provided a sense of solidarity, binding them as a team. Many nurses were German, some Austrian, a few French, and one Jew. Rebecca wondered if Ms. Eppes' fate would soon befall the only Jewish woman working in the hospital. The thought took her to Eli and her worries for him cooped up in the apartment alone.

Ezekiel told Eli to take off whatever time he needed under the violent circumstances that engulfed Germany. His main concern was for his son's safety, not for the law firm. Ezekiel said he would give Eli's work to some of the other staff until attacks in the city abated.

Rebecca was grateful to Eli's parents for their understanding, except in the case of her. She wished her own mother could support her the way Eli's family supported him living in Munich and helping with everyday needs.

If Rebecca had chosen to live at home and marry according to her mother's wishes, Rebecca would be doted on by her father and mother alike. If she wanted a trip to France, her mother would not hesitate to arrange it. Instead, Rebecca decided to go to Munich, study an unapproved profession, and be with a man who displeased her mother. This overt disobedience came at a cost and, if Rebecca wanted to follow her own will, she would also have to arrange her own life.

Sometimes when Eli slept, Rebecca wandered to the photo of her as a baby in her mother's arms. She tried to remember how wonderful and secure that feeling must have been, knowing her care was certain. Now, she still longed for her mother's acceptance, but refused to pay the high costs to acquire it. She gave Eli up once and she would never make that mistake again. Nursing and Eli were her life, a life that took her four years to create in Munich and she didn't want to regret it.

As she bandaged and tended chipped teeth, abrasions, cuts, and broken limbs, she knew this was where she needed to be, helping the people who could not help themselves. She was called into one of the back rooms to assist the doctor whom she had aided once before with the convulsing old man. She slid on her gloves and took out the doctor's supply kit filled with instruments for cutting and sewing. She clutched each instrument, waiting for the doctor to complete each cut and stitch, switching instruments as the need arose.

After an hour long procedure, the doctor finished with the boy lying on the hospital bed with a slash in his arm. The doctor looked up to her with a glimmer in his eyes and asked her to escort the boy to the front office. The doctor helped her lift him, grazing over her hand. Rebecca followed the instructions and ignored the encounter. She did not want to create any problems for herself at work; the country offered enough of that for her. But when she returned to clean the instruments, the doctor interrupted her.

"You did a real good job in there. Not many people can handle the sight of blood."

"Thanks." She glanced up, smiled and looked down at her work. After collecting each instrument, she placed them into the kit and began to walk toward the sanitation counter for washing and sterilizing. The doctor brushed up behind her and rubbed his hand over her lower back.

Startled and unsure of what to say or do, Rebecca abruptly turned to face him. "I'm with someone."

The doctor stepped back. "I'm sorry. I thought…I was told you weren't married." He answered in a polite manner.

"I'm not." She placed the tray on the counter and turned on the water. "But I'm in a serious relationship."

"Excuse me," he said with sincere intonation and retreated into a patient's room, leaving Rebecca relieved the incident did not escalate.

After work, Rebecca arrived at her apartment. Upon opening the door, Eli whisked her into his arms and swung her around while a sweet giggle escaped from her mouth. He returned her to the floor and she shook her head, smiling at his antics.

"What's gotten into you?" she asked and headed to the bedroom, slipping off her white top and unzipping her hospital skirt. Eli curled his hands around her arm and slid it from her wrist to her shoulder bone and then up along her collar bone. "You've really got to get out more," she grinned, "all this keeping you cooped up can't be good for a young man." She tilted her head into his hands and then darted into the bathroom.

"What do you suggest?" Eli plopped on her bed, filled with an energy out of character.

"I thought maybe we could go to the park this weekend. I have Saturday free."

"That sounds perfect." Eli threw his head back onto the bed, frustrated with an unsatisfied appetite to stroll around Munich and smell the fresh air, hold hands with the woman he loved and spin her around in his arms for the world to see. But he knew he had to wait. He had to be patient. He had to be still.

Rebecca finished her bath and sat next to Eli lying on the bed with a book in his hands. "What are you reading?"

"Heinrich Heine." Eli read silently, occasionally closing his eyes, imagining the pictures from Heine's words. Rebecca fell over, lying side by side with him.

"You always have such a serene expression on your face when you read him. Promise me you'll bring the poetry when we go to the park this weekend," Rebecca whispered. Eli turned to kiss her forehead.

"I promise." The sun dropped and the evening trickled into Rebecca's window and over their bodies until an abrupt knock at the door startled Rebecca in the comforts of her bed.

"Who is it?" Eli asked her while his chest puffed, stroking her back with his finger. A wrinkle broke on her forehead.

"I don't know." Rebecca leapt to her feet and threw on a chiffon pink robe over her silk beige nightgown. When she opened the door, Aaron stood on the other side with sweat dropping from his forehead to his jaw line. "What is it?"

"Is Eli here?"

"Yes, yes, come in." Rebecca opened the door wider for him and then shut it. Aaron sat on the sofa across from the television, the only television in the building. "Eli?" Rebecca called to him from the living room.

Eli went in after pulling on pants and a tee shirt. "Aaron, what brings you here?"

Aaron's face tensed and his eyes became unusually serious. "I thought you should know today the electoral campaign has turned into civil war."

"What?" Eli needed clarification. Rebecca sat on the sofa with Aaron and Eli remained standing.

"The Nazis wanted a fight and they got one. Under police escort, the Nazis barged into Communist Hamburg-Altona, Prussia. Street fights and shooting broke out and eighteen died, including two SA storm troopers." Aaron shook his head in disgust. "More than a hundred were wounded."

"Oh, my God." Rebecca's hand instinctively covered her mouth.

"And that's not the end," Aaron said and Eli wiped his forehead in frustrated thought. "Papen, the new Chancellor, proclaimed martial law in Berlin and took over the government of Prussia as Reich Commissioner." Aaron brushed his hands through his short curly hair and Rebecca gasped.

"Oh, no." Eli took a seat on the wooden stool across from the sofa. His words were more like a second thought to the concerned pondering of his mind.

"One more step toward a dictatorship." Aaron shared his news with his head in his hands. "The German youth worship Hitler!" His face contorted. "You know he speaks to audiences of over a hundred thousand at a time." The room lapsed into silence.

"Hindenburg isn't going to make it, is he?" Rebecca's voice cracked and her lips curled under. No one answered, because Eli and Aaron both knew it was a real possibility.

* * *

The weekend gave Rebecca and Eli time to spend together and they both promised to not talk politics or country. Every citizen of Germany felt this strain, which only strengthened whenever people discussed it. They strolled toward the park, past buildings and apartments and, on many of the walls, they could see Nazi posters.

They stated, Bring down the system and other political testaments, anything denoting the current system under Hindenburg failed and Hitler's change was necessary for Germany to survive.

In this cacophonous climate, Eli and Rebecca clutched hands, bodies as they moved toward the park, holding up together something they could never hold up apart, the weight of prejudice. The air on the street felt different. Caution for their lives, once the furthest thing from their mind, now leapt to the foremost, denying them their past naïve closeness. Though they tried to not let the prying eyes and callous whispers into their space, they knew this time, this year, the invasions invited danger.

They passed the crowds of buses and cars rushing to and fro. They passed buildings stained with the blood of men brawling. They passed bushes hiding the park that held their secret passions. When they turned the corner to enter, they noticed the park unusually empty. An elderly couple brushed past them before exiting. Another couple sat on a bench a few yards to their left. But neither mother nor child was seen, the life that once saturated the green grass gone. Deafening silence replaced the warm motherly affections and the sounds of children giggling and kicking balls across the green.

Eli took Rebecca's hand and whirled her around on the grass dance floor, with her for his muse. She laughed despite the tensions and emptiness around them. He whisked her toward the closest bench, laid his head in her lap and sang a song she knew well. At the end of the first line, Rebecca joined, and with a lack of proper harmony they sung words into the breeze and to each other.

…I do not know what haunts me, what saddened my mind all day;

An age-old tale confounds me, a spell I cannot allay…

They giggled over themselves and Rebecca raked her fingers through Eli's hair.

"I love that German song." Her expression, once a mix of fondness and fear, melded into memories of childhood.

"It is by Heinrich Heine."

"I never knew."

"German politics don't want you to." They laid in each other's comforts in the quiet emptiness of the morning, watching the sun become full, and listening to the birds chirp in the trees until the afternoon when the sidewalks became busy. Eli knew the change of expression on her face and reacted with prompt care. "We ought to get back. It's late and people are filling the city." Rebecca slid off the bench with Eli beside her.

* * *

On July thirty first, Aaron, Jacob, Robert, Rosalyn, Eli and Rebecca huddled around the radio in Eli's apartment, listening to election results. Every eager ear and every taut emotion stilled, waiting for the results. Robert and Rosalyn held hands with eager anticipation, staring at the radio. Eli and Rebecca stood close. The radio voice, rough in the sporadic static, spoke with hesitance as if reading over notes.

"...The results are in... with the Centre Party commanding 12.3 percent, 75 seats." Eli clapped his hands once and made an approving guffaw. "The Communist party holding 14.6 percent of the votes, 89 seats."

Robert and Rosalyn grabbed each other and smiled. The voice paused, "the Social Democratic party has 21.9 percent of the votes, 133 seats." Eli looked to Aaron whose eyes had a hint of smile at those results. "The National Socialist German Workers Party receives 37.8 percent, 230 seats."

The faces in the room crumbled. "The Nazi party is now the largest party in parliament," the voice shouted over the air waves. "But wait, the other ten minority parties make up..." the voice paused again to read his papers. Jacob's hold on Aaron intensified and he shouted, "Go liberals!" "...19.7 percent, giving them 81 seats in parliament." The eyes in the room became hopeful, "Combined with the Communists, the antifascist parties hold the majority of seats." The voice on the other end became low, "a disappointing day for a divided parliament."

"What does this mean?" Rebecca asked.

Robert answered in a heavy soft voice. "It means, with the Nazis on one end, the antifascist parties on the other, and President Hindenburg in the middle, the parliamentary government won't be able to function."

After he finished, Jacob interjected, "Papen's minority government will continue until another election."

The air in the room became a little harder to breathe as everyone realized the elections did not solve anything and the country was still at a violent standstill.

FRIDAY, AUGUST 5, 1932

While Schleicher and Hitler battled for the position of Chancellor, Hindenburg's grasp on his country wavered, but his persistence on cooperation from Hitler finally prevailed and Hitler put the SA and SS on a two week furlough. This gave Eli the chance to enjoy being outdoors without the fear of being attacked or the fear he heard in Rebecca's voice. It also gave Eli's father, Ezekiel the courage to open his firm again and he called Eli back into work on the following Monday.

Eli found piles of papers on his desk waiting for him, and the day was never long enough to get it all done. He never complained, being in his office brought him satisfaction second only to being with Rebecca. Focusing on his work made everything feel normal again, like the country could push through all this mess and soon things would go back to democracy and liberty.

Eli's office showed an arrangement of family photos, degrees and awards. He was a well accomplished young man for someone of only twenty five years.

Ezekiel knocked on Eli's office door before letting himself inside the room.

"Papa." Eli grew a tender smile, desperate for family since the woes of the attack in Hamburg which made him essentially a prisoner of his own home.

"Eli," Ezekiel smiled warmly. He opened his arms to embrace his son and Eli welcomed the gesture. Ezekiel held Eli for a few moments and then continued, "I am worried for you, son." He sat in the chair across the desk from Eli. "Everything has gotten very bad, for Jews especially. Hitler won't keep the ban for long and the Nazis will soon be up to their old tricks."

Eli grabbed his father's hand. "Don't worry, Papa, everything will be fine."

"You say that, but you forget I'm older and have seen more than you. I know the nature of men. I know the nature of politics. None of this looks like it will end well." Ezekiel's voice cracked, "I don't want to see you getting beaten, thrown in jail or worse, killed."

"The Nazis have no grounds for jailing me."

"Do they ever need grounds to do as they please?" Ezekiel scratched his head. "Hindenburg is old and won't be able to retain power much longer. The parliament is failing. New elections are continually called, but when this leadership is finally achieved, I'm afraid it will not be in our best interest, in your best interest."

"Papen will still be chancellor, Papa," Eli comforted himself with his words, "He is a National Socialist. He isn't as devious as the other parties."

"Papen is weak and he's got two vultures circling around him. How long do you think it will take to have either one of them in Papen's seat alongside a President who is also weakening?"

Eli glanced to the papers at his desk, the one thing he could do something about and control.

"Son, you must be careful, you know…" Ezekiel stared into Eli's eyes, "with your lady friend. The world we live in now is not kind to Jews who take German ladies away from them."

Eli was glad to hear his father's concern and, instead of disapproval, advice.

"Yes, Papa." Eli nodded and they established an unspoken understanding between them. Eli knew Ezekiel could never fully accept his choice to take a non-Jewish woman, but he would also never abandon his son.

Ezekiel knew Eli had an independent mind and followed his heart above all else. Ezekiel kissed Eli on the forehead before leaving.

Eli returned to his work and, though Ezekiel had appointed others to complete Eli's load in his absence, many employees could not finish all that needed to get done. This came either out of their own hectic schedules or out of a covert selfish sense of pride in doing a Jew's work, so Eli found he had more work than anticipated. Each day stretched well into evening and a few times he didn't get back to his apartment until ten.

Rebecca also kept occupied with her work at the hospital. Though the attacks had lessened, patients from the previous months still needed intense care. So, the two of them only saw each other sporadically until the weekend.

With the two week breather from the assault troops dedicated to Hitler's tyrannical views, Eli and Rebecca needed to enjoy life again and joined Jacob at their swing house in Hamburg the following Saturday night. Though many German youths filled the floors, Eli and Jacob could also remember the freedoms their country once afforded them.

As Rebecca swung the doors open to the loud boisterous sounds of swing, the music flowed over their spirits, lifting them out of the chaos of the country and inside to the dimly lit room, a room that didn't care who was Jew or German, Communist or Socialist, Catholic or Liberal, because under this roof they were all swingers. The high pitched violins whistled over the thumping of drumsticks beating against soft fabrics pop, pop, pop and combined with guitar strumming and occasional pats on the guitar wood frames. The mixed crowds cheered in gratitude. A room of youth and young adults from every political party, except the Nazis, clapped in unison to the sweetest sounds, melding them all into the counter sub-culture that defied the country.

The stage speaker said, "Get up hubcaps! Get ready to jump up and down for the jazz of Artie Shaw." The stage performers mimicked his sounds without missing a note or beat and much of the crowd moved in various boogie-woogie and jive movements while another portion swung through the air.

Eli stood and twiddled his fingers, calling Rebecca to him with his eyes and holding her in a deliberate trance-like state. Rebecca rolled her shoulders back as she approached and he grabbed hold of her, swinging her into his long, sturdy arms. He spun her before lifting her and swung her through the air like the many other young ladies around her. Her once cautious demeanor morphed into a carefree girl.

Jacob noticed a young lady with a long, elegant nose twisting her long blonde locks with her fingers under the soft lights spread around the borders of the room. Her bright pink blush and lipstick blended with the dazzling silver out of place flapper dress. She smiled ostentatiously at Jacob and he took it as a sure gesture. Strutting across the dance floor, he grabbed her hand much like he had with Rebecca the first time he met her. He spun her wildly in the excitement of hopping, sliding, and bouncy rhythms of the music. The two made a spectacle of themselves, as if there were no social boundaries to keep.

Aaron laughed at the sight of Jacob and his free spirit, wishing he could lose himself like that, but never could with so many concerns on his mind. The dancers kept to the beat of the music on the floor and at least forty swirled about, clad in all variants of color and makeup. The inside of the room stood in stark contrast to the country outside, dark and gloomy. The streets that used to have life had been replaced with fear and the days that used be filled with social gatherings had been replaced with Nazi attacks.

Eli and Rebecca sat down at a table they secured with drinks, expressing their affection and enjoyment. A tall blonde approached from behind and tapped Rebecca on the nape of her back. Rebecca spun her head around and shouted, "Rosalyn," her voice high pitched with excitement.

Rosalyn sat next to Eli across from Rebecca, who asked, "How are you? I didn't hear from you after the rally in June. Did you get home alright?"

"Fine." Rosalyn shrugged as if she attended rallies and fights all the time. "Robert came home with a couple of bruises on his cheeks, but we made it back." Rosalyn reached her hands out to hug Rebecca's like a sister.

"Where's Robert?"

"He's somewhere around here, probably getting a drink." Rosalyn lifted her head, gazed around the room and refocused her attentions back to Rebecca, sliding into the seat next to her, whispering into her ear.

"So, how are things with Eli?" Rosalyn's eyebrows rose in anticipated gossip. Rebecca smirked and her face flushed a hue of pink.

"Very nice."

"Because I heard you broke up in May and then, when I saw you at the rally, we didn't really have much time to talk." Rosalyn grinned and her cheeks puffed under her pursed lips.

"Yes, we broke up." Rebecca recalled her decision to ask Eli to leave, a decision she could not hold to emotionally. "But we're fine now.

Better actually." Rebecca spoke in a low voice to ensure privacy, but over the loud music it would not have mattered.

"I'm glad. The two of you are so perfect together," Rosalyn said and Rebecca smiled with relief. Aaron tapped his foot near the table, bouncing his shoulders back and forth and Rosalyn leapt and dragged him onto the wooden floors. Eli laughed and threw his head back at Rosalyn's brazen attempts.

"Come on, Aaron. It's real easy. You just gotta let it all go." Rosalyn wiggled her body, her hips swayed side to side. Her dark skirt and beige top caught the friction in the wind and ruffled over her figure. Aaron almost let out a smile, trying to keep up with a girl who had been swinging for seven years. The two of them relaxed in each other's arms. Robert strutted over to Eli and stood near the table, watching his girlfriend swirl in the freedom of the room.

"She's really something," Robert said and his stare glistened at the sight of her, patiently waiting for her to finish so that he could have his dance.

"She is," Eli agreed.

Not socially adept like his friends, Aaron rarely danced or socialized with young woman. His mind was astute and he spent most of his time in his work and on the politics of the country. But Robert always told Aaron to take advantage of his young age, to find someone he cared about and settle down before time caught up to him and he found himself old.

Rosalyn and Robert believed everyone should be equal in treatment and assets which is why they both joined the Communist party. Since the influx of racism, prejudice and brutal treatment against many of the Jews, Gypsies, Africans, homosexuals, and even the crippled of Germany, Robert and Rosalyn's sympathies grew even more for Aaron.

When the song ended, another one followed, but Rosalyn glided back to the table with Aaron and sat next to Rebecca. Robert joined Rosalyn and sat across from her while Aaron stared off into the dance floor, watching Jacob persuade his new lady. Eli laughed at the sight of Jacob swirling close to their table and then to the dance floor.

"He meets someone new every time I go out with him," Eli chuckled.

"He's got a spark the girls can't resist." Robert joked without a hint of jealousy, because both of them came into the dance room with the woman they wanted.

When the night slowed and the crowds dwindled from sixty to twenty, Eli and Rebecca headed back to their apartment. Jacob road home with Aaron, and Robert drove Rosalyn home.

"Thank you for coming with me, Rebecca," Eli said with great pleasure.

"I had a good time. I hope you did too."

"I did." Eli let the words escape like he couldn't resist them. He slept in Rebecca's room as most weekends they tried to make their own.

After the good news of the two week hold on SA activity, towards the end of the month, Hermann Goring was elected as chairman of the German Senate.

This weighed heavily on Eli and his friends for it meant one more man for the National Socialist party. His nuances of agreement would more likely fall under Hitler's persuasions than Schleicher's, because he worked under Hitler's orders in the twenties. Though more humane than Hitler, it was a faltered sense of humanity. But, Hindenburg now had two influential members for National Socialism (Papen and Goring) who were preferable still to the National Fascism of Hitler and so Eli hoped like many, this would be good for the country.

Thursday, September 15, 1932

Rebecca called Eli as the morning broke through her window because, after sitting down with a cup of tea and her morning paper, violence covered the front page. The two week hiatus of the Nazi SA activity ended. On September twelfth, messages flew between Göring and Papen. The Reichstag, under Göring's chairmanship, gave Papen's government a no-confidence vote. In response, Papen dissolved the Reichstag, resulting in a call for new elections.

The country grew tired of elections and campaigns, wanting results rather than promises. Added to this frustration, the Nazi party's fervor exploded. Rebecca's hands shook as she put down the paper and picked up the phone.

"Eli," her sweet voice woke him.

"Rebecca," he didn't have to wonder; he knew her voice like the back of his own hands.

"I don't want you to go into work today. One hundred and fifteen people have been killed in political riots." She emphasized the numbers. "Violence is escalating."

After a long pause, Eli spoke with a firm, soft tone. "Rebecca, I can't hide because of the Nazis. I'd be turning my back on my father and the business. I'd be giving into them, telling them they've beaten me. Forget my body. I won't let them crush my spirit and mind." At Eli's strong words, Rebecca knew he was right, but couldn't bear the thought of him in danger. She continued in her persuasions for her lawyer to stay indoors, but Eli's will dominated.

"I worry about you. How will I be able to concentrate on my patients when I'm worrying about you?" Her voice became desperate.

"I'll be inside my office the entire time." His voice rose high with his next sentence. "I won't even go out to lunch. I'll bring it with me. We all have so much to do to keep the firm alive. I can't bail out on my father when he needs me." With the last words, my father needs me, Rebecca retracted her desire for him to stay in his room.

"Alright, but, Eli, promise me you'll stay in the building and won't leave for anything, not even to go to the courthouse. It's crazy over there."

"I promise." Eli made the sound of kisses and Rebecca smiled and hung up. She had a day free from the hospital and, while Eli tried to get back into the habit of work despite the violence, she decided to meet up with her old friends from University.

Bernard and Louise waited at a coffee shop in downtown Munich. Traffic and people filled the busy streets even though poverty and hunger saturated the overcrowded cities of Germany. The streets left Rebecca feeling guilty for the affluent life style she was raised in and accustomed to.

She never lacked for food on the table or warm clothes to wear and, even when she couldn't afford something she desired, her father on occasion would slip behind her mother's back and buy her the luxury.

Rebecca dropped her change into the hands of a poor man in unwashed, ripped pants and tee shirt. He thanked her as the coins hit his worn, tired, outstretched hands. Strolling to the table where Bernard and Louise waved to her, she thought of ways she could help the poor. When she saw her friends, she rushed to them, feeling like she'd returned to her days at University.

"It's been too long," Bernard said, "where have you been hiding?" He brushed his fingers through his stark blond hair.

"I've acquired a nursing position at the hospital near the courthouse. You know the one?"

"I do," Louise interjected, "I pass it every day on my way to the clinic."

"You work at a clinic now?" Rebecca smiled wide, "So you've accomplished what you wanted."

"Well, not completely." Louise rolled her eyes to Bernard. "I still haven't been able to get him to ask me to marry him."

Bernard laughed in a way that seemed calloused, and then responded, "I will, Louise. You know I want to get things settled with work first." Louise nodded, wiping the smudge from Bernard's mouth.

"Please, Rebecca, order something to eat. I'm having a chocolate croissant. They are delectable." Bernard waved the waiter over.

Rebecca pointed to the croissant in front of Bernard and said, "I'll have one of those," and just as the waiter turned around, she finished with, "and a large coffee, please." Rebecca looked at Louise. "I'm so glad to finally be doing this with you two."

"Yes, very glad," Louise agreed.

"I was just thinking how sad it is that so many are on the streets without food and shelter. I thought maybe a few of us could collect a pile of old clothes and donate them to those in need."

"What a splendid idea," Louise responded.

Bernard rolled his eyes, "The unemployment rate is rising because there are simply no more jobs."

"Because businesses are running out of money to pay employees." Rebecca added, "so many unjustly."

"There are no more jobs because the Jews have stolen them all." Bernard raised his glass of juice to his mouth.

"Some of the unemployed are Jewish, Bernard, fired for no reason," Rebecca implored, remembering her friend Aaron and the name Ms. Eppes from the hospital.

"If you consider freeing up jobs for the hard working Germans no reason. The Jews are a crushing presence," Bernard said with his chin raised and his shoulders squared.

Rebecca bit her lip, trying to control the urge to smack him. The waiter set her croissant on a white plate in front of her and she stared at it in loss of appetite.

Louise tugged on Bernard's shirt to keep him from instigating an argument. Louise and Rebecca had been good friends at University and, though they had drifted apart, she still enjoyed Rebecca's company. Never one to cause strife, Louise followed Bernard and his Nazi ideals without giving it too much thought. Bernard appreciated the Nazi's growing influence and the youth growing in rapid numbers toward their ideals. Louise appreciated Bernard.

Though the Nazis redefined what it was to be German, Louise would not be troubled with semantics. She would inevitably follow without question what her country folk believed. But neither her politics nor lack of them bound her to Rebecca. They shared a compassion that led them both to the field of Nursing. Rebecca and Louise did not like to see others suffer and, on this point, she vehemently differed with Bernard and the Nazis.

"You can't think what is happening is good, all this violence and prejudice. You can't be on the side of the Nazis, Bernard?" Rebecca asked in innocent naivety, unable to grasp a friend from University could differ with her on such fundamental matters.

"I'm sorry to offend you. Are you still dating the Jewish lad I saw you with at the New Year's Eve party?" Bernard's words simmered to courtesy.

"Yes, I am." Rebecca folded her arms.

"Well, I'm not going to pretend to dislike the Nazi party just because you do, Rebecca. I voted for them. You are a German; you must be able to see their logic, the good they want to bring to the German country?"

"What logic is there in hate?" Rebecca responded, pushing her croissant away, her uncomfortable demeanor obvious.

Louise placed a hand on Rebecca's arm. "Do stay, Rebecca. Simply because we vary on politics doesn't mean we can't hang out together."

Rebecca offered a taut smile to Louise, knowing she was not at least in thought a Nazi, but her actions kept her close to their activities, which repulsed Rebecca.

"I'm sorry, Louise, but I don't feel right speaking with the two of you if you support the violent brutality and racism of the Nazi party. They're destroying people's livelihood and beating innocent people on the streets."

Bernard's upper lip curled at her words and his brows pulled back like a rabid dog about to bite. "But consorting with Jewish men is perfectly acceptable." Bernard tore a chunk out of his croissant.

Standing, Rebecca stared at the two of them and then darted her eyes in Bernard's direction. "I'm sorry you've forgotten your Catholic values, Bernard. I know our parents are members for the Centre's Party. It's a shame to see you lost in the fascism of Hitler."

"My father is weak. That's why he can't see the future of our country rests in the hands of the Nazi party. I pity him and you." His cheeks reddened with his flaring nostrils.

Rebecca smiled at Louise before turning away and walking to her car.

The Day the Flowers Died

* * *

Rebecca planned a special evening for September twenty-fifth, Eli's birthday. She phoned him at the office to come back to her place after work. Eli's forehead wrinkled in thought and his eyes widened with anticipation. She typically didn't contact him at his office to invite him to her room; they usually only spent Friday and Saturday nights together. But this sudden interest in spending Sunday evening with her, excited him and he wondered if it had anything to do with his birthday, though he didn't remember her talking about it.

"But what are we going to do Sunday?" Eli inquired.

"There is something I must share with you," Rebecca whispered.

"Must share with me? That sounds desperate."

"It is desperate, because if I don't get to see you Sunday, I don't think I will ever be the same again."

"Well then, I'd better be there."

"Yes, you'd better be." Rebecca mimicked the smile Eli had on his lips on the other end, both filled with anticipation.

After work at six, Eli locked his office and drove home in his car, with its taped windshield cracked by the thrown bottle. Eagerness hurried his feet up the stairs to her room and he knocked a few times.

"Come in," her sultry voice invited.

Eli slid the unlocked door open and stepped into a room lit only by two candles on each end of her table. A meal she'd stayed home to make sat in the center, its enticing aroma sharpening his hunger and its decorative colors pleasing to his eyes. Eli shut the door behind him and embraced her with outstretched arms. Taking off his coat, he followed her to the table and sat down with her.

"You did this for me?"

"It is your birthday, isn't it? You mentioned it a few months back."

Eli stood and stretched over the table to kiss her on the lips twice, his tie dangling unnoticed in the center plate, and then he returned to his seat.

"Thank you."

"You're welcome, and I'm not finished," she said in a sensual tone. "I also have a gift for you. Its small, but I think you'll like it."

Eli smiled, the corners of his lips almost found their way to his eyes. He dug his fork into the mashed potatoes, broiled beef and corn. "It's delicious."

"Thank you."

Upon finishing the meal, she carried out a small rectangular package encased with silver wrapping paper and handed it to him before kissing him on the lips. He unwrapped the gift and found a book of poetry from Penina Moise, an American Jewish poet of the eighteen hundreds. His eyes glanced over it with a mix of tears and enthusiasm and then he stood to hug her.

"Where did you find this?"

"My father bought a collection of poetry books on a visit to England when I was young. He gave me a few, which I brought with me to Munich. But I didn't remember I had it until I was weeding through my closet to find clothes for the poor. I knew you would appreciate it so consider it yours."

"I am so elated. I've been looking for this and can't find it anywhere. Most Jewish books aren't stocked anymore in Munich."

"I knew you were looking for it." Rebecca grinned, "which is why I was so excited to find it for you."

He put the book on the table, running his hand over the cover, then turned to her. "You are too good to me. With all the insanity around us, you are my one bright light."

"Sshhh." She raised a finger to his lips, the falling sun wrapping their bodies in shadow. "Let's not worry about anything outside my door...not tonight."

Rebecca laced her arms around Eli and he whisked her off into her bedroom.

* * *

Towards the end of the month, the radio reported that Eva Braun, Hitler's girlfriend, had attempted to commit suicide by shooting herself in the neck. The attention starved young woman craved spending time with the Nazi leader consumed with leading a political party. Upon hearing the news, Hitler rushed to the hospital and sat by her side until her recovery.

The distraction slowed the Nazi party further which was already losing momentum from a constant demand of re-elections, a siding with the Communist party to attack transport workers, and the violence of the SA. The party alienated much of the middle class.

Eli's room filled with delight at the news of it all, knowing it would affect the number of votes for the Nazis in the upcoming election in early November. Frail hopes grew and people started to believe that the National Socialist and Nazi parties might collapse. For the Social Democrats or Centre Party, both more supportive of Jewish people, a win became possible.

SATURDAY, OCTOBER 1, 1932

Rosh Hashanah, Jewish New Year: Eli told Rebecca a week in advance about the upcoming Jewish holiday Rosh Hashanah, the beginning of their New Year. He invited her to participate in it with him at his family's home.

Ezekiel, though disapproving of their relationship, was proud to see his son remember his heritage and invite Rebecca. Ezekiel was also glad to see Rebecca willing to observe and learn a new tradition.

Last year on Rosh Hashanah after synagogue, groups of Nazis waited outside to brutalize the Jewish fellowship. Brawls broke out, wounding many. This year, Eli and Ezekiel worried something like that would also occur.

Rebecca rode with Eli to the Levin home on Saturday afternoon after they ate in Munich.

Ada opened the door, welcoming both Eli and Rebecca inside and then, out of social decorum, guided them to the living room where Eli's family awaited.

When Rebecca turned the corner after a long walk through the corridor, she saw Miriam's bright eyes shine out from under her mama's arm where they sat on the sofa. Sarah sat on the far sofa with her posture upright as Rebecca had been shown many times by her own mother.

"Welcome Eli and Rebecca," Deborah said with warm affection and rose to hug her son and then Rebecca. The hospitality surprised Rebecca since their last visit ended after an argument between Eli and his father. Rebecca accepted the hug and followed Eli to the sofa across from Deborah. After Leah's big brown eyes became bored of staring at the new guest, she returned her focus to the game on the floor.

"How was your trip, Eli?" Deborah asked in a curt tone, her attention divided between him and Miriam. The girl put her fingers inside her mouth and wiggled them around until Deborah pulled her hand away from her face and held it down on her lap.

"It was good, Mama, always a pleasant journey. Rebecca enjoys the scenery too. It's quite different from the busy city of Munich."

"Which is why your father and I chose to live in this house, away from all the hustle." Deborah's words carried an air of sagacity.

Eli told Rebecca a couple months back that his mama was a soft hearted woman and did not much disapprove of him with her, but that his father, the strict center of the family, would rather Eli date a Jewish woman. This soothed Rebecca's nerves while she sat in the room with Deborah. In fact, Rebecca began to feel more acquainted with Eli's family than with her own.

Compared to this, her own home felt quite barren and, besides Mildred, who mostly raised her, and Rueben the chef, she did not have much of a childhood. The time spent with her mother involved formal classes and direction, teaching her to be a lady, a German woman of sophistication. On occasion, she could steal a few laughs from her father when she managed to escape her mother's rigid grip.

Rebecca rose from the sofa and sat on the floor with Leah, familiar with the game, one of the few she played as a young girl. Leah looked up with her short bob swaying and smiled.

Rebecca reached her hand towards the jacks. "May I play?" At Leah's nod, Rebecca lifted the jacks up high and then released them, letting them dribble to the wood floor. Leah bounced the ball once and lifted one of the scattered jacks into her hands before the ball hit the floor again. They played this game for a few moments with concentrated efforts while Sarah, Eli and Deborah watched in amusement. Eli even saw Sarah sneak a smile at Rebecca and her childlike demeanor.

The entire Levin family planned to attend the evening service for Rosh Hashanah. Eli had warned Rebecca about the violence from the Nazis the previous year, but she insisted on going, explaining, if he was going to put himself in harms way, she wanted to be there by his side.

Ezekiel made an appearance, wearing a traditional Jewish garb, a kippah, on his head and Eli pulled his kippah out of his pocket and dressed his head. The family, along with Rebecca, walked to the nearby creek and tossed bread crumbs from their pockets into the water to symbolize the casting of sins. Knowing what to do from Eli, Rebecca took crumbs from him and threw them in. They then walked to the nearby synagogue. Deborah had folded over her arms a few shawls of white with the blue Star of David embroidered on them for covering her and her daughter's heads during the service. Eli brought a shawl for Rebecca and handed it to her upon entering.

When they entered the large room, Deborah helped Rebecca place the shawl over her head and then aided Miriam before leading them to wooden benches on the right separated from the men and boys. Women greeted Rebecca with shalom and L'shanah tovah, peace and good year. Eli and Ezekiel departed to another area in front of the room where all the men stood.

The Shofar, the ram's horn, sounded like air filled with all the souls it passed over. Rebecca enjoyed the softness it made, especially in contrast to the clamorous noise and shouting on the streets of Munich.

Rebecca sat in awe at Miriam and Leah, sitting upright in their seats and keeping their mouths closed. She could never achieve that type of discipline as a young girl growing up in Catholic Church.

When the family left the building, a small but determined group of Nazis waited for members underneath a tree on the lawn. The members ignored the ill minded youth, the disregard bothering the privileged boys. Two of the young men ran up to a tall Jewish man, with a long beard and the kippah over his head, and hit him from behind as he walked down a sidewalk.

Eli jerked in reaction and darted across the lawn and street in defense of the innocent man. Ezekiel called out, Eli, hoping to draw his son back into safety, but Eli didn't hear him and pressed forward. He leapt onto one of the Nazis and pulled him to the ground while the other hit Eli in the face.

The tall man stood back, stunned and unsure of how to fight. Two more blond Nazis in their early twenties pushed through the Jewish crowd to get to the fight. They dragged Eli away from their wounded compatriot and continued to punch him in the face, kicking and spitting on him even when he fell to the ground.

Jacob and Aaron exited the synagogue, noticed the fight and dropped their books to rush to Eli's aid. The three fought hand and foot, fist and spit against the four Nazi men, scraping their skin, blooding their noses and mouths until more Jewish men, including Ezekiel, ran to the sidewalk and pulled the Nazis away. Kicking and shouting, the four young Nazis did not go quietly, but they eventually left, realizing they were outnumbered. It left Rebecca in a silent hysteria at the cruelty of the country and unfair treatment of the people living there.

The Levin family briskly walked to their home with Ezekiel on one side of Eli and Rebecca on the other, holding him up with his arms around their shoulders. Of the three, he was the most badly wounded. Jacob and Aaron wobbled with Eli's three sisters and Deborah until they reached the Levin home.

The family, along with Jacob and Aaron, plodded up the driveway to the front door where Ada, peeping through the window, saw them coming. She opened the door with a few wet towels in her hands and pressed them to the faces of the bruised, shaking her head and whispering audibly to herself, "Just like last year. What has gotten into the German youth these days?" The family followed behind Ada, and Ezekiel helped Eli to the living room where he laid down on the far sofa. Jacob and Aaron only had a few scratches on their faces, and blood from their noses ran across their mouths.

They entered the kitchen to wash it off and returned to the living room. Miriam shouted and cried, clinging to Ada. At first glance, Sarah seemed calm, but closer inspection showed her jaws clenched and her eyes locking up tears. Leah sat next to her brother, stroking his hair while Sarah washed his face with the wet towels Ada provided.

Deborah shook her head and exited the room to talk with Ezekiel. Eli and Rebecca heard discord between his parents in the next room, but couldn't distinguish the words. At that moment, Eli's health concerned Rebecca more than the approving or disapproving parents and she helped his sister tend to his needs.

Rebecca brought in a glass of water and when she returned, Eli's face looked much better cleaned of the blood and dirt. When Rebecca tried to lift his shirt to look at his abrasions, her soft hands gently brushed against his skin.

"Rebecca, don't," Eli responded, blocking her with his hand.

"Eli." Rebecca pushed his hand away, "this is my job. I'm good at it. Let me do it." Eli nodded and looked away while Rebecca curled his shirt up and gasped at the extensive red and blue she knew would bruise blue-black. She prepared ice wrapped in towels and requested help from the sisters. "Sarah, could you please get me some ointment. Leah, if you have alcohol?"

The sisters followed the simple instructions while Miriam sat on Jacob's lap in the next room. Aaron entered the living room to check on Eli, but his stern expression and shake of his head told Rebecca he had seen enough for today, and after Aaron aided Eli's injured jaw, Rebecca gestured for him to return to Jacob and help Miriam find comfort.

The sisters eventually went to bed and Aaron and Jacob returned to their homes. Rebecca rested on one sofa while Eli recuperated with bandages and medicines dressing his body on another in the living room. Almost asleep, Rebecca saw Ezekiel watching them from the hall, then turn away to go back to his room to join his wife.

* * *

Monday, October tenth, Eli observed Yom Kippur, the Jewish Day of Atonement, another important holiday ten days after Rosh Hashanah. Rebecca had to work at the hospital, so Eli attended the occasion alone with his family. But Saturday, October fifteenth, she took the day off for the final Jewish feast of that month, much like Passover with food and drink. Eli had enticed her with his mama's elaborate menu.

Rebecca wanted to spend more time with Eli's family and demonstrate her commitment to this relationship between them. She hoped with a fragile hope that her participation in Eli's traditions would open the emotional doors into his family. Eli called it the Sukkos, but Rebecca had a hard time remembering all the Hebrew names and simply called it the feast.

Every time she tried to pronounce the name Sukkos, her German accent spoiled it and Eli giggled at her diligent determination. She could not say the word without mispronouncing it and so had resorted to sticking with feast, a word she knew well. Eli told her she could call it the feast of tabernacles or booths if she was more comfortable with that terminology and she nodded her head in exasperation, all the while knowing feast was all she could muster for the moment. Upon approaching the house toward the evening, Eli reminded her of the nature of Hebrew tradition.

"This feast is going to be a lot like Passover for you with lots of words, prayers and lengthy patience before eating."

Rebecca nodded, understanding the formalities with a patient expression. "It's a lot like Catholicism. We have many particular rituals to abide by as well. It's nothing a lifetime of growing up in the Catholic Church can't handle," Rebecca teased and pinched Eli's puffed cheeks, which had become so from the cold.

The family decided to forgo going to synagogue since the last appearance presented risk to Eli's well being. The two entered the quaint home and made their way to the dining area with Ada by their side. Like at Pesach, Deborah had prepared many dishes for the family to enjoy; however, on this occasion Ada was able to assist in the kitchen after having fully recovered. After leaving Eli and Rebecca to sit at the table, she returned to her duties with Deborah in the kitchen.

The white cotton table linens with maroon silk napkins decorated the large room. The table groaned, loaded with decadent dishes of apple cake, beef stuffed peppers, chicken soup, brisket, Peacock vegetables of zucchini, squash, onion, peppers, garlic, parsley, and spices. The palatable smells seeped from the platters and over Rebecca's nostrils, leaving her mouth watery.

Ezekiel opened with prayers from the prayer book. Eli glanced at Rebecca and spoke in a quiet manner, "the Hallel," knowing she wanted to learn the correct wording. The recitation came from the book of Psalms and read in hebrew, a reading which Rebecca would have recognized from Catholic school if read in German. The wood stool to the left of the dining table held a collection of three green plants wrapped in bamboo and a fruit. A date palm branch, a willow branch, a myrtle branch and a citron fruit. She pointed to it and nudged Eli's shoulder.

"What are those for?"

"For tomorrow morning, the Four Species are bound and waved to symbolize dedication to God....We normally would have a tabernacle dwelling outside the home to eat in during Sukkos, but times are too dangerous for such traditions." Eli lowered his eyes to Ezekiel.

After the Psalms reading ended, the family performed the washing of the hands and Ezekiel gave the blessing before eating, much like

Rebecca had observed at the Passover. After all the rituals, Ada served the food and Rebecca and Eli both filled their plates.

After the feast, Ezekiel walked with Eli and Rebecca to the living room and sat down to talk. Deborah swung out of the kitchen after putting a few of the dishes in the sink and joined the conversation. Despite the comfortable easiness Rebecca enjoyed with them, the sight of Ezekiel's worrisome face agitated her nerves. Her body became tense and her hands squeezed Eli's thigh.

"You wanted to talk with us, Papa?" Eli began the conversation.

"Yes, I just wanted to tell you, Eli, that despite my disapproval of wanting my only son to marry a Jewish woman and, despite my belief that the emotions between the two of you would fade, I can see now that your feelings for each other are strong. I can also see Rebecca is a sweet and lovely young lady who loves you, and I would rather have the two of you as part of my family then push you out," as he said you he looked into Eli's eyes, "and never know if my son is safe and alright." Rebecca's body relaxed and her hands softened their grip.

"Thank you, Papa." Eli stood and kissed his father on each cheek, then Ezekiel returned the affections to his son's forehead.

"With all the chaos of the country, it makes no sense for us to not stand together. There's enough division already." Ezekiel grabbed hold of his son's hands and squeezed them before letting them go. The wrinkles from Ezekiel's hands showed a long life.

Deborah stood, hugging Eli and then Rebecca before speaking, "I'm so glad to see you, Eli, join us this year, remembering our traditions. You've been quite neglectful in the past. Maybe Rebecca is good for you. It's important to never forget where you come from." As Deborah nodded, affirming her statement, Eli recalled the many times in the past years where he had skipped observing the Jewish feasts. Of late, though, the violence and persecution created an urgency to reaffirm who he was to himself, to his family, and to Rebecca.

Eli and Rebecca departed from the house late, heading back to their apartment. This ride home was different from previous ones because the approval from Ezekiel warmed and eased their hearts, making them believe their love could survive this country.

SUNDAY, NOVEMBER 6, 1932

The week filled with political unrest, continued violence and disruption on the streets, especially with the anticipated upcoming results of the election Sunday. Cheers from thousands lined on the streets echoed for Hitler throughout Munich and Germany whenever he spoke. Rebecca and Eli tried to avoid his presence along with his supporters, but living in Munich gave ample opportunity for the two to collide.

Eli came to work midweek to find a window in his father's office smashed. Ezekiel entered a few minutes later and saw Eli with a broom and dustpan, sweeping up the glass.

"Good morning, Papa." The sound of glass rattled into the dustpan and accompanied his greeting.

"Good morning." Ezekiel paused for a moment to study the situation, hands on hips. "I hope that's a gift from the Nazis."

"What? Why?" Eli's head jerked and brows furrowed.

"Better them than a client mad at us." Ezekiel and Eli chuckled, then Ezekiel turned toward the door. "I'll get some plywood to board that up."

"No. Let me. You've got a client in half an hour. After I take care of this, I'll get the Scholtzen brief ready for you."

Ezekiel nodded, placed his hat on the coat rack by the door and went in search of a morning cup of hot tea.

Towards the evening, Eli's room filled with Rebecca and his friends listening in on yet another set of results from the Reichstag elections. Bodies moved to and fro, anxiously awaiting the news.

Though Robert and Rosalyn wanted to see a Communist government emerge, they would be content if any party but the Nazis took control. Jacob thought a Liberal government might be best, but had never been one to focus on politics if it took time out of his swing. Eli had voted for the Social Democrats every time elections had been called. Rebecca normally followed her father's persuasions, but this year had been alongside Eli in support of him. Rebecca's parents were Catholic and Rebecca knew her father would want to vote for the Centre party, but her mother enjoyed appearances, and the Nazi Party had power and her mother had influence over her father.

This November election differed from the elections of July, because the Nazis lost much of their momentum from middle class citizens. So, when Eli, Rebecca and his friends sat around the radio to hear the outcome, the faces in the room displayed a sense of achievement.

The radio announced the results with a different speaker from July's elections. Eli and Aaron stood while Rebecca and Jacob sat. Robert and Rosalyn gripped each others hands.

"The National Socialist German worker's party loses two million votes with one hundred and ninety six seats." A heavy cheer filled the room and then quickly quieted to hear the rest of the results...

"The Social Democratic Party drops slightly at one hundred and twenty one seats." The voice paused and then answered... "The Communist Party gains 2.6 of the votes to one hundred seats and the Centre Party drops just slightly to seventy seats." The faces around the room shifted in stunned disbelief for a minuscule moment and then filled with long grins.

The announcer finished..."A good day for antifascists, a bad day for the Nazis."

Everyone's pleased faces with the Nazis losing two million votes lightened the room. Eli passed around tall wine glasses and Jacob poured a bottle of bubbly white Champaign. Drips of the bubbles slipped over the sides of the glasses and washed over the fingers as each took a sip and cheered the demise of the Nazis.

"To knocking those Nazi bastards out of parliament!" Aaron said and his face filled with relief instead of his usual stress and intensity, because though there was still no working government in Berlin, the Nazi Party just fell thirty four seats further from leading it.

"To the Communist and Social Democratic rallies which tested the streets of Germany!" Robert said and Rosalyn clicked her glass to his.

"To a hopeful Democracy and liberty!" Eli shouted and Jacob responded, "Hear, hear!" The clinking of glasses filled the room like a musical game.

The Nazis slid down the ladder rungs on November sixth, but they found a way back up to power. On November seventeenth, Chancellor Papen told President Hindenburg he was unable to form any working coalition and resigned. Two days later, Hitler requested he be made Chancellor, claiming only the Nazis could be relied on. He was denied. On November twenty-first, Hitler approached Hindenburg again with the support of the country's most influential industrialists, bankers, and business leaders, signing a petition to appoint Hitler Chancellor.

Hindenburg called Papen and Schleicher into his offices to help him find a solution. Papen suggested eliminating Reichstag altogether, using military and police to control crowds and suppress political parties, much like the days of the Empire with conventional, upper-classes ruling.

Schleicher disagreed, demanding he would get a majority in Reichstag with Nazi support.

The two fought for power until Hindenburg nominated Papen to take back control. But Schleicher had the support of the military and, if Papen insisted on his plan, Schleicher warned the country would fall into chaos. Hindenburg declared Schleicher Chancellor with tears plummeting from his eyes and handed in Papen's resignation, which shocked the country.

My dear Papen, you will not think much of me if I change my mind. But I am too old and have been through too much to accept the responsibility for a civil war. Our only hope is to let Schleicher try his luck.

- President Hindenburg.

Schleicher made a better choice than Hitler for Hindenburg, and Papen did not have enough power to gain a majority in parliament or retain the Chancellorship. It was the only decision the President could see with the military in Schleicher's pocket. Hindenburg preferred Papen to Schleicher, though. When Schleicher still offered no movement within the standstill government, behind the scenes, Hindenburg encouraged negotiations between Papen and Hitler to find a resolution.

Ami Rebecca Blackwelder

* * *

At the end of November, on Saturday the twenty-sixth, after all the political intrigue, Ralph and Deseire drove through the city to arrive at Rebecca's undersized apartment. Rebecca expected them early and prepared a few soft muffins and tea for their arrival.

The previous night, she tidied up her room, hanging clothes which had been ignored and giving Eli back some of his garb which had found its way into her closet. She spent much of the last night washing and dusting her tables and cabinets, refusing to settle for clean. Immaculate. It had to be immaculate or she would never hear the end of it from her mother.

Rebecca clad herself in a long flowery dress of purple and pink and wrapped a heavy pink scarf around her neck because of the cold November chills passing through her window.

Ralph pulled up into the parking lot in his expensive vehicle. Next to the other cars, it sparkled in elegance, yet with haughty contrast. Ralph walked alongside his wife to the front door with its broken latch. Deseire fiddled with it before they stepped through, rolling her eyes at the condition of the place. Though not unsuitable for Munich, she didn't want to be seen someplace like this: unkempt, common.

Their knock startled Rebecca in her seat near the kitchen table which she decorated with a vase of lilies. Deseire slid the door open and Ralph lifted out his arms to embrace Rebecca.

"Becky! Come here." Ralph rushed toward her and she leapt into her father's arms.

"Papa, it's so good to see you!" It had been years since their only other visit when Rebecca first moved to Munich. Their arrival now strained her words.

"The place looks much different from what I remember. You have so many more flowers around your room."

"I've bought a few new pieces of furniture and have decorated it. I have Marigolds, Edelweiss, Cornflowers, Roses and many more." As Rebecca mentioned each flower, she showed them off with a gesture of her hands. Ralph followed her, admiring all the varieties she had taken care of in winter. "When you first visited, I didn't have any time to do anything to the place."

143

"Well, it looks pleasant," Ralph complimented. Deseire's eyes darted around the room, partly disapproving and partly suspicious, looking for any sign of Eli.

Ralph walked up to the unique box along one living room wall. "Does the television still work?" He rubbed his hands over the top and played with the knobs.

"Yes, thank you, Papa. It works quite well. Everyone enjoys it."

"And your Jewish friend…Eli…he enjoys watching it too?" Deseire questioned, but her tone was not rough and displeased, but rather surprisingly curious.

"Yes, sometimes, he and his friends come over and we all watch it or just listen to the radio…or talk." Rebecca answered, remembering the many lovely evenings she spent here with Eli and his friends.

"That sounds nice, dear," Ralph commented.

"Please, sit down for tea. I made some muffins for you two. I wasn't sure how hungry you'd be but I know how you get, Papa, when you travel." Rebecca scurried to the kitchen and arranged two plates on the table while Ralph took off his heavy brown winter coat and hung it by the door. Deseire lifted her white wool scarf off her neck and let it dangle in her hands over her shoulders and cream colored lace dress which wrapped around her slim arms.

"There's a chill in your room, Rebecca." Deseire grimaced and adjusted the cold pearls around her neck, "I feel it over my body." A gust passed the window.

"Sorry about that, Mama, but the landlord hasn't fixed the crack in the window yet and some of the cold air from outside seeps in."

"I'll talk to the landlord before I leave," Ralph said in protective pride. He and Deseire sat at the small table, sipping their hot tea, the only item besides the temperamental heater that gave off any kind of warmth in Rebecca's room. Deseire returned her scarf to her chilled neck.

"Thank you, Papa." Rebecca kissed her father on the cheek with sincere gratitude and then kissed her mother on the cheek more out of obligatory observance. "It's nice to have the two of you finally come down to visit me." Rebecca said, feeling like a child again.

Deseire cleared her throat. "Well, we wanted to talk to you and thought this would be the best way."

Rebecca's lips tightened at her mother's tone and she fidgeted with her hands, walking to the kitchen sink to wash a few dishes and to keep her mind busy. She knew her mother wouldn't come all this way without declaring her opinions. The sound of Deseire's voice echoed through the room, over the still table and over the quiet air like an avalanche about to crumble over Rebecca's fragile demeanor.

"I know you love Eli," her mother began, straight to the point, and at the sound of his name, Rebecca whisked herself around and faced her mother. "But the country is at a very delicate time. Parliament has been divided in the hands of Hindenburg, Papen, Schleicher and Hitler. Schleicher has been declared Chancellor by Hindenburg himself, followed by Papen's resignation."

"I know, Mutti. I've read the papers." She tried to keep the edge out of her voice.

"Then, you must know Schleicher is sympathetic towards many Nazi players and ideas. If he's going to be in charge of the country, your relationship with Eli will not get easier and, with the Nazis roaming the streets, it will become worse." Deseire stood and held her daughter's shoulders. "I don't want to see my only child fall to the wayside in the midst of all this disorder."

With Deseire not acting as a dictator ruling her life, but as a concerned mother, Rebecca softened her stance for a moment. She searched Deseire's face and recognized the motherly façade for what it was, knowing what her mother would ask next.

"Where will you be in the middle of all of this?"

Rebecca shrugged her shoulders out of her mother's hands, knowing in that moment there would only be one place she ever could be. "At Eli's side."

For the first time, Ralph spoke up in the middle of the argument between them, the two women in his life. "Rebecca," he stood to hold his daughter's hand, "you must learn to conceal your feelings. You wear your emotions on your sleeve. It's not safe in these times to be so transparent."

Deseire's demeanor became forceful. "Rebecca, if you aren't going to heed our words then, for your own sake, we have to take more drastic measures to show you we are serious. We will cut you off financially if you stay with that Jewish man."

"You mean for your own sake, don't you, Mutti? You wouldn't want me to put shame upon you." Rebecca straightened her posture, not out of aristocratic habit, but out of inner strength, willing herself to separate from her need of her mother's approval; knowing she no longer needed it. "I won't leave him, so if you can't accept he is a part of my life, then it may be best that you leave."

Deseire's face flushed with disappointment, but Ralph's face crushed with sadness. He hesitantly smiled at Rebecca as he put on his heavy coat.

"Papa?" Rebecca's heart broke at his expression.

His eyes reddened, but he squared his shoulders and whispered, "Goodbye," before walking out.

Deseire tightened her scarf around her neck and stepped into the hallway beside her husband. "Rebecca, you never know what is best for you. We love you. We are your parents. I wish you could just see that."

"I know you love me, but sometimes love means letting go," Rebecca said with soft intonation and initiated a final kiss on her father's cheeks before shutting the door, dividing them. Rebecca let go of all her hopes for her parents' acceptance of Eli. She let go of all the angst between her mother and herself. Rebecca collapsed on her sofa in almost a faint. Curling her legs beneath her, she held her head in her hands, tears falling without restraint.

Her father siding with her mother weighed heavily on her mind and that bothered her more than cutting off her inheritance, more than the Nazi's violence against Eli, more than anything else. She would have to adjust to a new life: a life where secrets became a part of the everyday, a life where love hid, and the friends and family once relied on now stood distant and unreachable. The life she grew up knowing ended when she closed that door.

FRIDAY, DECEMBER 16, 1932

Kurt von Schleicher became Chancellor of Germany on December 2, 1932, with Hitler and Papen negotiating behind his back. The country didn't know it at the time, but a Hitler-Papen government would eventually change the face of the country in a second World War that included deliberate mass human extermination.

But, despite the uncertainty the country faced even after elections, Eli woke up excited today, Friday, which meant Rebecca had this weekend off. The heavy drizzle pounded like beads on Eli's umbrella as he walked Rebecca out of the apartment. He tucked his pale blue tie under his light brown suit coat and then held her hand. They stood on the sidewalk with rain sliding over Eli's nose as he held most of the umbrella over Rebecca.

The crowds of people, moving, marching, breathing, shouting, kept the streets noisy with vibrations. Nothing was still in Munich anymore. Nothing was quiet. Whenever they walked on the streets, alone or together, the sense of fear hung like a cloud in the storm-filled sky pouring over them.

Raindrops bounced on the sidewalk and splattered against shop windows. People pressed to the sides of buildings, trying to afford their shelter. A stooped over elderly woman, dressed in dark gray, approached Eli and Rebecca who stepped away from the wall to allow her to continue on. Rebecca smiled and nodded a silent greeting into the woman's sharp brown eyes.

"Jew lover!" The woman hissed then, passing behind the couple, spat on Eli's coat. He clenched his eyes shut and felt Rebecca's hand tighten on his.

"Honey?" She whispered to him.

"Let it go. Just let it go."

They strolled to a small shop he found down the block. Eli opened the door and gestured her in.

"Have you found some new swing records?" she asked, scanning the store.

"No. Christmas is coming and this year it will be just the two of us, so I've made a ruling."

"A ruling?" Her eyes widened. "Are we in court?"

"Perhaps. Depends on your behavior this afternoon."

"Ah, I see. Then what is your ruling?"

"We need our own traditions and it starts with Christmas music."

"Sweetheart, how did you know I was feeling melancholy about this holiday?"

"I see your eyes staring at the window displays, your mouth watering at the hams hanging in the butcher's window, and sighing at the Christmas tree in the toy store."

"You are perfect, Eli. Just perfect."

"Yes, I know. Now, come on."

Eli walked Rebecca to the empty listening station and slipped on the earphones for her. He slid in the Christmas recording by Shumann Heink singing Silent Night and Rebecca's eyes lit up as her cheeks lost their pinked hue in the warmth of the store and Eli's wool coat. While Eli searched the counters, she found The First Noel and Come Let Us Adore Him, Christ the Lord on a record and clicked it into the record box.

The two sat side by side, their expressions serene, with Rebecca listening and Eli watching until she tossed off one of the ear phones from her right ear for him to put up to his own. Eli swayed to the soft melodies of a reminiscent time which seemed like ages ago. Somehow in this closed room, with a wooden record player and earphones, they transcended from a time where racism and hate dominated the streets to a place of peace and liberty, hoping this future would become their own.

The music faded and they jolted back to Munich, 1932. Rebecca tilted her head and kissed Eli's lips with a small innocent peck. "Thank you, Eli." Her voice was sturdy and her hands no longer trembled from the fear she felt on the streets.

Eli never practiced Christmas in his strict Jewish home; his father Ezekiel would have forbid the trees and foreign traditions, but Eli knew its importance to Rebecca and her traditions became important to him; after all, Eli reasoned, she has done the same for me.

* * *

Sunday, December 25, Christmas, was Rebecca's birthday and, though her parents usually blended the two dates into one, Eli had promised her this year he would do something special. Both were free from work, Eli because of the chaos of the country and Rebecca because she had asked for time off. Rebecca waited with eager delight at Eli's arrival. Her phone rang and she answered it with anticipation, believing it to be Eli.

"Rebecca?"

She recognized the rough voice. "Father?"

"I just wanted to wish you a happy birthday and Merry Christmas." He rushed his words, then cleared his throat.

"Oh, Papa, Merry Christmas to you too." Her tone softened.

Her father cleared his throat again. "I have to go now, but I love you...we both do."

"I love you too, so very much." The line went dead, leaving her staring at her phone, tears welling up in her eyes.

The knock at the door startled her and she patted her cheeks dry. When she opened it, her low cut red dress which fell above the knees, swayed when she swirled into Eli's arms. Her dark hair curled over her left shoulder and hung just below her left breast.

Coughing, he raised his arm and looked expectantly at her. "Well?"

"Well, what?" She glanced up and saw mistletoe dangling from his fingers above her head. "Ooohh." Pursing her crimson tinged lips, she kissed him once and leaned in for another when he pulled back.

"No. There's no time. Come on."

He accompanied her to his apartment and made a show of opening the door. Candles placed on top of tables and bureaus brightened the room. Next to the window stood a Christmas tree decorated with silver tinsel, red ribbons, green and red glass ornaments, and a big gold star on top.

On the windowsill she could see the outline of his golden Menorah for Chanukah holding eight white candles with the center candle being

149

the longest. Rebecca stopped in the doorway, stunned at the attention to detail.

"It's…it's like a fairy tale." She motioned her hand in the direction of the tree. "Breathtaking." The moon hung through Eli's window behind the Christmas tree, it also shone of reflective light from the evening stars. The winter sky became dense and hail started to fall. Bit by bit, the scene reminded Rebecca of a story her father used to read to her when she was a child on Christmas Eve and, for a brief moment, she missed him. Presents nested underneath the tree and food covered the table: two plates of roasted ham and turkey, mashed potatoes, peas and corn.

"Cranberry sauce! You remembered!" She clapped her hands in delight. "How…when did you have time to do all of this?" Rebecca pointed to the table, admiration on her face.

"Rosalyn and Robert helped me last night." Picking up a small piece of turkey, he fed it to her. "Good, huh?"

"It's delicious!"

Rebecca curled into Eli's chest after they enjoyed the meal and the two hung like Christmas lights in each other's embrace, beaming, circling around the room in a slow dance without music. When they circled the room once, Rebecca took Eli's hand and guided him to the sofa.

"I was thinking, your lease is up at the end of the year and, instead of renewing it," she pulled his hand close, "why don't you move in with me?" Her eyes tickled with delight. "It would make more sense, with everything going on. We would save on rent and could keep a close eye on each other."

Eli's disposition lightened even more, and he held her hands in his. "I'm glad you have a question for me, because I have a proposal of my own." Eli lifted the small gift wrapped in silver paper from under the tree and handed it to her. He sat next to her while she unwrapped her Christmas gift.

The box was square and small, smaller than the box her father had given to her when she received the keys to her new Audi. Lifting the top off, she found a silver band with a diamond at its center. Her blue eyes widened and her rose lips opened in awe.

"Eli..." She said his name with tender appreciation and approval. He bent on one knee and held the tiny ring in his manicured hands.

"Will you marry me?" Eli's words brought tears to Rebecca's face, tears of euphoria. She grabbed his hand holding the ring, "Yes," she kissed his hand and pulled the ring to her, "yes." Eli slipped it on her ring finger.

"We're officially engaged." Eli stood and pulled Rebecca to him in one motion, lifting her over the floor. Her body slowly slid down his while their lips locked, their hands caressed each other's hair, and Rebecca's legs saddled around Eli's waist until they fell backward onto the sofa. Breathing for a moment, Rebecca pulled away a bit.

"Did you...do your parents approve?" Rebecca asked in a coy manner.

"My mama is elated...but my papa told me you would have to convert to Judaism for him to wholly accept you into his family." Eli confessed and Rebecca's elevated spirit descended. "But he will learn to love you all the same." Eli brushed his fingers over her chin. "I told him you would think about converting." Eli answered with a tinge of hope in his own voice.

"I will think about it. I want to be a part of your family in every way I can...to be close to you." Rebecca's soft eyes met Eli's. "But this will take time. The country. My family. My mama will never approve. When she hears about this wedding...she will be furious."

The next day they used the time off of work to move items from Eli's place into her own. They combined both their sofas to form an L-shape in Rebecca's living room, put his radio beside the television, and moved his wooden table to her porch next to the banister.

With the table moved, Rebecca twirled on the porch floor on her tiptoes in ballet motion, holding onto the banister. She emulated the ballet dancers she had observed growing up, and remembered a few of the steps from her early ballet classes. Holding one leg up horizontal to her vertical body, she drew her leg back in a circle, reconnecting her toes to the floor and beside her other foot. Her blue skirt whirled with her and with the breeze.

SUNDAY, JANUARY 1 1933

Eli arranged the wedding to be held at the synagogue near his parent's home with Rabbi Yosef on a Sunday. Neither Rebecca nor he wanted an extravagant wedding and chose something quaint and simple.

Saturday evening after Shabbos, prior to the wedding, Eli took Rebecca to the synagogue to meet Rabbi Yosef and, with her acceptance, the rabbi gave a blessing by the Torah for their future. Eli then performed the Mikveh, washing and preparing his body for marriage, followed by Rebecca who became more comfortable with his traditions.

Aaron acted as Eli's shomer, or best man, and Rosalyn as Rebecca's shomeret, or maid of honor. They assisted the bride and groom in every way they could with arrangements, but since the wedding was small and hurried, they only needed to arrange the quick construction of the canopy, the simple décor and the reception.

Sunday, Rebecca sat in front of the dresser, its round mirror reflecting her thoughtful expression. Deborah put the finishing touches on her hair and Rosalyn stood beside them.

"You look beautiful," Deborah smiled into the mirror. "I only wish your parents could be here."

Rebecca flicked a sad smile at her and shrugged. "I know. I'd always dreamed they'd be here for my wedding day. But…things change." In silent reflection, she recalled those girlhood dreams of wearing an elegant long white dress with its lace train. The flowers would be voluminous and abundant and the chairs would be filled with over two hundred guests.

She turned to look directly at Deborah. "Thank you so much for helping me today, for making me a welcomed part of your family. I don't just love your son. I love all of you."

"Stop it!" Rosalyn protested. "You're going to make me cry."

Deborah leaned forward and kissed Rebecca's cheek. "You are a beautiful bride and a welcomed daughter." Straightening, she stepped back. "I must take my place out front now." With a wave, she left the room.

Rebecca stood and nodded to Rosalyn. "I'm ready for my dress."

Rosalyn took it from the garment bag and helped her into it, then went to tell the rabbi the bride was ready.

Eli's parents sat in the front next to Miriam, Sarah, and Leah in chairs on the left side. Behind them sat many of Eli's friends from synagogue, including Aaron and Jacob. Robert and Rosalyn sat on the right side in support of the bride, along with a friend from the hospital Rebecca knew she could trust.

The synagogue members decorated the outside with a variety of foliage: Orchids, Roses, Marigolds, Edelweiss, and common mosses, since Eli had informed them of Rebecca's adoration of gardening and flower décor. The stained glass of the synagogue in the background sparkled in winter sunlight. The chairs were adorned with white and green plastic vines a few of the members had in a box at home. The chairs lined up on either side of the center aisle covered with a long white cloth leading up to Rabbi Yosef under a canopy. The musicians of the synagogue played their instruments with slow elocution.

Eli waited in a white tux with a white kippah dressed over his dark short wavy hair, standing next to Rabbi Yosef. His palms grew sweaty and the words he memorized to say over and over again had muddled in his brain and he struggled to remember each word.

Rebecca stepped toward him over the white cloth in a simple white gown she had worn once for a business dinner a few years ago and the sight of her drew every memorized sentence to his lips. Keeping her eyes locked on the handsome man before her, she walked to her future and everything from her past washed away. The soft music moved her towards him in each romantic step of vocal silence, a sacred silence, until she found herself face to face with Eli.

They stood in the midst of a cool breeze surrounded by winter white and barren trees. Rebecca's lace veil had been interwoven with white lilies and covered her face. Her hair dangled in a braid with white silk interlaced and tied at the end.

They stood together under the assembled canopy ready to be joined in this union.

"Now that the bride and groom are together under the huppah, I will begin," the rabbi intoned, then scratched his heavy beard before taking the ketubah, marriage contract, into his hands for Eli and Rebecca to sign. Rosalyn and Aaron stood at their side to sign it as witnesses.

Eli opened his palms outward and Rebecca mimicked his gesture. The rabbi recited the kiddush, the blessing for the wine, while holding the cup in his hand. "Baruch atah Adonai Eloheinu Melech haolam borei p'ri hagafen' (Blessed are you Lord our God King of the universe Creator of the fruit of the vine)," and sipped before giving it to Eli and then to Rebecca.

Deborah aided Rebecca in holding the glass as was custom. Eli and Rebecca gazed into each other's eyes, knowing every moment which preceded them led them to this fated event. Eli held the silver ring up for Rebecca's hands to grasp and they both clung onto it as Rebecca circled around Eli three times in Hebrew ritual. Eli then slipped the silver band with a small diamond over Rebecca's index finger, tears welling up in his eyes. Rebecca whispered, "I love you." After Eli said each phrase of the vow, Rebecca repeated it.

"Behold you are made Holy to me. Through this symbol, in accordance with the customs of the Jewish people, I commit myself on every level. I commit myself to share both challenges and resources. I will try my best to be just. I will flow loving kindness your way without judgment. I will be faithful to you so that you will know God."

The rabbi gave seven blessings before sipping from the wine glass again shared by both Eli and Rebecca. Ezekiel's face lit up when Eli took the glass wrapped in cloth and laid it on the floor to be stomped with his feet. When the glass broke, thunder crackled and grey storm clouds rolled through the winter sky. Before the rain fell, Eli, Rebecca and the crowd escaped to the inside of the synagogue where the reception waited.

When Eli pulled Rebecca to him and kissed her, neither one expected this new emotion. A spark ran through both their bodies simultaneously and unapologetically, uniting them to each other like Adam's eyes fell on Eve. This love, this wedded love, would not be ripped apart, would not be threatened and would not be told it couldn't exist.

Eli stepped back, whispering, "I'll only be a few moments." Then he departed to a private room separate from his new bride to take time to contemplate, a time he called yikhud. Eli spent time alone with his thoughts, in partial disbelief they had preformed the ceremony without interruption from Nazis patrolling the area. Their union to the rest of the country was a secret he and his wife would have to keep, even from her parents.

In spite of the necessary secrecy, Eli beamed for what the day had given him.

Rebecca knew she could rely on Rosalyn like a sister. Though Rebecca loved both her parents, she did not fully trust Deseire to keep such news quiet. Rosalyn sat by her side in a room outside the reception hall. The two hugged each other with an embrace Rebecca once longed to receive from her mother. Then she sighed.

"Are we going to make it?"

Rosalyn knew what Rebecca meant, not just her and Eli, but the entire country.

"I don't know." Rosalyn shook her head once and then looked into Rebecca's eyes with a hint of inspiration, "But we have today."

Rebecca saw Eli from the corner of her eye walk down the stairs to the reception. She scurried to him, holding the white used gown so that she didn't trip, and fell into his outstretched arms.

The Day the Flowers Died

MONDAY, JANUARY 2, 1933

Eli whisked Rebecca away for a romantic honeymoon outside of Munich, passing through Nuremburg in its elegant Bavarian architecture and then to Frankfurt. They caught a boat traveling on the Rhine River through Germany's Reign Castle District.

The medieval designs once owned by feudal landlords in the nineteenth century left them both nostalgic of German history. The variety of castles adorning the mountain tops clouded the landscape with mystery and splendor, forgetting the strategic war-bent functions of the castles along ago. They circled around the Schloss Stolsenfel castle which stood magnificent with a terrace bordering the outside mountain, offering a view of the Rhine River. Holding hands, fingers interlocked, they gazed over the terrace and watched the white blue waves crashing onto the shoreline.

They sojourned on the boat to another castle called the Marksburg. Its structure, thick and rounded, provided a solid military defense. Light grey fog swirled in an eerie formation as they peeked at the castle from the boat. Rebecca leaned forward on the boat's railing for a better view while Eli held her sturdy with his hands snug around her waist.

Continuing onward to the Burg Katz castle which sat like a crown of jewels for a queen and provided one of the best views of the Rhine, they exited the boat. They sauntered up the steps to the castle and stared at the Rhine River for twenty minutes before for Eli and Rebecca departed to find a nearby lodge to stay the night. Despite various inauspicious glares upon their jubilant faces from hotel guests and passersby, they forgot for a blissful moment they lived in a country divided.

They headed out of Kohn the morning of January second to catch the boat back to Frankfurt. Rebecca snapped photos with the camera Eli taught her to use. She didn't want to forget anything about their honeymoon, however brief. In Frankfurt, Eli drove to where the countryside stretched to the horizon and the sky bled into yellow-green grass.

The tall trees hung high in the blue sky, dropping their branches and leaves to the earth as a blanket. Light and dark hues filled the countryside as Eli swooshed down the winding street in his car. He drove off the road to an isolated location which provided transcendence to another time, another place far from where they had been.

Eli laid a wide chocolate brown blanket over a plot of grass underneath elongated trees of evergreen fanning above them. This peaceful place reminded them that the nature of Germany was still alive and untainted by the terrible violence of the Nazis. They'd found an oasis. Hidden. Secluded. Private.

Rebecca in curtsey-like fashion dropped to the center of the blanket with her legs underneath her puffed up skirt and awaited the surprise behind Eli's jaunty smile. He lifted a basket from the backseat, carried it to the blanket and plopped next to Rebecca with his legs crossed.

Rebecca smiled out of the right corner of her mouth, lifting the basket open and finding a variety of cheeses, meats, breads and a bottle of red wine. Eli ran his fingers through the grass.

"Eli, this is perfect," Rebecca gushed. This location provided them the unadulterated time they longed for since the wedding.

Rebecca broke the rye bread and filled it with goat cheese and salami. Eli broke the wheat bread and stuffed in chicken, goat cheese and rolled it.

The delectable sandwiches were only surpassed by the hidden box of strawberries Eli had at the bottom, which he revealed after they both finished eating. Rebecca wiped Eli's face of crumbs at the corners of his mouth and he pulled out a strawberry for her. She opened her lips and let him place it between her teeth. He watched her savor the flavor before she bit down and pulled it into her mouth.

The next strawberry Rebecca placed into her mouth herself, but not without temptation from Eli. He pressed his lips on the other end of the strawberry and they bit the fruit at each end until their lips touched. They could feel the strawberry seeds brush up against their lips as they kissed. Eli poured the red wine into one tall glass while his eyes caressed her skin. He balanced the glass next to her mouth while she sipped and then he sipped himself, reminding her of their wedding.

Eli declared in whisper, "I've loved falling in love with you, every morning, every hour. Every day you become more of my life and I can't wait for our life together to begin." Eli had a way with words, perhaps from the years of training in law school and debating in court, but next to Rebecca, they became passionate and full of emotion.

Their lips lingered in quiet spaces for moments, before Rebecca didn't feel anything but his lips chasing away everything that hurt inside of her until passion compelled her to lunge toward him, knocking him back onto the blanket. His hands caressed her arms; her fingers outlined his eyes, his nose, his lips. His fingers brushed her long dark hair dangling over her shoulders and then they brushed her high collar bone and the white lace of her pale blue silk blouse until he found her supple breasts.

Her lean legs wrapped themselves around his body and Eli rolled her over so that they lay side by side. A breeze blew through the trees, ruffling the leaves and tousling their hair. Rebecca's orange scented perfume filled Eli's sensations and he drew a breath of ecstasy before Rebecca delighted him with her lips on his chest. His hands moved up her legs under her fluffy white skirt. Her stomach rose and dropped, rose and dropped in anticipation. Their bodies twisted in configurations the trunks and roots of trees had only ever seen.

The prudish upbringing of Rebecca's life disappeared. When she lay next to Eli on the brown blanket she felt anew. A part of her sank when her mother and father left her that day from the Munich apartment, but within Eli's arms, a new piece of her grew and at the wedding she could feel all the pieces inside of her making sense. Here with him sharing this picnic, she felt whole again.

Fate brought all the pains to her for a reason, for this reason, to be with him now. They held each other as the afternoon sky shifted its brilliant colors into darker shades of evening. They needed no conversation between them. They needed no other sounds. They only needed to be close to one another, to feel each other's touch and rest under the peaceful German sky.

* * *

A new fervor in the air of German streets came from many Nazis hoping for the success of their party in Reichstag.

Schleicher's inability to offer the answers needed in parliament sent the desperate public searching for new leadership. Reichstag was a teetering canoe in a stormy sea. Throughout December and January after Schleicher's appointment as chancellor, Hindenburg wanted Papen in governmental office, trusting him above all the others. Consequently, in secret meetings, Hitler negotiated to have Papen share power with him if he was declared Chancellor.

On the twenty-ninth, Hitler perpetuated a false rumor that Schleicher was about to arrest Hindenburg and stage a military coup. This pushed Hindenburg to give the chancellorship to Hitler. Schleicher's inability to obtain dictatorial powers kept the country at the brink of anarchy. Hindenburg reluctantly accepted a Hitler Government on the contingency that Papen retained power in one of the eleven important cabinet posts, all dominated by conservative parties, thus balancing the Nazi's power. The Nazis retained only three of those posts and Hindenburg hoped for the best.

January thirtieth, 1933 a new face of German history began. Adolf Hitler, with tears rolling down his cheeks, emerged from the presidential palace as Chancellor of Germany. Admirers surrounded like a flock of seagulls all wanting a taste of him. The car drove away with Hitler shouting, "We've done it! We've done it!" The Nazis flaunted their troops and power in a sea of marches smashing into the country like a heavy storm.

Days and nights of celebration continued with burning torches casting ominous light on red hooked cross symbols of racism and terror clad on tan shirts. Red and gold Nazi banners reminded everyone Germany now belonged to them and, like shadows of darkness they stretched, covering the German country. The slow beating drums in the cities trembled in the minds of all those who opposed Hitler. He took an oath heard on the radio by all of Germany. Eli and Rebecca cringed at his insidious deceptions. His words would not fool the many already suffering discrimination and brutality by his hands and the hands of those he controlled.

Adulation poured from the crowds when he vowed, "I will employ my strength for the welfare of the German people, protect the Constitution and laws of the German people, conscientiously discharge the duties imposed on me, and conduct my affairs of office impartially and with justice to everyone." Hitler marched through the Brandenburg gate and along the Wilhelmstrasse to the Presidential palace.

Cops, once his adversaries, wore swastika armbands like wielded weapons. The rhythmic pounding of jackboots, drums, and military parade music beat into the dizzy minds of everyone at the ceremony and everyone clinging to the radio.

The month ended with words from various men denouncing Hitler as Chancellor, witnessing the sinister violence of the man. Strasser, a former leader alongside of Hitler, broke away from him, declaring, "Whatever happens, mark what I say. From now on Germany is in the hands of an Austrian, who is a congenital liar (Hitler), a former officer who is a pervert (Röhm), and a clubfoot (Goebbels). And I tell you the last is the worst of them all. This is Satan in human form. Göring is a brutal egotist who cares nothing for Germany as long as he becomes something."

A telegram delivered to Hindenburg from Ludendorff, who had been for Hitler in the military in the twenties and had since changed his mind, stated, "By appointing Hitler Chancellor of the Reich, you have handed over our sacred German Fatherland to one of the greatest demagogues of all time. I prophesy to you this evil man will plunge our Reich into the abyss and will inflict immeasurable woe on our nation. Future generations will curse you in your grave for this action."

But despite the words from various opponents of Hitler, the Chancellor within weeks would become absolute dictator of Germany and propel a series of events resulting in World War II and the eventual deaths of approximately fifty million humans, many of whom he deliberately exterminated in concentration camps on German soil. The fertile grounds that once offered life for many would become graves to bury the increasing dead.

Upon the announcement, many vacated Germany: writers, musicians, great thinkers, doctors, scientists, including the pacifist Albert Einstein who would effectively help end the war to come with his scientific efforts. Einstein fled the country, vowing never to return, asserting that he "shall live only in a country where civil liberty, tolerance, and equality prevail."

The floods of influential people in vehement disagreement at Hitler's successful Chancellorship emigrated west, finding a refuge that would eventually turn many others away and send them back to the feared German country they had departed.

The heated news brought Rebecca to her knees and Eli picked her up and held her against his chest her breath labored. Pushing away, she walked downstairs, taking each step in disbelief at the turn of events from November to January, somehow yielding Germany to Nazi power.

No one could have seen and no one expected this. Her body became tense and muscles froze as she felt starved for fresh air; air she knew wouldn't be fresh much longer with the rank words from the Nazi party unfiltered in the streets. She scraped across the cobblestones in her black shoes while her black button up dress swayed over the sidewalk and then over the grass. Gazing at the flowers that once brought her peace, she discovered the flowers were dead, trampled by Nazis in their celebratory parades. In place of spring's budding flowers, they left behind only dirty prints of heavy jackboots.

The Day the Flowers Died

MONDAY, FEBRUARY 27, 1933

The crackling fire from the burning Reichstag building woke everyone. The attack on Reichstag equaled an attack on Germany for many citizens. Despite Nazi plans to destroy German democracy, Hitler blamed the Communists for this wanton destruction, which many willingly and naively believed. Regardless of who was to blame, parliament burnt to ruin and along with it, the republic.

The hands of one man wrote a new instrument for government — suspending civil liberties, freedom of speech, freedom of assembly, freedom of press, accomplished by the issuance of a Reich Presidential decree. Those who opposed this new legislation were brought to a set of special courts which Papen enforced by signature to the decree, including revoking the right to appeal.

Nazis paraded on the streets. Considered pests in Germany before the chancellorship of Hitler, now citizens welcomed them as the police. No one who despised them tested their impatience, lack of mercy or brutality, or one would be beaten or disappear.

Harsh words poured from Nazi tongues and often they kicked and punched like undisciplined children who wanted candy. They dragged rebellious citizens off to jail. Unwanted shops, offices and business were vandalized and discouraged. The mark of the Nazis, like slaves branded, burned into the minds, the streets, the cities of Germany. Their presence overshadowed the lives of German citizens and even the air seemed heavier to walk in, strangling those who wished to depart from it.

* * *

Rebecca awoke the next morning and brewed tea for herself and Eli while he slept. They had to ready themselves for the work day ahead. When the kettle whistled, Rebecca poured them each a cup of tea and sliced a bit of lemon to drop into Eli's. She admired the diamond ring on her finger, clenching her hands together and caressing the ring with the palm of her other hand. Though small, the diamond symbolized their commitment and their love, a silver band, a circle that never ended.

She smiled as she set the cups on the table and called out to Eli, "Rise and shine. Your tea is ready." Eli rolled over, swinging his arms, pushing himself out of the comforts of the double sized bed.

"Coming, my dearest Rebecca." Eli enjoyed emphasizing his adoration for her and had been referring to her as his dearest Rebecca since they returned from their honeymoon. Rebecca loved hearing it. Eli threw on his long black robe and wobbled to the table to sip his tea before washing in the large bath basin in the bathroom.

She waited for him on the sofa in her white hospital attire and, when he exited the bedroom dressed in his grey suit with a white button up shirt, she placed his plate of eggs and toast on the table in front of her rare television. They ate breakfast before he drove her to the hospital, then continued to his father's firm.

Another office window was smashed; its broken glass littering the floor. Eli picked up the stone and set it on his desk. Only a few lawyers stayed with the firm and they remained in their office, finishing up work. The firm's carpeted hallways were barren of the life it once knew, quietness and stillness taking its place. Ezekiel hired Aaron a few months earlier and now Aaron sat in the office across the hall from Eli with the door closed. Eli invited himself into Aaron's new office where Ekkehard used to sit.

"How are things with you?" Eli inquired and Aaron faked a smile of contentment, a smile Eli knew too well, stretched across his face like hard clay.

"Good."

"What's wrong?" Eli insisted.

"What do you want me to say? Things are terrible. I don't have the job I was hired out of University to do because I'm a Jew. Our country is being dictated to and controlled by fascist racists. The parliament has been burnt down and, along with it, our civil liberties. Who knows how much longer we can continue working without being attacked by the Nazi patrol."

Aaron took a deep breath and then glanced out the window behind him overlooking the breaking city. "I'm not like you, Eli. I can't look at people and see the best. I can't look at Germany and have hope for the future." Aaron shuffled the papers in front of him. "I'm a realist and it's time to get out of Germany."

"What do you mean?"

"Einstein left, Jewish musicians, artists, writers, thinkers have all left Germany. They can see what's coming. With Hitler in charge, there will never be equality for Jews. There'll never be peace for you and Rebecca."

Eli's face grew stern and red and Aaron went on. "What will become of the two of you? What happens when the Nazis find out about your marriage?" Eli's thick brows twisted in concern, of thoughts he long had himself.

"What do we do?" Eli sat in the chair across from Aaron.

"I know you love her. So, you need to do what's best for her. The two of you need to get out of here. You need to get her out of here."

"How?"

"There's a ship, the Hamburg American Liner, that leaves for America every month, but you won't be able to purchase a ticket without the proper paperwork."

"What do we need?" Eli wiped his forehead.

Aaron rubbed his chapped lips before speaking. "It will be easy for Rebecca. She doesn't have a passport, but her mother is American and her father is German. You can request her American passport from the America embassy, disclosing her dual citizenship." Eli's lips released their clenched form. "Then you present her passport to purchase her ticket and she must show it again before boarding and at immigration upon entering America."

"And myself?" Eli worried and Aaron moved in close.

"You will need to apply for an American visa. You'll need your birth certificate, a certificate of good conduct from the German police which includes the police dossier, your prison record, military record, and any other government records as well as a German Police permit allowing your departure."

Aaron pondered in thought like he often did in court. "Additionally, you will need to obtain two affidavits from American citizens sponsoring your entry into America and give proof of a substantial savings in your bank account." Aaron spoke like he was reading a list, a list he himself had become familiar with in his own inquiries.

"How am I to acquire affidavits from America citizens? I don't even know anyone in America." Eli's brows arched.

"You told me Rebecca has an aunt. You could request a sponsorship letter from her. You said Rebecca speaks of her aunt highly, that she is a compassionate woman." Eli nodded. "If she'll write the letter for you, then you can present it to the American Embassy in Germany. In the meantime, while waiting on the letter, you must assemble all the other documentation."

"What about my marriage to Rebecca? Won't that help?" Eli asked.

"You've only just married her. For American citizenship, you'll have to demonstrate your marriage to her for at least a year or two." Aaron shook his head and continued, "Even after all the paperwork, you'll still need to convince the American consuls and the state department officials that you will be a benefit to their economy, not a burden."

Eli looked out the window, watched a few youths pass and then returned his thoughts to Aaron. "What about my family, my parents and sisters?"

"They'll have to undergo the same process and, even if you all comply with the regulations, it doesn't guarantee your visa will be approved." Aaron played with the papers on his desk, avoiding the inconvenient truth. Eli laid his hands over the mahogany desk and moved close to Aaron.

"What does that mean?"

"There has been a steady increase in immigrants to America. Roosevelt has tightened restrictions on immigrant policies to protect national safety and guard against an influx of foreigners. The President is fearful of the swollen unemployment rates in America and doesn't want immigrants taking jobs from American citizens. The quotas are low at just over one hundred and fifty thousand immigrants for the year."

Aaron's face grew weary. "This number includes everyone from every country wanting to enter America." Eli looked down at his hands in Aaron's response, hands once manicured but now neglected.

"Compassion takes a back seat to protocol when the majority of American citizens are opposed to refugees. Anti-Semitism is rampant in the general public and in many key governmental offices." Aaron stood and walked to his bookcase against the wall to browse with his finger, tracing over the titles of books.

"But there is another way." Aaron's eyes hinted of a devious idea.

"What?"

"The documentation can always be forged." Aaron whispered the last few words as if others might overhear.

"Forged?"

"If it comes to that; if you don't hear from immigration or if they deny your visa."

"If I don't hear from them?" Eli looked confused.

"I've heard visa processes have been slowing. Immigration is not inclined to do you any favors."

"What about my family?" There was a hard swallow in Eli's throat.

"They should all start applying for visas now," Aaron said, "but if I were you, I wouldn't wait on the American immigration office. I know the legal system like the back of my hand and I would talk to Mr. Reiner." Aaron whispered the name, but his insistent tone led to many more questions in Eli's mind.

"Mr. Reiner?"

"I will take you to him if you need me to."

"Thank you."

"Just promise me the two of you will get out of here."

"I promise."

* * *

Rebecca left the hospital on her lunch break and strolled up the road with her friend who had become like a mother to her. The woman's dark hair was rolled into a braid and she wore spectacles for distance. Rebecca guided her along the German cobblestone sidewalks to the flower shop she frequented.

Rebecca wanted to pick up more of her favorite varieties since the flowers she had were fading and the baby flowers outside the apartment were mauled. Upon arriving, loud cries from an elderly woman of the shop pervaded outside the shop's broken glass window. Glass was scattered all over the sidewalk and inside the shop. The elderly woman sat wailing on her stool with flowers torn and ripped up around her. Rebecca rushed to her side, shielding her with her own arms in an embrace.

"What happened?" Rebecca's voice shook in panic and anger. Her friend stared at the destroyed shop, shaking her head in disgust in the corner behind Rebecca.

"Nazi boys. My business ruined!" The woman's jagged nose reminded Rebecca of the nose she adored on Eli. "They had such sinister smiles on their faces when they threw my flowers and pots against the cement floor." She held her mouth with her hand and then told the rest of the story. "They laughed while stomping all over them. My precious plants." Her sobs kept her for a moment. "How can anyone delight in destroying a livelihood?"

The older woman burst into more tears, but Rebecca had no answers to offer and could only hold her in her arms, consoling her in silence. After a moment, Rebecca began lifting the broken pots off the floor and her friend helped sweep the dead flowers into a bag. The broken glass cracked underneath their feet until they swept it into another bag. The woman's shop stood empty of flowers as she sat in hushed agony while Rebecca and her friend departed to return to the hospital for work.

Work only provided a whole new set of problems for Rebecca.

Upon learning of her wedding to a Jewish man, her boss had given her the snub nose every time he passed her. Eyes that once held a healthy respect for her now dimmed with slanted, tightened edges of revulsion. Rebecca would cordially smile and look away, pretending to not notice the change in his demeanor. She wasn't sure if he felt this way because she married a Jew or because she married at all. During the few encounters she had with him, he hinted at being single and wondered if she was available. Rebecca had said no.

On top of this, an overflow of patients depended on a declining staff, some of whom were asked to leave because of complaints to their character or personality, though Rebecca knew it had more to do with their heritage or sympathies. The woman with long blonde hair rarely said anything to her anymore, though they had once been close friends.

Most of the doctors avoided her, except for one who on occasion still enjoyed her discourse.

The hospital felt like the streets of Munich to Rebecca. There was no longer the fellowship among equals. Care for the patient no longer came above all else. Rebecca would see certain patients fitting the Aryan profile given treatment first over non-Aryan patients, though they may have entered the hospital earlier. She would see preferential treatment to blond haired men and women to those with dark hair.

She couldn't justify the rationale, though, not officially law, it was practically a mandate by the Reich Chancellor. Then she wondered how long it would take for the Nazis to make it law, not just social prejudice, not just something done because everyone else did it, not just something done because you felt threatened.

On her way home from work, she saw the streets mauled with Nazi soldiers clinging to their structured forms, red twisted crosses, and perverted ideals. The streets to her smelled repugnant, like raw sewage or burnt food, and she wanted to throw up. Looking at the German youth idealizing this man, this god to them, marching in perfect rows up the streets made her want to weep.

She thought about all the generations of young boys and girls who would grow up with ideas as twisted as the crosses they wore and wondered how they would ever be taught something different, something that would tell them this is not right. The cab drove her to her apartment building and she plodded up to the steps, gazing at the dead flowers in the grass bed as she opened up the door with its broken latch. Her fingers fiddled over the latch, reminding her of the first time she met Eli and how long ago it seemed. That thought stayed with her all the way up to her room and kept her smiling.

She walked to her kitchen sink, wanting to fill her flower vases with new water, but the flowers wilted and new water couldn't revive them. Even the spring sun could not save them. She waited for Eli to come home from work and prepared dinner of boiled potato and beans. Meat was expensive and, without her parent's financial support or her father's occasional slip of money, she had to save every penny.

Eli also tightened his finances. Though he worked for his father so long as his father had the firm, Eli's paychecks also had to be cut. Ezekiel's firm had steadily declined since early 1932 and his employees felt this lack of income. When Eli walked into the room, the air lifted and the heavy weight of the day disappeared. Rebecca ran up to her Eli and allowed herself a brief visit at his chest before he took off his trench coat. He could smell dinner and his nose enjoyed the fragrance.

"What are you cooking?" Eli inquired.

"Nothing special; just beans and potatoes."

"Still, it is the best beans and potatoes I have ever smelled," Eli joked and nudged Rebecca in the shoulder, drawing a taut smile from her. It was difficult for her to let go of the sadness of her days.

"It will be ready in twenty minutes."

"Good, gives me time to wash up first." Eli washed his face in the sink and then gave himself a mock bath with a washrag and a little bit of water in the basin. They tried to conserve water usage. He sat in the tub, mulling over what Aaron had told him and considered if forging his family's passport documentation would be the best course of action. He could wait on his own papers, but he didn't want to put their lives in danger.

He needed to know they would be safe. After he finished his wash, he wore a comfortable tee shirt and pajama pant. He sat the table where two plates were ready to be filled with dinner. Rebecca carried the platter of food to the center and plopped comfortably into her seat.

"Bon appetite!" She attempted a failed French accent which sounded a cross between the hard German sound and the soft Dutch. Eli smiled and then his face froze in seriousness.

"Rebecca." At his tone, Rebecca sat motionless in her chair.

"Yes?" Her eyes widened.

"I need to talk to you."

"I'm listening."

"I love you, and it is because I love you that I need you, I need us to leave this country." Rebecca reached, stretching her hands to him.

"I'm not leaving without you." Though he had said us, she needed this fact to be very clear to him.

"I wouldn't want you to." He consoled her worry, "but I need to request your passport from the American Embassy to show you have dual citizenship. Your passport is the only way you can get out of Germany and to America. I will need documentation to verify it is you."

"America?"

"You have family there, your Aunt Martha. I remember you telling me about her once."

"And what about you?" Rebecca's concern quickly transferred to Eli.

"Aaron and I've talked about it." Eli cleared his throat, "I'll send another letter to your aunt for her support in sponsorship to say I'll be staying with her. While I wait for her response, I'll send my documents to the American Embassy here in Germany. I have to show my marriage certificate contract and my financial statements and acquire some papers from the German police."

"What if it's not enough?" Rebecca's heart jumped and her calm disposition became nervous.

"It will be," Eli encouraged, but he knew the chances were slim.

Since the 1930's, immigrants had been leaving Germany by the shiploads to land in other European countries or on liberal Western soil, carrying their dreams and hopes. Since Hitler's Chancellorship, the numbers doubled and the visa immigration departments everywhere began furthering already stringent restrictions. The number of anti-Semitic men in the immigration offices and the increase in fraudulent claims of marriage for green cards added to this problem. Eli knew he would have to get his paperwork into the immigration office as soon as possible to be approved.

Rebecca's head lowered and Eli reached for her hand, clasping it in his own. "It will be enough."

They finished their dinner in a haunting silence only disturbed by the sounds of chewing. Rebecca pondered over this information, trying to figure out what it all meant. Eli thought about his letter to Martha and the right wording for his request. After dinner they sauntered into the bedroom and Rebecca rested for the evening. Eli stayed up writing and rewriting his request to Rebecca's Aunt Martha and preparing the documents he would have to drop off at the immigration office, as well as thinking through his visit to the German police.

Ami Rebecca Blackwelder

Dear Aunt Martha,

I am writing on behalf of Rebecca Baum, your niece, and myself, Eli Levin. As you may or may not have heard, we have been married since the 31st of December. You may already know of the troubles in Germany under the new Reich leadership, but I will inform you of some of the hardships. Social prejudice is rampant with more and more Jews being asked to leave their place of employment. Violence against Jews is increasing and, sadly under the Nazis power, is overlooked and even expected. I have been a victim of a couple fights while living here and the initiator of a few myself. However, Rebecca and I hope for a world where liberty and equality is foremost and one does not have to fight to survive.

We hope to receive a letter of sponsorship from you for myself, Eli Levin, in hopes of soothing the legislation of immigration that dictates visa approval. Rebecca tells me you are a fair minded and compassionate person whom I look forward to meeting. Within the letter, we would need confirmation of your approval of us living at your home until more suitable accommodations can be arranged. I will be forwarding my information to the immigration offices soon and, when I receive your letter, I hope to add it to my documentation.

I thank you in advance for reading my personal letter and for considering the writing of a letter of sponsorship for me. I hope to see you soon.

With love,
Eli Levin & Rebecca Baum Levin

Eli showed the letter to Rebecca and without pause she signed under her name. The next day he dropped it off at the post office down the street.

WEDNESDAY, MARCH 1, 1933

Eli took a few days off of work to get the required documentation from the German police and, with the Nazis in favor of Jews exiting Germany, fulfilling the request was not difficult. He scurried to his Audi with the file containing Rebecca's documentation for an American passport and the documentation he acquired for himself, including bank statements, photographs of the wedding, and the signed contract, with the signature of both witnesses.

Eli also included a personal letter describing why he wished to immigrate to America.   Among the reasons listed were his and Rebecca's desire to live close to her aunt and grandmother and raise a family, though Eli knew as well as Rebecca that her grandmother was harsher than her mother, Deseire, and they probably would not spend much time with her.   Much of Deseire's values and discrimination stemmed directly from her mother, Adel.   Her older sister, Aunt Martha, like Rebecca, always had a mind of her own.

Deseire met her husband Ralph on his business trip to America, then moved to Germany where she lived ever since.   Up through her fifties, Adel would visit her daughter and granddaughter.   Rebecca distinctly remembered Adel commenting on how many Jews lived in the cities of Germany and remarked to Deseire and Ralph, how do you deal with it?

Only six or seven, Rebecca didn't know what Jew meant, though, by the negative tone in her grandma's voice, it might have meant a lot of traffic or robbery.   When Rebecca grew older, she began to see the little biases and discriminations exclusive to Adel and passed to Deseire, though Martha and Ralph did not seem to share the same discontentment.

At the American Embassy, fenced in with the America flag blowing in the wind behind the metal gates, the soldier requested Eli's identification and reason for entering before opening the gate.   As Eli waited in line, he noticed a number of Jews like himself with files of papers and reasons for a visa to America. The Americans were business oriented, shuffling through people like they were shuffling through papers. When Eli approached the desk, the lanky clerk grabbed Eli's files with robotic motions and then handed Eli his application form, took his fee for processing and then dropped Eli's file in a stack behind him with many other records. The office was tense under the lengthy immigrant restraints. Government moved with a slow, stern hand and Eli drew back in his seat with a distaste for the compassionless regulations.

"How long will it take to hear from the immigration office?" Eli asked.

"It could take a couple months or more. It's difficult to say for sure. If we get backed up, it could take longer." The clerk raked his fingers through his blond hair, cooling himself in the upcoming summer heat. With the cooler broken, only one fan wobbled back and forth, offering little relief.

Eli narrowed his eyes to concentrate on the clerk's thick American accent. Once he understood, he asked, "You think I will be able to procure the visa?" His throat tightened.

"There are quotas. If you don't make it in this year, you could be on a waiting list for next year. But there are no guarantees." The clerk's grey eyes became empathetic and he lowered his head, calling the next in line. Despite the clerk's attempts to lighten the unlikelihood of his obtaining a visa, Eli could not help but worry his paperwork wouldn't be enough and he would end up sitting in Germany until next year or later.

He walked out of the office, considering the possibility he and his family would be left behind. Aaron's suggestion about a forgery came to mind. He considered the shaky response of the clerk despite his hopeful expressions and couldn't bear the thought of his family being denied.

* * *

When he arrived at the law firm Thursday, he saw Ezekiel pass through the hallway heading to his office.

"Papa?"

Ezekiel turned his head. "Eli, did you accomplish what you sent out to do?"

"Yes, and that's what I want to talk to you about if you have time."

Ezekiel nodded and they headed for Eli's office.

"Let's talk in here." Ezekiel sat in the mahogany chair near the desk and Eli leaned over the desk towards him. "What is it, son?"

"I know you're comfortable in Germany and I know you hate to disrupt your life, but Germany is being ravaged of all its civil liberties. It's not the Germany you or even I grew up in. It is no longer the fatherland of Germans." Eli grabbed his father's folded hands and held them across the desk. "You know as a man who studied law what these legislative actions can lead to. You know better than most how delicate our lives now hang in the power of the Nazis."

His voice grew stern. "There's no more legislative balance. There's no more parliament. There's only Totalitarianism." Eli closed his eyes and opened them again in hope. "Papa, we must leave for the safety of those we love. You must leave for your family. I must leave for Rebecca."

Ezekiel rubbed his chin and lowered his head. "I've thought about it, son, but I've talked to clerks at the immigration office and they tell me it's risky. They say it's very difficult to acquire the visas. Even then, the country we enter may reject us and send us straight back to Germany. It also costs a lot of money for the ship, the visas, and the travel arrangements, as well as money to start up a new life."

"But, Papa, we have to try." Eli's eyes filled with desperation for his father to hear him, for his father to waive the stubbornness and agree to leave with him.

"I don't know if it will be better to uproot the entire family to a country we've never been to. I just don't know." Ezekiel rested his head in his hands, wiping his forehead. "There are prejudices everywhere, Eli."

"I dropped off my paperwork at the immigration office. I'll let you know how it goes, but, Papa," Eli's voice lowered, "even if the immigration office rejects the visa, Aaron knows of someone who makes forgeries. If we have to, we could…"

"No, no, son. That could send me to jail, you to jail and what then? What good will you or I be to our families then?" Ezekiel shook his head and Eli knew he would have to wait on hearing from the immigration office and hope his father changed his mind before he and Rebecca departed.

* * *

Sunday March fifth, Eli and Rebecca joined a spontaneous Jewish anti-German boycott. Jews throughout the world held mass rallies and marches proclaiming their rights. Eli built a sign reading: Be Free of Fascism! He and Rebecca marched through the streets with other Jews and those who sympathized. Unlike the violence of the marches from the red hooked-cross Nazis filling people with fear and dread, these marches evoked humanity and dignity and yielded its participators, previously stomped and kicked by jackboots, a way to combat the maltreatment. This gave a voice to many whose businesses were being vandalized, closed down and abandoned by once faithful employees.

Rebecca and Eli marched side by side and, unlike the earlier demonstration with the Communists and Social Democrats, Rebecca was not in the least bit intimidated or afraid. The protest boycott empowered her as she watched Eli and his Jewish friends fill the streets with their heads held high, with determined voices and a sturdy will. The boycott allowed those being denied their livelihood a refusal for the perpetrators. Felt all over the world, German efforts led organized movements across Europe.

Wednesday March twenty second, fifteen kilometers northwest of Munich, the first group of prisoners made up of mostly Liberals, Communists, Social Democrats, and homosexuals was taken to a concentration camp in Dachau. The sounds of marching soldiers and military trucks dragging men away from almost every German community echoed in Rebecca's mind, sounds of resistance, struggle, and ultimately of free thought suffocating.

Political leaders and rebels threatened the Reich and Hitler's ideas for government. They believed in liberty and equality above all. The Nazis had no use for those values and systematically executed influential political leaders.

Part of Dachau held prisoners in row after row of cots inside buildings. Another part conducted medical experiments. In total, the camp held two hundred thousand, one third of them Jews.

Some German citizens became concerned at the recent brutality, but Hitler assured everyone his totalitarian government had every right. After all, the Communists burned down the Reichstag parliament, leaving the country helpless. The Nazi party grabbed the reigns and began leading the country again. This soothed some and worried others. Eli and his friends were not fooled.

Rosalyn and Robert stopped by Eli's house the evening of the twenty third to discuss the country and the options left for people who did not agree with its course. Rebecca had warmed tea for everyone.

Rebecca answered the door; Rosalyn and Robert entered briskly and headed straight to the table. They did not have time to waste. In their minds the country's downfall was imminent and they were in its wake. Rebecca filled three cups with mint tea, and then handed a cup of lemon tea to Eli who exited the bedroom.

"What is so urgent?" Eli inquired. Robert shook his head and stood, unable to sit in his anger.

"I can't believe it. I just can't believe it."

"What happened?" Rebecca sipped her tea and sat next to Rosalyn.

"Didn't you listen to the radio news?" Rosalyn asked.

"No, we haven't had time. I've been busy at the hospital. Eli's been focused on work at the firm. They've lost many employees."

Rosalyn spoke with calm, a calm beyond Robert's capability at the moment. "The Enabling Act was passed." She said her words with slow methodical motion, almost freezing towards the end of the sentence in disbelief. Then her tone became inflamed. "Hitler promised the Act would in no way be harmful to the Presidency, the Reichstag, or municipal government. The majority of Germany bought into his conservative national leader's façade, believing him at the ceremony where he pretended not to be in charge of a radical party."

"Oh my God!" Eli reacted. Robert eased his angered wounds and sat down before Eli continued almost as calmly as Rosalyn. "This gives them the power to dissolve political parties altogether and grants him dictatorial powers."

"The Parliament is now just paper for the Nazis to hide behind and play puppet master," Rosalyn said with disgust. As Rosalyn finished her thought, someone pounded on the door. Rebecca opened it, delighted to see Aaron.

"Aaron, glad you could make it." Rebecca invited him in, her hands motioning him forward.

"Thank you, Rebecca." Aaron took off his dark blue suit jacket and laid it over the sofa. He surveyed the room and noticed the tension in the faces of everyone. "You all heard the news."

"Yes," Eli confirmed.

"What are we going to do?" Rosalyn's voice shook. Robert and Rosalyn steadfastly supported the Communist party. The idea of not being able to participate in protests, rallies or marches in support of their beliefs was unfathomable to them.

"It's incomprehensible what is happening to the country," Robert said in a forceful, unabated declaration. "What is more incomprehensible is that the citizens of Germany are allowing it to happen!"

"The country will be ruined under the hands of an evil brilliance," Aaron insisted.

"Brilliance?" Rebecca questioned.

"Hitler is no fool. He knows exactly what he's doing, what he wants and how to get there," Aaron responded in a confidence he carried in the courtroom. "A sociopath, but brilliant."

"So, how do we get there, to what we want?" Eli asked Aaron.

"I wouldn't wait too long. I'd look for all the possible routes out of Germany." Aaron's eyebrows clenched upward and his lip curled underneath.

"What do you mean?" Robert interjected.

Rebecca sipped her tea and answered, "Eli and I have decided to leave."

"You're leaving?" Rosalyn's mouth dropped open and she darted her eyes to Rebecca. "How come you didn't say anything to me earlier?"

"It's not finalized yet. We have to wait on Eli's visa from the immigration office and then we'll make arrangements for the ship."

"I wouldn't rely on the immigration offices." Robert confirmed Eli's fears.

"Why not?" Rebecca inquired. Eli shook his head out of Rebecca's view, telling Robert to close his mouth.

"Nothing." Robert cuddled Rosalyn close to him.

Everyone left after tea and, with a long face, Rebecca followed Eli into the bedroom. Eli sat on the bed with his head down and eyes staring at the sheets. He glanced up at Rebecca, knowing she would ask, but not wanting to answer, not wanting to bring more worry to her. His eyes tore away from her to avoid the conversation.

"What did Robert mean, 'I wouldn't rely on the immigration offices.'?"

"Don't worry about it, Rebecca. You know Robert. He's just looking at it from all angles."

"Should we worry about it?"

"It will do no good, will it? Whether they approve my visa or not, worry will not change it." Eli rubbed Rebecca's hands as he spoke to her and Rebecca slipped into bed under the thin silk sheet she bought for the summer sun. "Let's not think about this much and rest now."

Rebecca nodded and Eli pulled her to him with his arm around her neck. Rebecca nestled her head in between the sheets and Eli's chest, a comfortable position which they had grown to enjoy.

The rest of the month, radio stations lost their right to broadcast and the Nazi paper, Voelkische Beobachter took their place, filling the news with their propaganda.

The twenty fourth, Eli sprinted downstairs to pick up the morning paper before heading off to work. The newspaper's front page spelled out a historic day for the Nazis. The day of the Third Reich has come! Eli ripped the paper in half and tossed it in the trash can in front of the building while a neighbor from across the street watched him with careful eyes.

SATURDAY, APRIL 1, 1933

Saturday morning, Rebecca awoke under her thin silk sheets in Eli's arms just where she wanted to be. She curled her shoulders and rolled into Eli's chest, his comforting chest that provided warmth like the sun and protection like a soldier. She longed for nothing more in this moment, this perfect moment. The sunlit air was warm and the wild flowers outside were beginning to blossom and grow on their own again. Her wide smile bunched up into Eli's face in need of a morning shave and she brushed her cheek across his chin and giggled.

"What's so funny?" Eli squished his face up to hers as he rolled toward her body.

"I'm just happy, in this moment with you, despite all of it, all of the chaos around us."

Eli traced his fingers across her brow, down her jaw line to her lips. "Me too." He only needed to say two words to delineate the feelings between them, to make them real and alive. Though Eli and Rebecca were in the habit of skipping many Synagogue services for sleeping in and spending the day together, Eli wanted to take Rebecca to service today. They slipped out of bed and bathed. Rebecca lifted the water drenched sponge and squeezed it over Eli, watching the water trickle down his back. She dabbed soap on his body and Eli rubbed the scented cleanser into his skin and then squeezed the saturated sponge over Rebecca's back and chest, washing her.

Rebecca twirled her hair up and pinned it on top of her head and dried off before slipping on a cotton lavender skirt draping over her knees and a white silk blouse with the lace enveloping her neck. Eli pulled on beige slacks and a caramel brown shirt with well ironed sleeves and collar. Rebecca tended to his clothes when she could despite her busy schedule at the hospital and despite the insistence from Eli to forget the ironing and allow him to do it. But Rebecca enjoyed tending to Eli and aiding him in his comforts.

The Day the Flowers Died

They sauntered over the street in the cool April breeze. With the Synagogue just blocks away from their apartment, they preferred walking to driving. Many shops along the street were closed because of the Shabbos. Eli pulled Rebecca close to him with a tug on her hand. Rebecca's heels clicked against the pavement and Eli's loafers softly patted the cement.

From behind, the sound of jackboots disturbed the rhythm Rebecca and Eli had between them. As the sounds approached, they pushed past the two of them. The SA soldiers stopped in front of the closed shops and businesses, their hands filled with pamphlets. A few couples walked ahead of Eli and Rebecca and, as they passed one of the shops, two members of the SA pushed pamphlets into their hands. The soldiers declared, "Protect German blood and German honor! Don't buy from Jews!" Across the street, several SA members no older than Jacob painted a sign in red ink across the window, Don't buy from Jews!

The streets flooded with picket signs and demonstrations boycotting Jewish businesses and Jewish products. Some who held the signs were teenagers and young boys with smiles on their faces like they had achieved something great — the acceptance of their country and government.

Eli kept Rebecca close with an upheld confidence, a forceful will pushing him forward into morning Synagogue. Rebecca's hand clenched Eli's. Her smile dropped and tightened. They briskly ambled past a few shops decorated with newly posted derogatory Jewish remarks. Two SA guards handed out pamphlets, the taller one fixing his grey blue eyes on Eli and shouting, "Jew boy!"

Ignoring him, Eli reassured Rebecca's safety with a touch of his hand to her lower back. They hastened around the corner to the Synagogue before a fight broke out. The synagogue service provided both Rebecca and Eli with a comforting peace not accessible on the streets of Munich anymore.

Rebecca had grown accustomed to the long service, and today felt most grateful for that fact. She didn't want to return to the streets where discord waited on every corner, where at any moment she or Eli would have to fear for their safety.

Sometimes she awoke in the middle of the night in terror with images of Eli being dragged away in one of those Nazi vehicles taking him to the Dachau Concentration Camp. For Rebecca there were only two places she could entirely feel like herself anymore, two places that offered sanctuary, synagogue and her apartment. The streets held an uncertain future.

On April seventh, a new Nazi law forbade employment to all non-Aryan civil servants. Silent frustration and anger lingered in the minds of many non Aryan workers now out of a job, but the German citizens complied. Opinions divided. Some Germans held sympathies for the non Aryans, yet many remained adamant in the Nazi's convictions.

The decline of civil liberties affected everyone. Life would only get worse for non Aryans. This theft could be tasted in the air. It could be heard in the whispers. It could be felt in the stares. No longer a place for business and strolling Sunday mornings, the streets became a maze for many, with roads leading to fear, some to retreat, and some to Nazi beatings.

On April twenty-second, Nazi law prohibited Jewish lawyers from practice throughout the country and, without tears, Ezekiel boarded up his firm and locked it for the last time. He had a few boxes filled with important papers and his black briefcase. Eli, along with Aaron and a friend Kevin, helped his father lift the boxes into the car. Not many supporters remained for Ezekiel by the time he locked the doors. Employees he had worked with, some for many years, departed month after month until he had very few employees left to pay.

When the firm closed, so did Eli's ability to earn his living, and the weight of the country fell like a heavy stone upon his already wavering shoulders. Eli arrived at the apartment with a forlorn look of desperation and defeat. Already hearing the news at the hospital, Rebecca rushed to his side as he plodded through the door. Rebecca was used to comforting and aiding patients so, when Eli's face lost its color and he slipped in a faint, she caught him before he hit the floor.

"My papa had to close his firm today, a firm he managed and owned most of his life." The words flowed heavily out of Eli's lips. "There was such sadness in his face."

Rebecca walked him to the sofa, pulled off his coat and laid it across the sofa's back. Then she hugged him, drawing his tired face to her chest. A few minutes later, she boiled a pot of tea and Eli sat in a worrying daze. When Rebecca handed the cup to him, he drank slowly and began to warm up. The gold brown hint of color replenished the earlier paleness and he refocused on Rebecca.

"We have to get out of here. Things are only getting worse. Papa might listen to me now and take the family to America." Eli's reasoned tone returned and Rebecca could see the lawyer in him pondering his next moves. "I'll look for forged visas for my family. We don't have time to wait for all of us to be approved."

"Is it safe?"

"What else can I do? Papa hasn't turned in the family paperwork for a visa and the chance of immigration approving all five of us is unlikely." Eli's voice scratched, "Roosevelt is tightening the quotas. The immigration rate is rising. If we had a famous scientist or athlete in the family, we could rely on being approved, but we have no one influential." His words flowed like he argued a case before the courthouse.

"You must be extremely careful, Eli." Rebecca squeezed his arm. "It would be very dangerous if you were caught. Jews opposing the Nazis are already disappearing. If anyone found you out, you…you…" She couldn't say the words. She couldn't think the words. Her eyes teared at the unbearable thought.

"No one will find out. Aaron knows what to do. He has a Jewish friend who's good with documents. He'll be able to find something for my family."

"And you?" Her eyes watered and wrinkles stretched over her forehead. "What if your application is denied?"

"If it is, Aaron will find the paperwork I need." Eli whispered the sentence as if someone might hear and Rebecca rested her head on his shoulder. The evening drew upon the country and Rebecca closed the curtains over the kitchen window. They rested in the bedroom that held their secrets and that had become their sanctuary.

Saturday morning, many shops and restaurants refused service to Jews. Placards placed around businesses stated, Jews not admitted and Jews enter this place at their own risk. Because of Nazi insistence of public school overcrowding, they limited Jews in the number that could attend. Many knew this meant Jews would eventually be banned altogether.

They [the Jews] have no business being among us true Germans, explained one Nazi teacher to his students. A dark cloud situated itself over the country and the country succumbed to its darkness. Those not especially adverse to Jews still followed the Nazis out of fear for their own livelihood.

Some parts of the country banned Jews from public parks, swimming-pools and public transport. Laws prevented universities from keeping Jewish educators, and campuses across Germany removed Jewish teachers from the buildings. Teachers who had spent most of their adult life educating were no longer welcome, and the sting like a wasp did not end with the simple request from the Nazis.

The sting stabbed much deeper as feelings wavered among non-Jewish students. Some felt the discriminations in the new laws were unjust, unfair and yet many felt them necessary to ensure Germany returned to the hands of German blood. The very students who many Jewish educators dedicated their lives to teach turned against them.

A secret police began watching the citizens. Gestapo. If they found anyone not abiding Nazi decorum, the Gestapo assaulted them or they disappeared, assumed to have been tortured and left at a concentration camp. The Protestant and Catholic press described the papers' ambivalent feelings towards Hitler's anti-Semitism. They denounced banishment of Jews, violence and persecution and yet, argued Germany's Jews had brought these consequences upon themselves because of their dominating presence in the press, as well as in the economic and financial world.

* * *

While Rebecca was at work, Eli met with Aaron at an archaic building owned by an older Jewish family, long time friends with Aaron. They had operated a legal advice office, but the business closed and chains lay across the doors. Eli followed Aaron into the back alley and saw a man with a cigarette standing beside a door. The man nodded at Aaron in recognition and squeaked the door open. He dropped the cigarette and twisted it under his foot while Eli and Aaron slipped into the building.

183

Eli followed Aaron through the corridor and into an office toward the front. The room, musty from a lack of operation in the past weeks, carried the sounds of distraught and frustrated voices. Two men with short dark hair and heavy mustaches sat on a short sofa against the left wall. An elderly woman holding a cup of tea stood in the right corner where a kettle sat on small table. Three younger men sat on a long sofa against the right wall. An elderly man with a grey mustache and grey hair directed the meeting from the middle of the room. As Aaron and Eli entered, the loud discourse softened and eyes focused on them.

"Aaron, come in, come in," the older man said and gestured for Aaron and Eli to sit on the middle sofa. The man stood next to a small coffee table with papers spread over it. His long black trench coat dangled below the table. "This must be your friend, Eli." He reached to shake Eli's hand. "I'm Mr. Reiner." He then returned to the papers. "I guess we are all here for the same reasons."

One of the men on the right sofa spoke, "Our visas were denied and we were told the quota has been met for this year. But we have to get our wives out of Germany."

"This is not a guarantee," the director said. "You have to realize this is dangerous."

"We know, but there is no other way for us," one of the two men implored while the other cleaned one of his fingernails with his other nail.

"And Aaron, you two are here for the same reason?"

"Yes."

Eli cleared his throat and declared his predicament. "There are five in my family and they won't have the time they need to get the documents required to exit Germany this year."

The older man nodded and his heavy brows quirked. "And this family, does it include yourself?" he asked.

Eli shook his head. "I'm waiting on my paperwork from immigration. It shouldn't be much longer."

"And if you're denied?" The older man said these words as if they were a certainty.

"I'll have to come back to you."

Mr. Reiner spoke to the room. "I'll need pictures of everyone requiring visa documentation. I will also need birth certificates and

passports and three hundred marks for each manufactured approval."
Eli's brows arched at the request of money.

Aaron patted Eli's shoulder. "It's alright. The money isn't for him.
It's for the officer in immigration who'll help with the documents. He'll
stamp the passports with the needed visas and approvals and provide a
forged letter from the American Embassy."

"I'll get everything you need. Just help my family get out of here,"
Eli declared. Mr. Reiner adjusted his mustache and then handed Eli a
paper from his coffee table.

"Drop off what I need at this mailbox address. Come back to this
building in June and the paperwork will be ready for you."

"In two months?" Eli's voice stressed.

"It is as soon as I can get it done." He laid his wrinkled hand on Eli's
shoulder. "These things take time."

* * *

The Passover fell on April eleventh and, though the synagogues
closed and Jewish services were refused acknowledgement, the Levin
family made a feast to celebrate much like they had the previous year at
their own home. Rebecca clung to the invitation with delight. She
missed her own papa, Mildred, and Rueben and, despite her mother's
faults she missed her as well. She had hoped in time they would come
to accept her decision to stay with Eli. Then she would be able to
confess their marriage.

But no call since last Christmas arrived for her from her mother or
her father and this disappointment weighed on her spirits. The Jewish
holiday of Passover came for her as a needed interruption, providing
the warmth of family again, though not her own.

The distance she felt sometimes between herself and the Levin
family vanished at their wedding. Any resistance she felt in Deborah
and Ezekiel had melted into affection and acceptance. Sarah, Leah,
and Miriam became like her own sisters and Eli's Jewish friends like her
own brothers.

Rebecca clung to Eli's warm hand as they walked into the Levin
home for the second Passover together. More familiar to her than the
last time, she knew what to expect and how to behave. She knew how

long everything would take and what culinary elegance would be present. Though this year was laden with financial burden, political unrest and social uneasiness, the Levin family managed to provide a lush course for the dining enjoyment they called the Seder. All the expected food was present, cooked by Ada and Deborah with some help from Sarah.

The rituals had become like second nature to Rebecca and she even remembered many of the colloquial expressions and Hebrew words used during the feast. Many of Eli's other relatives arrived for this feast, contributing to the food and drink. Outside the house, the country crumbled under a façade of righteous persecution. But inside the Levin home, familial tenderness shrouded each child and each adult, making this country still feel like home.

WEDNESDAY, MAY 10, 1933

"All the authors that we had treasured — and of course still do treasure — were suddenly supposed to be valueless." Elfrieda Bruenning, aged 93.

Rosalyn and Robert stood on the outskirts of a fire blazing into the once quiet evening German sky. Oxcarts crammed with forbidden books traversed throughout the German streets to various bonfires for destruction. University students, considered some of the finest in the world and once well studied in a variety of intellectual persuasions, plundered unwanted books and threw them into bonfires to the ominous sounds of Nazi music.

They poured gasoline over the books, torched them and watched them go up into smoke. Bands and parades marched and their sounds permeated cities across Germany. The music surrounded the crackling fires. Students took oaths and sang Nazi songs, declaring their disregard of unGerman ideas. Freud, Einstein, Thomas Mann, Jack London, H.G. Wells, and many others went up in flames to Nazi anthems and salutes.

Fires burned January evening on torches of Germans parading at the announcement of Hitler's chancellorship. Fire burned the Reichstag down in February. Now fire destroyed ideas and words in May.

Towards the end of the book burning, Rosalyn and Robert heard Joseph Goebbels, the Reich Minister for Public enlightenment and Propaganda, speak at the bonfire in Berlin. "German men and women! The age of arrogant Jewish intellectualism is now at an end! You are doing the right thing at this midnight hour — to consign to the flames the unclean spirit of the past. This is a great, powerful, and symbolic act. Out of these ashes the phoenix of a new age will arise...Oh Century! Oh Science! It is a joy to be alive!"

Rosalyn grabbed Robert's hand and pulled him back when he attempted to make his way to the bonfire.

Robert turned his head to her and tilted left in a weakness he had for her desires. "I have to try to save some books," he whispered.

She held his gaze for a moment and then let him go. Robert tunneled through the crowds until he pushed his way to the fire. He pulled the book of poems by Heine Henrich out of one student's hands and brushed off the ash. The blond, young student stood firm in his perverted ideals and, with a strained grimace, lunged forward at Robert and knocked into his shoulder.

"Give back the book!" the student said.

"No!" Robert pulled the book of poetry to his chest like he was protecting a wounded bird. The student lunged forward again, grasping for the book but, in Robert's retreat backward, only grabbed air. A few other students noticed the scuffle and joined their peer's efforts to retrieve the book for burning.

Robert surveyed the area and saw four students stare at him with eager intent to harm. Seconds stood still and then Robert twisted around in Rosalyn's direction, pushing and clawing his way out of the maddening crowd.

The four students followed Robert and shouted, "Get him! Get him!" Their jaws clenched and they hissed their words like an animal about to kill its prey.

Rosalyn stretched her arm toward Robert as he stumbled forward onto the street. He grabbed hold of her hand which pulled him away from the chaos. They raced down the dark street full of exuberant Nazis, and the students followed. A few street lights and Nazi torches carried by the marching parade broke the night. The crooked red crosses glimmered under the burning light and the wave of Nazis and German citizens flooding the roads washed over them. Robert grabbed hold of Rosalyn's arm, clinging to her dark wool jacket, and pulled her into an alley.

"Stay quiet." Robert held her close. The four students plowed through the parade, pushing forward until they stopped on the street. The sounds of the band's Nazi anthems pervaded the roads until they turned the corner and left the street in silence. Robert watched them before retreating further into the alley and ushered Rosalyn inside an open door.

The dark room smelled musty. Robert clicked the door shut and locked it. He clutched a table and squatted next to Rosalyn, then brushed his hands over the saved book. From the moonlight seeping through the cracks in the door, he admired its simple cover.

Rosalyn stared into Robert's eyes and pushed herself closer to him. His fingers caressed her blonde hair pinned up in a pony tail and he then returned his attention to the book. This quiet moment between the two of them and a forbidden book reminded them of the many clandestine meetings of children and adults gathering to read their favorite banned authors, many reprimanded when caught by Hitler's youth leaders.

"I think they're gone," Rosalyn whispered. Robert peeked out of the crack in the door and eased it opened, noticing the streets had become more silent and still.

"Let's get going," he said with uncertain anxiety. He grabbed Rosalyn's hand and helped pull her to her feet. The two of them walked out through the alley and returned to their car parked a few blocks from the bonfire.

* * *

Sunday morning found Rebecca up early in the kitchen, preparing a basket of food. She wanted to go on a picnic at the lake Eli had taken her to for Valentine's Day. Eli awoke to the sounds of her dressing and watched her lace her legs with nylon and clad her breasts with a silk blouse and pale blue skirt.

"What are you doing up so early on Sunday?" Eli squinted his eyes and yawned, struggling to cover his mouth with his hand currently nestled under his leg.

"We're going on a trip to the lake. I'm in the mood for swimming." Rebecca braided her long hair.

"We are, huh?" Eli leapt out from under the sheets and ambled to the bathroom. "Then I'd better get ready." The sounds of the falling water complimented the sounds of the tea pouring into two cups by Rebecca's hand. She shouted to him from the kitchen area, "I've put your swimming trunks in the basket with my swimming garb and two extra towels."

"Thank you, my dearest Rebecca."

"Hurry up. I want to get there early," Rebecca scolded as she put the homemade sandwiches into the basket. Eli appeared in the kitchen and picked the basket up from the counter.

"Well, let's get going then." They walked down the steps to Rebecca's car which Eli drove whenever they went anywhere together. Rebecca did not enjoy the stress of the road.

Eli found it a pleasure to sooth her concerns and provide a state of comfort for her if only temporary. Rebecca relaxed while Eli chauffeured her to the lake. Eli pulled into the park and situated his car next to one other car in the lot.

The park was quiet and the early morning air fresh. Eli and Rebecca changed in the changing rooms marked for women on one side and men on the other. Eli left the room first and then Rebecca met him out in front by the lake. The short grass softened against their feet. The turquoise water glistened under the morning sun and shimmered with little waves washing up to the shoreline and over the white, brown sand resting just outside the border of the short blades of grass and sun capped shrubs.

A distant couple snuggled in the water. They twirled together before swimming side by side further off. Eli drew Rebecca to him with a tug of her hand and they splashed as they dove into the water in unison. Blue jays chirped in trees and sometimes as they flew over the lake. Wind rustled branches and leaves. Clouds hid the intensity of the sun and provided a welcomed shade.

They swirled together arm in arm in the blissful freedom of the water and, on occasion, Rebecca splashed Eli's face with a kick of her foot or childlike movement of her hand. Eli dove underneath, disappearing and Rebecca swarmed around the lake looking for him. He popped up next to her and grabbed her shoulder. She screamed and then splashed Eli's face again in retribution.

As the afternoon approached, more cars piled into the park's lot and the lake soon filled with children and adults playing beach ball, Marco-Polo, and wading in the water or relaxing on the park grass. The distant couple whom Eli noticed earlier vanished and so did the quiet stillness. Two young ladies swam past Rebecca and Eli, their long blonde hair pulled tight into pony tails.

They glared at Eli as they swam and then returned to the shore where two young short blond haired men helped to towel dry them. Eli noticed one of the young ladies pointing in his direction and his lips tightened. One of the young men sped to a lifeguard and the discourse lasted a few minutes before the lifeguard hastened to the edge of the lake and called out to Eli.

He gestured with his hands and said, "You need to come out of the water, young man."

Rebecca turned her head to Eli. "Is he talking to you?"

"You need to come out now," the lifeguard demanded.

Eli complied and swam to the shore. Rebecca followed closely behind him. Pulling himself out of the water, he walked over to the lifeguard and asked, "What's the problem?" Eli's smile curled down in reluctance.

"No Jews aloud. You need to vacate the area."

Rebecca's mouth gaped and her disposition became agitated. "You can't do this! He has a right to swim here."

"The Nazis have made it clear he has no such right and, unless you want to talk to the SA about this, I would prepare to leave, Miss." The lifeguard spoke with military rigidness. His short trimmed, blond hair and blue eyes told Eli he was one of Hitler's Youth and Eli yanked Rebecca back.

"It's fine. We were just leaving." Eli placed his hand on the small of Rebecca's back and pushed her in the direction of the car. He lifted the basket of food and towels from the picnic table and wrapped Rebecca in one of the towels. The once rhythmic cadence of the park's sounds of nature had been disturbed and became like the streets of Munich, ripping the two of them back into the world they tried to hide from if just for a moment.

"They can't do that," Rebecca declared and she slammed the door shut.

"They can and they have." Eli reasoned with his lawyer tone and laid a towel over the seat before he started the engine.

"This isn't right," Rebecca insisted as Eli drove them home in silence. The walk up to their apartment felt long and heavy, each step in a direction they had not chosen and did not want.

Eli shut his eyes and plopped on top of the bed. Rebecca sighed like the lungs within her constricted and she found it hard to breathe.

"Are you alright?" Eli asked and sat up on the foot of the bed, watching her in the living area through the open door.

"I'm fine, Eli. Don't worry about me." She brushed his concerns off her like she brushed the dust off the objects in her room. She did not want sympathy or unwarranted fret. He was the one in danger, the one whose civil rights were violated every day since the chancellorship of Hitler. He needed her sympathies. She climbed into the bed with him, though it was still afternoon. They snuggled like the couple at the lake in the distance, swirling and twirling and swimming toward the shore.

But the bedroom only offered a momentary peace, passing hours that soon fell into the next day when Rebecca needed to report to work and Eli began to feel cooped up inside the apartment. He needed to feel normal again, busy with work for his father. He didn't graduate University to lie in bed all day and he didn't enjoy the lack of intellectual stimulation from being absent from the courtroom. He did not want to become a prisoner in the country he was born and raised in. He felt as German as his Aryan neighbors and, with exception to his observance of Jewish Holy days and Shabbos and avoidance of pork, he was very much German.

But the days filled with an absence of many things for Eli, an absence of Rebecca, an absence of the courtroom, an absence of his office, and an absence of fresh air. Since the boycott and riots in April, fear and violence escalated with Jews the primary target. Eli swore to Rebecca he would not linger outside for too long in the mornings without her and he would not walk the streets unless necessary. Gestapo, SA, and Hitler's Youth patrolled the streets now.

He spent much of his time reading from banned authors and reviewing the law. This law no longer existed under Nazi control and radical reform, but he grew up with and knew it, and hoped it would return someday. He sipped his morning tea which Rebecca prepared for him before a succulent kiss on the lips and a wave goodbye for the day.

He went downstairs, slid his coin into the vender and pulled out the day's paper, Hamburger Tageblatt newspaper, Friday 31. The Nazis not only controlled parliament, the streets and public opinion, but controlled journalism, too, to ensure no one spoke against them. As Eli read the paper walking back to the apartment, he realized no words were untainted anymore. Nazi propaganda slanted all the news on the radio and in the papers and he ripped the paper in half before tossing it into the waste basket in the corner of the fourth floor. He headed to the room, vowing to never read the paper until the Nazis no longer held power.

MONDAY, JUNE 16, 1933

Rebecca drove to the hospital in her car, the Christmas gift from her father, and her mind wandered back to the last Christmas with her papa and mother. If she had explained her feelings more tactfully about Eli then, could events have occurred differently between her and her family? She remembered the warm embrace her papa gave her when she thanked him for her present, and the indifference he showed while she and her mother engaged in volatile discourse.

She regretted not asking her papa at the time what he thought about her dating Eli, before her mother could inject him with her poison. But nothing could be done about it now. Her mother shaped and influenced his actions. He was a wise man when it came to business and naïve when it came to matters of his heart. He always intended to do the rights things, but usually managed to become muddled between social expectations and his wife's desires.

Rebecca pulled the car into the hospital lot, turned off the engine and locked the door. Her thoughts returned to the present day and she focused on the events about to unfold at the hospital. Always a hectic place to work, since her wedding and moving in with Eli, gossip about her personal relation with a Jew only made days at the hospital more stressful. But Rebecca ignored the idle words that floated inside those walls and concentrated instead on her duties to help the victims and heal the ailments. The injured and sick flooded the front office until nurses escorted many into exam rooms in the back.

A few patients remained waiting for care. An elderly woman, with a wrinkled face, angular nose and heavy brows, hunched over in one of the chairs. She coughed in her tissue held tightly in her hands. Next to her sat an unusually tall man with dark blond hair and sky blue eyes who held his left arm, grimacing in pain. On the other side of the room sat two young women in their twenties. Their dark hair, twisted into braids, laced around their head and contrasted against their light blue eyes. They sat with their hands clasped in their laps over a German designed dress. Though not identical twins, they had similar features. The secretary at the front desk called to the tall man and gestured for him to come to her.

"The doctor will see you now." She reached her hand out to help him with his paper for signature. A doctor in a long white coat appeared at the swinging door dividing the front office from the patient rooms and then the tall man disappeared. The elderly woman coughed again, her tissue becoming twisted in use, and she tossed it into one of the trash bins near the door. Rebecca stood from behind the front desk, away from her filing work and handed the elderly woman a few more tissues from the box on the counter. The secretary glared at Rebecca and then returned to her own duties of answering phone calls and arranging doctor schedules.

Thirty minutes later, a nurse ushered in the twins through the swinging door and led them to a patient room. The elderly woman remained still in her seat. An hour later, over five of the patients who had received their care finished their visit and left the hospital. Rebecca gazed into the waiting room where the elderly woman remained and two new patients sat down in once empty seats. The secretary played with her blonde curls under her nurse's white cap and called out to one of the young men sitting in the waiting room. Rebecca swung her head around in the secretary's direction while her lips twisted and her eyes grew sharp corners of disbelief.

"That woman has been waiting for over three hours," Rebecca fumed.

"A few more hours isn't going to hurt her."

Rebecca stood too close to her and, as if to explain her actions and return Rebecca to her seat at the other side, she said, "We don't see Jews before Aryans." Rebecca looked away from the counter and at the elderly woman still waiting in unprecedented contentment for someone to call her name or gesture for her to move forward. Rebecca fell back into her chair, disgusted at how Nazi perversion affected the hospital.

Rebecca could not sit easily in her chair, knowing the disregard for this elderly woman and quickened her step through the swinging doors. She marched over to the doctor standing nearby at the sink, the same doctor who made unwanted advances at her. The doctor stepped back at her forceful advancement.

195

"Is anyone going to tend to the elderly woman who's been waiting more than patiently for the past three hours for care?" Rebecca demanded.

The doctor's mouth fell open and his words lingered in an uncommon silence, uncertain of how to respond to her brash request. He was not a particularly cruel man and yet, he didn't fight against the grain either. He knew Rebecca loved a Jew and to him this made her all the more sensitive to their plight.

Still, when he gazed into Rebecca's eyes, he remembered all the feelings he had for her while they worked side by side. When he learned of her relationship with Eli, he managed to conceal those feelings, but only if he kept his distance. At this confrontation, he was unequipped to handle the rush of emotion that exuded from him. Any quarrels he might have had about tending to a Jew faded and he only desired to assist Rebecca in whatever way he could. Words slipped from his lips unchecked.

"Bring her to me," he said.

Rebecca smiled at the doctor in a silent smile behind her eyes where only he could see it, then she returned to the front desk to retrieve the patient. Rebecca wheeled her into the room she had shared many times with the doctor. He waited for her to arrive and, though Rebecca suspected his kindness had more to do with herself than with the patient, she felt grateful nonetheless.

"Thank you, doctor," Rebecca responded while helping the patient out of the wheelchair and into her hospital bed. She positioned her head on the pillow and caught her grey eyes.

"The doctor will take care of you now." The wrinkled chin of the woman stretched with her smile as she closed her eyes. Rebecca assisted the doctor with each request more attentively than she had with other patients, knowing the doctor risked his own reputation caring for this woman.

By the end of the day, Rebecca was exhausted and eager to arrive at her apartment where Eli would draw a warm bath and have a nice dinner ready for her to eat. The way they had reversed roles was unconventional, but it worked for them in this time, this place where everything seemed to be turning upside down. Upon entering her apartment, the gust of wind from the open door blew a paper off the side wall table and onto the floor. Rebecca picked it up with her tired hands and sat on the sofa to read it.

Rebecca,

I have gone to collect my immigration documentation for my family. Dinner is in the fridge and I will be back soon. Take Care.

Love You My Dearest,
Eli

Eli met up with Aaron outside the apartment and drove in Eli's blue car to the old building they had stopped at in April. The haggard man in the back smoked his cigarette as he opened the door for the two of them to enter. Mr. Reiner and his wife were present. She poured Eli, Aaron and her husband a cup of tea before returning to her seat on the middle sofa with her husband.

Mr. Reiner adjusted his spectacles and then looked over the documents one last time before closing that file and handing it to Eli. It contained stamped passports with all the paperwork required for Aaron and his parents, and likewise for Eli's family. The tall, grey haired man bent down to retrieve eight more forms from his desk.

"These are letters from the immigration office declaring your approval to enter America. The birth certificate information is included along with a photo of each family member in the passport," Mr. Reiner said.

Eli opened the file and caressed the passports as if he held Rebecca's own hand.

The first page was marked with a J for Juden and the following page held a photo. The next page was a visa approved for America and the fourth page was a German police permit allowing departure. The forms that followed were a German police record of each individual and two affidavits from American citizens whom Eli had never heard of.

"Thank you so much." Eli stretched his hand out to shake Mr. Reiner's.

"Yes, thank you," Aaron said with easiness in his words. The wrinkled and serious form Aaron's face usually held soothed.

"Take good care of your documents. We will not be able to forge them again if they are lost or damaged," the old man warned.

"I understand," Eli said and Aaron nodded. As Eli and Aaron turned to exist the way they had come, a loud screech from a vehicle sounded outside the front of the building.

The man's wife drew back the curtain and hissed, "Gestapo!" Moments blurred with the four hurrying and orchestrating their movements. The old man pulled Eli by the arm to the back of the room where a table blocked a closet. Aaron followed.

"Quick, you must be unseen, unheard. Stay here." Shoving them into the closet, the old man's voice whispered against the cacophony of the soldier's jackboots pounding hard on the road as they marched toward the building. The entire event didn't take two minutes. Eli and Aaron squeezed close as they listened.

"Herr Reiner, you and your wife are under arrest for falsifying government documents and for aiding and abetting Jews in illegal exit of this country. Make it easier on yourself and give us your files and names."

"I...I have no files."

The two men heard a slap and Mr. Reiner groan.

"Don't hurt him!" Mrs. Reiner screamed. A scuffle ensued and they heard the elderly woman hit the floor, her nails scratching the table where the immigration papers just sat.

Aaron gripped Eli's shoulder, his eyes wide with fear. Eli shook his head for silence.

"Helga!" Mr. Reiner cried out just before a Gestapo officer growled.

"Names, old man! We want names!"

"I don't know what you mean."

The next sound Aaron and Eli heard came from the old man crashing into furniture, knocking it over. It sounded like something wooden broke.

"Oh, god, you're bleeding," his wife whimpered.

"We have to do something," Aaron whispered into Eli's ear.

"What? We're locked in here."

Before they could arrive at a rescue plan, the Gestapo dragged the old couple down the hall and to the sidewalk.

The sounds echoed through Eli and Aaron's distressed ears, but neither heard the old man or his wife yell out in question or in defense. The jackboots pounded up and down the building in patterned search.

Moments later, the voice of the haggard man in the back of the building startled Aaron as he shouted, "Why are you doing this? Where are you taking me?" He screamed, running the words into one sentence.

"Who are the forged documents made for?" A sharp voice from the Gestapo asked. The haggard man shouted out in pain as if his arm had been twisted. "We want all the names," the Gestapo shouted again.

Aaron stared at Eli in fear, an expression Eli was not familiar with seeing on Aaron's face. He had often seen his serious brooding side and he had on serendipitous occasion seen his jovial side. But Aaron never let fear escape him, especially in the courtroom. Eli stood beside Aaron with trembling hands. Both of them breathed heavily and yet more quietly then they ever had in their lives. Their hearts raced and Eli felt he could faint except for the possible need to escape keeping him alert.

Another twist to the man's arm and then another agonized scream sounded before the front door slammed shut. Then silence. The screaming was gone and the raucous noise caused by fighting bodies smashing into furniture vanished. Eli and Aaron stood motionless, thoughts still caught in the disturbing events.

Eli's voice broke the silence. "Can we come out? Is it over?" He whispered to Aaron like a younger brother to an older brother. Aaron delayed his answer with a hesitant departure of his ear from the door.

"I think so, but the door is locked."

Eli ran his hands across the door, feeling for nails or hinges or anything to take the door down. "I wish I had a screwdriver," he mumbled. "I could remove the doorknobs."

"Will this work?" Aaron pulled a small knife out of his pocket and held it out. Enough light came from the crack in the door for Eli to see. After several moments of feverish work, he got the doorknobs off and the two men pushed their way to freedom.

Eli and Aaron walked to Eli's apartment rather than drive. They ducked down alleyways and side streets, hiding behind bushes or parked cars whenever they saw traffic. It took hours to get to Eli's home and they arrived after sunset.

With a sigh of relief, Eli looked to the fourth floor and saw the light on in his kitchen window. "Let's go."

He took one step out of the shadows across the street and Aaron jerked him back.

"Look." Aaron nodded with his chin to the far corner where two dark figures lurked. Every time a vehicle passed or someone walked by, the dark figures inspected each one.

"I'm being watched," Eli concluded.

"Then so am I." Aaron stuffed his hands in his pockets, his mind a flurry of panic. "Where shall we go?"

"We must stay away from our families. I would die if Gestapo arrested Rebecca." His mind fluttered in thought, but the only images he could manage were ones of Reiner and his wife being dragged into the back of the Gestapo's military truck.

"The swing club." Aaron's eyes lit up while his lips grinned. "There's always a mixed crowd to blend in with."

"But they're in Hamburg. We'll have to take buses," Eli groaned.

"There's a local club across town." Aaron gritted his teeth. "I've been there with Jacob."

As they prepared their escape from the looming grip of the Nazis on the streets and into the cloak of lights, colors, and sounds of the local swing club, Eli gripped Aaron's shoulder from behind.

"If we don't make it out of this, I want you to know you've been a good friend to me and I wouldn't want to be on these roads with anyone else."

"Don't say 'if we don't'. When we do, Eli, when we do." Aaron nodded to confirm his words and Eli returned the nod.

The swing sounds permeated the room and reverberated against the walls, seeping onto the nearby streets. The club was not full of swingers at this earlier hour, but a few couples danced to the practice routines of the band. Despite the elated music and lively atmosphere, a cloud of defeat hung over Eli. In the pit of his stomach his nerves twisted into knots as his mind panicked over the Nazis waiting by his apartment, so close to his Rebecca.

Aaron's stomach growled and they both knew they needed to eat something. They went outside and ducked into a side street to consider their options. The local markets offered an easy opportunity, situated on the sidewalks under canopies, but Nazi youth infested them and neither Aaron nor Eli could afford the chance of being seen. Eli stared at Aaron and they both knew what they had to do to eat. Hunger would only worsen and neither knew how long they would have to hide out on the streets before they could return home to their families.

"I'll do it." Aaron grimaced.

"No, I will," Eli protested. "I'm better at this kind of thing."

"No, I got us into this mess. I took you to Reiner." Aaron concluded and pushed Eli back, then darted off like a rabbit fleeing from bloodhounds. Aaron blended behind a family of four, passing the market on the sidewalk. He kept his eyes ahead while his fingers snatched an apple. It wasn't a full meal, but the two could share it to alleviate hunger pangs.

Aaron followed the family of four to the end of the sidewalk and twisted around the block, ducking and bending to keep out of the Nazis' sight as he made his way back to Eli.

"I'll do it next time," Eli stated. Aaron smiled in his nod and they both took a bite out the apple while they cowered on a side street. The clouds darkened, the heavens opened, and rain poured over Eli and Aaron.

"Can you believe this?" Eli groused and turned up his jacket collar. "What else can go wrong?"

"C'mon." Aaron tossed the apple core away and led his soaked friend back to the swing club.

* * *

Rebecca hurried to the sound of pounding on her apartment door. She threw on her silk white robe and eased the door open, familiar with the sounds of the Nazis. Dark hair swept high in a loose bun on her head wrapped with a white lace ribbon. Strong blue eyes complimented her porcelain skin. A sting of blood dripped off a cut on her left leg from a shave in the bathroom when they first pounded.

The Day the Flowers Died

The Gestapo, clad in black uniforms with breeches tucked into their polished black jackboots, didn't ask questions until they pushed their uninvited presence into her room. Their black hats hid their short cut hair. Visors hid their eyes. One of them pushed the door back into her arms and, even if she'd tried, she wouldn't have been able to stop it. Four men marched inside; one surveyed the room while the others rummaged through her personal belongings. Opening drawers, they dumped the contents on the floor. Pictures cracked when they tore them off the walls and threw them down. A baton swung for the television screen, and Rebecca gasped, but the thick glass didn't break.

One of the men kept her occupied with questions. "Where is Eli Levin?" The man's large blue eyes did not deviate from looking into hers.

"I...I...don't know," she said with thoughts of Eli circling in her mind.

He grabbed her arm, squeezing it. "Where...is...Eli...Levin!"

"I don't know," she said again with certainty to the contorted face towering over her.

"How long has he lived here?"

Rebecca knew a lie to the Gestapo would be found out and she could pay for it with her life. "Since January of this year." She answered curtly and her hands began to tremble at the inquiry in her home, her sanctuary, by what she and Eli both determined deplorable — the very presence of German perversion. At the sound of a plate breaking behind her, she grimace but refused to look.

Hearing the truth, he released his grip. "When will he return?" The man's words grew impatient and his face reddened.

"I don't know." Tears streamed down her cheekbones, highlighting their pink tint.

The man turned from her and marched towards the door. The other three followed, their boots crunching over broken glass, and the door slammed shut. Rebecca crumbled to the floor with her face in her hands and her body curling up into her legs. Her body shook and her face and lips became puffy with tears. Pushing herself off the floor after several moments frozen in fear, she ran to the phone. It rang twice and then a coarse voice answered.

"E...Ezekiel?"

"Yes, is this Rebecca?" He could hear the distress in her voice. "What's happened?"

"It's Eli…" She swallowed her tears. "Gestapo is out looking for him. They stopped by my house to question me. He mustn't come here. You need to warn him." The word Gestapo slipped from her lips with bitterness and disgust.

"They'll come by my house next," Ezekiel answered in a calm response, mulling over his thoughts. "He can't come here either."

"How are we going to warn him?" Rebecca's pitch heightened.

"I don't know," Ezekiel said. "Do you know where he is?"

"He wrote me a note." Rebecca began to sob again. "He said he was going to get the visas for everyone."

"Then, I'll drive down there. I have an idea where it might be." Ezekiel spoke in a fatherly tone like he had rescued his son from many mishaps before today. "Stay where you are in case he returns. I'll let Deborah know what's going on." Ezekiel sighed and then gave words of comfort to her. "If the Gestapo stopped by your house looking for him, then they don't know where he is either. Don't worry, Rebecca. He will turn up."

"Alright." Rebecca clung to Ezekiel's words that he would find Eli and return him to her. She waited all night for the call from Ezekiel, unable to sleep, tossing in the bed where only she lay. It felt unnatural for her to sleep alone anymore. She had grown familiar with Eli's masculine smell, and his heavy breathing before he fell asleep. She missed him. Every sound she heard, every creak and crack tossed her from the bed and to her feet, longing and yet afraid for it to be Eli at the door.

As her neighbor exited his apartment, the sounds of shoes against the steps swept Rebecca off her bed and she rushed to the door, whispering Eli's name. Flinging the door open and finding nothing but an empty hallway, the absence of Eli only drove her madder. Her hands clung to her forehead and she rubbed her temples, her fingers growing red and worn. Then, she dropped to her knees at her bedside.

"Please, God, return Eli to me. He needs to be home, warm and safe. I need him in my arms. Please, I beg you." Her prayer turned to tears swelling up her reddened eyes. Her head throbbed in dizzy thought. "Papa, is there anything you could do to bring him back to me?" Rebecca spoke aloud as if her father stood before her, as if her father wielded that kind of power. For a brief moment she thought he did and was there to grant her wish. But the mirage before her soon faded and she wept as she realized the only answer to her prayers was to wait.

* * *

Ezekiel drove frantically to the old building he knew his son had been. He knew the business of the owner there. They had known each other from Synagogue and from legal advice Ezekiel had provided him over the years. The Jewish community knew to talk to this man if one wanted forged immigration papers. His work began in 1930 and increased in popularity in 1933.

Ezekiel pulled his BMW behind the building and entered through the backdoor to find the latch broken and the door kicked in, hanging on a nail. He walked in haste through the corridor leading into the main room. The room was in disarray with furniture knocked over and broken. Papers and books sprawled all over the floor and furniture.

"Eli? Eli?" Ezekiel whispered. He stumbled over a fallen stool and hit the closet. His eyes fixated on the outline of the pine door and he squeezed his hands into the two center holes missing door knobs and pulled the closet open. Cloths hung on hangers, but the space was empty of his son. "Where are you?" he cried out. Ezekiel scurried through the building, searching in the bathroom and hallway until he found himself at the backdoor. He hung his head, ambled to his car and drove home. Hands trembled as they gripped the steering wheel and a few tears rolled from his eyes.

* * *

Rebecca awoke the next morning to call into work sick and then went downstairs to retrieve the mail in the cubby of the first floor lobby.

The box held only one small thin envelope. Rebecca slipped her hand in and her sharp fingernails scratched it as she pulled it out of the box. She read over the address as she plodded upstairs to her apartment.

The return address stated New York, America which meant the letter came from her Aunt Martha. Getting the letter opener, she inserted the end of the blade, slid it across the envelope and pulled the letter out in one motion to find two pieces of paper folded into thirds. She perused the letter twice until she was satisfied with the meaning and intent she drew from it.

Dear Rebecca and Eli,

I have received your letter with its request and must first congratulate you both on your marriage. I do wish the very best for both of you and, unlike my mother and your own mutti, Deseire, I do not hold any grievance upon your choice.

I am happy to oblige with a letter of sponsorship, suggesting the arrival of Eli Levin in New York City is both expected and requested. The letter is followed by this one. It has been certified with a notary and includes personal information to establish my citizenship (which took some time to put together).

However, please don't pin your hopes on this letter as I've been informed that many Jews have been turned away upon arriving by boat and a few of the boats were simply turned away without even so much as a glance at the passports the passengers carried.

The immigration offices and harbors are filled with immigrants from all over the world requesting permission to stay in America. Our President is restricting the numbers allowed entry to appease the angst of the public, which has only increased in fear of losing their own jobs to cheaper labor.

I hope this all becomes sorted out and, since the two of you are legally married, that Eli will be allowed to accompany you to America. I have heard horrible stories about the conditions of Germany today and if you are in any need of help from me, please do not hesitate to ask. You are my only niece and I love you dearly.

Sincerely,
Martha

Caressing the letter between her fingers, Rebecca recalled a time ten years ago when her Aunt Martha had sojourned to Germany to see her sister, Deseire. She had a memory of Martha frolicking in the park hand in hand with her while Deseire relaxed on the park bench with Ralph.

Rebecca remembered the smell of roses and squishing her nose in between a bundle of white lilies. A protective warmth radiated from her aunt, not like the suffocating rigidness of her own mother. Rebecca's lips pressed softly up into her cheeks as she held the letter, remembering Martha and, as she folded the letter and laid it upon the dining table, she hoped she would be seeing her aunt soon.

Still quietness filled her living room, and she hoped the ring of the phone or a knock at the door would shatter the silence. She sipped a cup of tea, too distraught in Eli's absence to make herself breakfast.

Had the Gestapo taken him? Was he being tortured? Was he at the Dachau concentration camp? Was he dead?

She wandered to her room and paced over the floor before walking outside onto the porch. She looked over the terrace, surveyed the area, and hoped for a glimpse, any sign of Eli. The phone rang while she stared over Munich. She was out of breath when she picked up the phone.

"Hello?"

"Rebecca?" the coarse voice asked.

"Ezekiel, is he alright?" Her words clung to hope.

"I haven't found him. He wasn't there." Ezekiel fell silent and Rebecca didn't respond. "There was a scuffle of some kind. Furniture was knocked over. But the room was empty."

"Oh god." Rebecca's throat tightened. They both thought the worst. "Gestapo?"

"It looked that way," Ezekiel reasoned. "But he may have escaped, which would explain them coming to look for him. We can't know for sure if he was taken," he said with a father's hope.

"What do we do?"

"I'll ask around. I know a few people who might be able to tell us if he was taken to Dachau." Ezekiel's sigh deepened. "I'll call you when I find out."

"Please do," Rebecca implored without realizing the intensity of the words falling from her lips or the outpour of emotion from her heart.

It brought some comfort knowing the Gestapo just last night did not know Eli's whereabouts. It gave her a shred of hope that he somehow escaped their clutches. But it was also possible Eli got lost in the shuffle of victims and already sat in a concentration camp without the Gestapo realizing this yet. She needed to know for sure.

"Take care of yourself," Ezekiel finished and hung up.

Click. The sound of the click on the other end pulled Rebecca back into a silent emptiness. Without Eli in the room with her, loneliness flooded in. Though she'd been alone throughout University, this loneliness felt more pronounced.

At the end of the week, Rebecca felt like she was going to die, as if her own heart would somehow stop in its rhythmic motion and her own lungs would collapse and leave her whimpering for air on the floor. Did she feel this way from being physically ill? Or, did the worry bombarding her mind do this? She didn't know. Fighting depression, she kept busy at work and tried to keep her mind occupied at home.

Ezekiel called midweek to inform her that, as far as his friends knew, there was no sign of Eli at the Dachau camp. This gave them both relief, but still no Eli and they both dreaded the answer could be far worse than Dachau.

* * *

On Saturday evening, Eli made his way upstairs, checking over his shoulder to make sure he'd remained unseen. Easing his door open, he slipped inside. The smell of home wafted over him, orange scented soap and dinner. His bleary eyes scanned the room and focused on his beautiful wife standing at the stove, her back to him, pouring tea. Pushing the door closed behind him so that it clicked, he watched her whirl around at the noise.

Rebecca dropped the teacup in her hand, where it smashed on the floor. Her heart raced and her eyes widened. She ran to him and felt his face, his chin with stubble, and his dirty hands that had grown coarse over the past five days. His beige trench coat was torn and navy pants damp.

He held her soft porcelain face in his and then pulled her to him, grabbing her, pressing her against his chest, needing to feel her heartbeat and her breath on his ear.

"God, I've missed you," Eli whispered after a moment.

"Where have you been?" Rebecca's eyes welled with tears and her lips trembled.

"I'm sorry. It wasn't safe. They were watching the apartment…my parents' house…Aaron's." He held his arms out. "I need to get cleaned up." Eli went into the bathroom, Rebecca following. He poured water over his hands and face. "Aaron and I had to stay hidden. They came to his house, too, looking for him."

"Aaron was with you?" This news brought relief that Eli was not alone on the streets for five nights. Rebecca pulled off his trench coat and her soft hands brushed over his rough ones, his nails embedded with dirt.

He poured more water over his face and arms. "Yes." Eli took a moment to answer before pulling off his torn shirt and shoes.

"What happened?"

Eli loosened his belt. "Aaron and I were picking up the documents for our families and the Gestapo pulled up to the building." He took off his pants and jumped into the bath for a quick wash, his skin moist with dirt and his knees scuffed. He poured water over his hair and raked his fingers through it. Rebecca bent down to the bath and cupped her hands through the water, gathering some to drizzle over Eli's soiled body. "We were locked in the closet to hide, but they took Mr. Reiner," Eli explained in a tone of agony, "and his wife…I can still hear her crying while they beat her." His strength shattered at the memory. Tears fell from his eyes over his cheeks, first one, then another, until they blinded him. He couldn't stop them.

Rebecca leaned in and pulled his head to her chest, getting her summer dress soaked. "You're ok now. You're safe now." Rebecca rocked him in her arms, leaning into the tub until his skin pruned and her dress was soaked from chest to waist.

Eli called his papa after his bath and Rebecca showed him the letter she hoped would bring relief to his face. But he knew as well as she did that this letter alone did not ensure anything. For the first time, Eli did not wear his façade in front of her, the face that told her everything would be alright, because he knew that she would not believe the lie anymore.

SATURDAY, JULY 22, 1933

Eli awoke to the sounds of heavy breathing. He rolled over to see Rebecca holding her chest as she lay sweating on top of the bed sheets, her head propped up on pillows and her silk white nightgown clinging to her damp body. The sounds of her struggling for air filled him with desperation. He threw himself over her and rested his head against her slowly rising chest.

"Rebecca! Are you alright?" Her blue pupils faded in and out as her lids closed and opened and the white of the eye consumed them. "Rebecca!"

"I feel weak," she struggled to whisper and her eyes closed again.

"I'm taking you to the hospital." He wrapped her arms around his shoulders and pulled her from the bed.

"No, it's too dangerous." She said each word slowly into his ear as she lay in his arms.

"I don't care. You need help." He set her down on the lounge chair in the bedroom as he heard her weakened voice whisper, Gestapo. "I'm getting you dressed."

"The Gestapo," she paused for breath to say it louder, "could see you." Her sentence sounded broken in its stretched intonation.

"I'll be careful." Eli's arms reached for a purple summer dress from the closet, revealing his defined muscles. Rebecca admired him with a light smile as she waited in the lounge chair for him to dress her. Her hair drooped around her face and her body appeared limp without much will of her own holding it there.

"Love you." She mustered two more words in an inaudible sound. Eli kissed her chapped lips and then slipped the summer dress over her nightgown and took a washrag dipped in water from the bathroom and wiped her face. He pulled out his black slacks and a salmon colored shirt and added his beige trench coat. He took out his knit beige wool hat, a hat he never wore, and pulled it over his hair and part of his forehead.

He helped her off the chair and she walked with one arm over his shoulder, draped around his neck. He braced her up with both his arms, one behind and over her back and the other positioned upon her delicate waist. They walked together down the steps and to Rebecca's car. Her vehicle was more reliable and inconspicuous. Eli's broken windshield invited questioning eyes and, as the car grew older, the engine grew temperamental.

Eli pulled into the hospital parking lot and carried Rebecca over the steps into the waiting room like he was cradling a baby. The secretary behind the desk noticed Rebecca at once and, despite her disapproval of Rebecca's choice in husbands, she grew alarmed at seeing her so despondent. She leapt out of her chair and rushed to Eli's side whom, unknown to her, was in fact Rebecca's husband. She rolled a wheelchair over to Eli to place Rebecca into and then wheeled her through the swinging doors.

Eli stayed close to Rebecca, following the secretary down the hallway into a patient's room and then she realized Eli must be the rumored man by the way he clung to Rebecca's side. She grimaced as she left the room, having to assist more patients in the waiting room. Rebecca sighed at the sight of the hospital bed, used to aid patients and now a patient herself. As Eli laid her in the bed, the doctor appeared at the door.

Rebecca gazed upward at his face and recognized him. A short smile crept over her and she closed her eyes to rest. Eli brushed his fingers through her hair and along her jaw line to her lips. He rested his head next to hers while the doctor entered the room.

His long white jacket swept against Eli's arm and he lifted his head. The doctor inserted a thermometer into Rebecca's mouth and she opened her eyes. He took the device out of her mouth moments later and took a step backward.

"How are you feeling?" he asked in a professional but concerned manner.

"I feel…exhausted. I…feel like…I can't…breathe." Rebecca spoke in short bursts and pulled her left hand up to her chest to hold her heart.

"Does this hurt?" The doctor pressed against her abdomen on one side and then the other. Rebecca grimaced both times. A nurse walked in with another instrument and wrapped it around Rebecca's upper arm to measure her blood pressure. Eli stood and put his face into his hands against the wall. The doctor walked over to Eli and put his hand over his shoulder. "We're going to have to run some tests. You may want to wait out front. It could be some time."

"No! My place is with her. I'll stay by her side." Eli walked over to her, kissed her forehead and then sat in the chair in the corner. Rebecca's eyes closed and she appeared to fall into a tranquil sleep. The doctor spoke in quiet with the nurse who rushed back with a tray of more medical tools. The doctor drew Rebecca's blood and peered in her mouth, pried open with a wooden flat stick. Eli watched her without moving from the room or taking his eyes off of her, except to address the doctor and nurse.

The minutes became hours as Eli watched the woman he loved, the only woman he ever loved this much, lay in the hospital bed, losing her vibrancy to feebleness and confined instead of free. His heart ached.

Though the thought of both of them losing their chance to escape Germany by boat this month weighed heavily on him, he could not think of much else but Rebecca. She would be in no condition to travel and they would have to wait until September to depart, if at all this year.

In the late afternoon, the doctor returned to the room. Eli rose from his chair to hear the assessment of Rebecca's declining health.

"I have good news," the doctor announced and Eli sighed in relief. "She's suffering from a combination of stress and a lack of nutrients, which is treatable. We have vitamins and an IV of glucose in her now. It should stabilize her. However she'll need to rest all day and preferably all week."

"When may I take her home?" Eli's wrinkled forehead straightened.

"Tomorrow, after I've made sure she's strong enough to travel."

"Thank you so much, doctor." Eli grabbed the doctor's hand and shook it profusely.

"There is one more thing." The doctor interjected midway between Eli finishing the shake and letting go of his hand. Eli's eyes widened at the doctor's words and he waited in silence for the doctor to finish his thought.

"Rebecca is pregnant," the doctor said matter-of-factly and tried to conceal his elation for treating Rebecca. No matter what he felt for her, he wanted her well and happy. Eli rushed over to her side and held her hand which dangled over the edge of the bed.

"You're having a baby," he said in a mixture of disbelief and exuberance.

"I heard." Rebecca spoke quietly under an elongated smile, revealing her teeth which she didn't try to hide. Eli placed his hands over her belly and they stared at each other for a few moments, gathering their thoughts, assimilating this new unexpected information.

"We will get to America. We'll start our family there." Eli said it with such assurance and confidence, like he spoke in the courtroom, that he left no room for Rebecca to doubt its validity.

"But we missed our boat," Rebecca sighed.

"There's another in September, if you're feeling up to it."

"What about your family? They should leave this month. They shouldn't wait on me."

"I'll talk to them later. But right now, I want to make sure you're alright."

"Has my passport arrived yet?" Rebecca tilted her head in Eli's direction over the hospital pillow.

"Not yet," he said with disappointment, knowing his own immigration papers were not yet completed either. "But it will. You are an American citizen through your mother."

"Yes, my mutti." Rebecca's thoughts fixed on her mother and her eyes rolled to the ceiling as they became teary. "She doesn't even know I'm here." Eli shook his head no to her question. "She doesn't even know I'm married." Eli rubbed his hands over her dangling arm. "Will she even be a part of this child's life?" Eli wrapped his hand around her own.

"I'll talk to her for you if you want me too. I'll let her know what's happening." Eli swept his fingers through her dark hair which, in this hospital light, concealed the honey hints.

She shook her head and answered, "No, I'll talk to her myself when I'm feeling better. She should hear it from me." Rebecca knew Eli speaking to her mother would only complicate matters. Seeing him while her daughter lay in a hospital bed, hearing the words of their marriage and her pregnancy and their soon departure from Eli's lips instead of her own would only sever the already thin bond between them.

"Ok." Eli kissed her lips. He stayed the night with Rebecca and the next day the doctor approved her for release, but insisted on her resting throughout the rest of the week. Eli wheeled Rebecca out of the hospital and to her car, lifted her in his arms, though she was more capable of walking this morning, and placed her in the passenger seat.

The new morning brought a new hope to each of their faces, easing their once worried expressions and festering anxieties, the kind of hope that crept into lives unexpectedly. Though the pregnancy meant Rebecca would be in a more delicate condition for traveling, they were both elated at the thought of starting a family.

The following day, Rebecca slept in while Eli drove to the Levin home to provide his family with the spurious documentation he had procured at a risk to his own life. Ezekiel took the papers from his son's hand with a reluctant tug and then sat in the living room to talk with him.

Deborah came in with a bowl of fruit and tea for the both of them and placed it on the table in the middle of the room. Ezekiel ate a strawberry before speaking.

"Son, I'm very grateful for the risk you have taken for us, but I don't want to leave without you and Rebecca. We can wait till she feels better."

"No, Papa, I don't want to be the cause of your delay. I need to know you and Mama and my sisters are safe. We'll come after your ship. I promise. Rebecca needs her rest. The stress of the country has worn on her physically and she should recuperate before boarding for such a long journey." Eli's eyes brightened with delight, "Rebecca is pregnant."

"What? When did this happen?" Ezekiel said, excited and yet taken aback.

"We just found out when she was at the hospital."

"It looks like you'll be starting your family early." He grinned and then ended, "I would feel better knowing you both were with us."

"We will be, Papa, just on a later boat. The visa is in the mail, but I can't worry about Rebecca's health aboard the ship. I have to wait till she feels well enough for travel. Please, tell me you'll take the family and lift the worry of it from my mind."

"Ok, ok," Ezekiel conceded.

"The Hamburg American Steam Liner left on the second, but you can catch the ship again next month. Here's the brochure." Eli handed Ezekiel a grey pamphlet with a figure of an American woman in a long dress gracing the cover. "You ought to leave tonight to pick up the tickets. You can stay at a hotel in Hamburg and purchase them first thing tomorrow morning."

"How much will the tickets cost?" Ezekiel's left brow rose.

"About two hundred dollars each."

"One thousand American dollars?" Ezekiel whistled in surprise and rubbed his forehead. "How long is the journey?"

"About ten days." Eli stood and carried his cup of tea with him. "I have to get back to tend to Rebecca soon."

"Yes, yes." Ezekiel took his son's face into his hands and kissed him on either cheek. "We'll miss you."

"I love you, Papa." Eli helped his father carry his overnight luggage into this car. He hugged his father and then Ezekiel started the engine and began his journey into Hamburg.

* * *

The following Friday on the fourteenth, the Nazis passed another law Germany would have to suffer, the Law for the Prevention of Genetically Diseased Offspring, initiated by the Interior Minister Wilhelm Frick. The law required the forced sterilization of German citizens with congenital disabilities such as feeblemindedness, schizophrenia, manic depression, epilepsy, and others. Doctors throughout the Reich performed the procedures on everyone fitting the descriptions. Following the sterilization law, the Denaturalization law stripped non German blood citizens of their citizenship. Jews were now no longer protected under the law with the little safety they received as German citizens.

Saturday morning after these new laws, Deseire came to visit Rebecca unannounced. Rebecca had rested the entirety of the week under doctor orders with meals provided by Eli and with readings of some of his favorite books of literature and poetry. The two lay arm in arm over the bed sheets when the knock at the door alarmed them.

Eli jumped off the bed and stood at a distance from the door.

The thought occurred to both of them that the Gestapo made a second trip for Eli's arrest. The knock sounded again and Rebecca hurried to answer it. She buttoned the top three buttons of her white blouse and straightened out her sky blue shirt as she approached the door. Eli concealed himself in the shadows of the room. The door squeaked open.

"Mutti?" Rebecca said not really as a question, but more in disbelief.

"Yes, dear." Deseire spoke in a polite, but clipped manner. Rebecca stood for a few moments gazing at Deseire. "Are you going to invite me in the room?"

"Yes, sorry, of course, Mother. Come in." Rebecca pulled the door further open and took her mother's caramel cashmere coat off her back as she entered. Eli hastened to the door with a sigh of relief and took the coat from Rebecca's hands before placing it over the sofa.

Deseire walked in regal grace to the sofa and wiped the seat a few times with her spread out hand before sitting down. She adjusted the gold necklace that hung over her silk white blouse. Rebecca pulled her hair back behind her, combing it with her fingers a few times before sitting down to join her mother. Eli prepared warm tea in the kitchen. The room remained silent except for the fidgeting of Rebecca's body trying to find a place of comfort, and the clinking of the kettle.

"Would you enjoy a morning tea, Mrs. Baum?" Eli suggested, turning his head in her direction.

"I would, thank you, but no sugar please." She answered cordially, but as if she spoke to her cook Rueben.

"What brings you here, Mother?" Rebecca inquired.

"A few matters have come to my attention." Deseire opened her beige colored handbag and pulled out a folded letter. She began to open it and look it over, "I felt I needed to address them personally." She handed the letter to Rebecca and as Rebecca's eyes fell upon its words, Deseire continued. "My sister Martha has told me about your marriage to Eli and your desire to depart Germany and sail to America." The cup in Eli's hands hit the counter and he turned his head toward her.

"You've come to scold me?" Rebecca responded.

"No, dear," Desire shook her head and then pulled Rebecca's chin with her forefinger, drawing her face to her own. "You are my little girl."

Her finger dropped back to her lap. "I know you think of me as a rigid old woman who doesn't understand you, but I'm not heartless. I don't want to see my daughter getting herself hurt or worse, killed." Deseire touched her throat as she said the last word and her voice wavered. Deseire reached for her daughter's hand and Rebecca didn't pull it away from her. Her mother rested her hand over her own and it felt uncommonly warm to the touch.

"So why did you come?" Rebecca inquired a second time.

"To give you this." Deseire handed Rebecca a miniature blue booklet with the words American passport embossed in gold lettering over the top.

"You had my passport?"

"After receiving the letter from your aunt, I knew you would need it."

"But when…?" Rebecca couldn't complete her thought before her mother answered.

"When you were sixteen, your father thought it would be a good idea in case we visited Grandma in America. We never did." Deseire spoke the last sentence in regret.

"Thank you, Mutti." Rebecca said mutti with tenderness as she embraced her with both arms. Deseire cleared her throat and arched her back as if to conceal her emotions. She patted her daughter a few times on the shoulder with her outstretched hand and then adjusted back in her seat.

"I've also brought you this."Deseire pulled out a wad of bills wrapped in a string from her bag and in clandestine manner as if the whole of Germany was watching, slipped it in between Rebecca's clasped hands. "You are going to need money to start a life in America."

"This is too much. You don't have to do this." Rebecca's face softened from the hardness it usually carried in the presence of her mother.

"I do," she said boldly with honesty. "I've been intolerable to you, to Eli," she said almost ashamed. "You won't have much if a life together in Germany with all the new laws. I'm afraid for your well being," she corrected herself, "for both of your well beings." Rebecca wiped a fallen tear from her eye which had made its way to her cheek.

"Thank you, Mama. Thank you so much." Rebecca embraced her mother again, this time letting go of all the barriers between them, of all the injustice and hurt from the past. The past did not exist between them anymore, only the here and now. Deseire held Rebecca's face in her hands.

"I love you," Deseire said with an unbridled emotion.

"I love you too." Rebecca kissed her mother on each cheek. She wanted to tell her everything, how much she loved Eli, how they were pregnant and looking forward to starting a family in America, and the word mama perched on her lips. But her mother stood and took her coat off the sofa, interrupting her before the thought formed into words.

"I need to be going. There's a lot going on today." Eli set the cup of tea on the kitchen counter that he had prepared for Mrs. Baum, holding it until the private conversation finished. He knew she had forgotten all about her tea. Instead, he helped her with her coat and walked her to the door. She turned to him and kissed him once on the cheek, "Take care of my little girl."

"I promise," Eli said, his words meant for two and opened the door for Mrs. Baum. Rebecca kissed her on the cheek one last time and, as Deseire turned to depart, Rebecca pulled her back into a warm extended hug.

"Tell Papa I love him," Rebecca said.

"I will," Deseire answered, smiled, then headed down the corridor and disappeared on the stairwell.

WEDNESDAY, AUGUST 9, 1933

Ezekiel Levin packed up the last of his belongings and walked with his family to a cab outside their home. They had decided to each carry only one piece of luggage and Ezekiel sold their car to have more money upon arrival in America. He put the house with its furnishings on the market and entrusted the profit of the sale to be put into his account by a German real estate agent who he had befriended over the years.

Ezekiel and Ada helped place the five suitcases into the trunk while Deborah wept on the driveway. Sarah wrapped her arm around her mother and walked her to the cab just after Ada finished with the last suitcase and hugged Deborah. Leah and Miriam were already sitting in the back with their faces to the window on either side of the seat. Eli drove up in Rebecca's car just as Ezekiel had gotten Deborah into the cab. He rushed up to his family and threw his arms around his father.

"Papa, I thought I was going to miss you." Eli squeezed him and then leaned into the cab to hug his mother and kiss each sister on the cheek.

"Promise me you'll be on the next ship out of here," Deborah implored.

"Just as soon as Rebecca is stable enough to travel," Eli reassured. "I love you and I'll see you all very soon."

"We love you too, son." Deborah reached out to hug her son once more before the cab drove off.

The Levin family arrived at the docks in the late afternoon. Trolleys road over rails in front of the large building and an exquisite tower clock stood high above to the right as they approached. Ezekiel led the family through the building with signs posted: Third Class on the S.S. New York of the Hamburg Amerika Linie from Hamburg, Germany to New York.

He followed the signs to the ship and, as they boarded, someone handed him a menu for their meals. A flowery decorated grey card with a picture of a mountain in water framed the words Hamburg Amerika Linie at the bottom. He flipped the card over and read the food items: Philadelphia Pepper Pot Roast, Ribs and German Puff Pastries. The words were in German with an English Translation. The steam liner featured game rooms with tables for playing cards, and a dining hall with black and white checkered floors. Standardized private quarters came with bed, mirror, and bathroom. Outside offered deck tennis, and long rows of chairs lining several wooden decks. The family stood on the deck to watch the ship sail away from Germany and to their future in a new land.

* * *

Rebecca's health had been fluctuating for weeks, yet she frolicked on her porch in ballerina movements for the past couple of days like she had after her and Eli first made love. The thought of her new child kept her spirits high, though her body went through many physical changes from her recovery and from the growing baby inside of her. Eli was relieved to see the hospital visit had not brought her to a state of melancholy.

Rebecca held her stomach and tried to feel the life made of part herself and a part of the man she loved. Every breath she breathed was not just for her, but for that tiny child. She knew she could not let her health falter in the slightest in order to keep her baby healthy and strong. She ate abundantly and slept in when she felt the need.

The hospital afforded her a savings combined with Eli's savings which they needed to live on in the months to come. The doctor who helped her recover put in a good word for her with the head of the hospital. Even so, rumors circulated that she had married a Jew and so her baby was a half Jew. Those two rumors spoiled her reputation for good, leaving no manager at the hospital allowing her to return.

Eli took care of balancing what savings they had. He bought food by the volume, but always inexpensive produce and usually at a Jewish market. German citizens grew particular with whom they bought from so, whenever Eli purchased from the local Jewish market, only fellow Jews shopped there.

He carried a wicker basket on one arm and filled it with apples and assorted vegetables. Stew was easy to prepare and healthy. Apples could be baked into a pie, fried, put into a salad and eaten whole. Rebecca adored the fruit and Eli could never purchase enough for her; however, her cravings for pickles and sauerkraut always kept him searching at several places before returning home.

Jacob met with Eli at the market and filled his own basket with fruits for the woman who accompanied him. She sat on a short wooden bench just outside the market, combing her long blonde hair with a silver plated comb and then started on a cigarette. Eli glanced to where she sat as Jacob smiled with a glitter of frivolity in his eyes.

"Is that her, the same girl from the swing club?" Eli gawked, remembering her flashy flapper dress.

"That would be the one." He answered in a confident manner that bordered on cocky.

"You two have been seeing each other all this time?" Eli asked in surprise.

"Off and on at the swing clubs." Jacob smirked and wiggled his eyebrows in jest.

"Good for you." Eli patted Jacob on the back and finished piling in the fruits and vegetables in his basket and then put in two loaves of bread.

"How are you and Rebecca?"

"We're good," Eli's grin widened, "really good."

"I've heard she's expecting," Jacob stated. Eli did not deny it and the widened smile only grew. "It's true then?" His voice pitched high and then he lowered it. "The two of you are going to have a baby?"

"Yes." Eli glanced back at Jacob's girlfriend and noticed her standing. "I think she may be leaving." Eli pointed in her direction and Jacob turned his head.

"One moment," Jacob rushed his words and then scurried out of the market to her side. "Are you leaving?" As he finished the sentence, the wrinkled brows in her forehead deepened and her lips tightened across her mouth.

The sound of a large vehicle screeched along the side of the market and seven Gestapo jumped out of the back of the truck. The pounding of their jackboots surrounded Jacob and, as Eli watched, they hit him across the jaw and his sides with their guns. Blood flew out of his nose and mouth and splattered across the long white summer dress his girlfriend wore. She dropped her cigarette and screamed.

Her hands trembled against her face and she dropped to Jacob's side where he lay curled on the sidewalk. Two of the Gestapo pulled him up and dragged him away while she clung to him until he was torn from her altogether. They threw him into the back of the truck.

The others followed, but not before one of them declared, "There will be no Jews consorting with German girls. It is forbidden!" He shouted forbidden and then the black hats, jackets and breeches disappeared into the truck and the engine revved.

Eli dropped his basket and raced towards the military vehicle pulling away. He chased the truck for several blocks before its own speed drove it far ahead of him and it vanished in the distance. Eli fell to his knees in the middle of the road, calling out to his friend, wailing. An elderly Jewish man limped with his cane over to Eli and helped him back to his feet.

"Don't make a scene, son." He walked with him back to the sidewalk. "No need to draw unnecessary attention to yourself." His voice sounded scratchy from years of smoking.

"But Jacob, my friend." Eli implored for someone to understand his pain.

"Your friend is gone. There's nothing you can do for him now. Go home. Be with your family." His words were short, brutal, honest. Eli glanced at him as if the old man knew and could sense that Eli was about to have a baby, and protected him from endangering all those he loved. Eli took a few heavy breaths, swallowed his tears and then ran back home to his Rebecca. He skipped two stairs at a time and upon opening the door to the apartment, stopped to catch his breath.

"Eli?" Rebecca grew concerned and ran over to him before shutting the door behind him. "What happened?" Her left brow quirked and the pink tint to her skin fell from her face.

"Jacob... they took him. They just drove up and threw him in the back of their truck for being with his German girlfriend." Eli's voice wavered in sadness and he stood stunned. He threw his arm across the empty vase on the small table which had not been filled with flowers for some time. The vase fell to the floor and the crystal glass shattered. He slammed his fists to the barren table and shouted, "What is happening to this country!"

Rebecca curled her arms around him from behind and drew his body to her chest. Eli fell into her and released the emotion he had to keep inside on the street. He turned his face into her sky blue blouse and sobbed until the sun fell and the evening brought them to their bed. Rebecca folded a wet rag over his bloodshot eyes and curled up beside him as they fell asleep.

The morning sun trickled over their bare feet and awoke them. Eli rolled his mouth over to her ear and whispered, "Forget me. Forget you ever knew me. Protect yourself. Protect our baby."

Rebecca rolled onto her knees. "I could never do such a thing! Even if my mind thought it wise, my heart would not be strong enough. I love you. I'll always love you." She braced her hands over his bare chest. "We are going to get through this. We are going to board the next boat. We are going to have our family." At her wishful words, Eli's expression became contemplative and he lingered in thought for a moment.

"I must find a way for us. I must get my visa for America."

"You haven't heard from the Embassy?" Rebecca bit her lips. "But you told your father..." Her body fell off of Eli and lay at his side.

"I told him what he needed to board the ship," Eli said, turning to her and then looking away from her lake blue eyes. "Aaron says they make promises of reviewing applications, but the truth is the papers simply sit in stacks for months before anyone even bothers." He returned his gaze to her. "There are just too many restraints and no one wants more refugees taking jobs in a country that's just coming out of its own depression."

"Why didn't you get the forgery for yourself with your family?" Rebecca's voice strained, but tried not to sound accusative.

"I...I don't know. I thought I would have heard from immigration. I thought if I hadn't, I'd have more time with Mr. Reiner to create the documents." Eli covered his face with his hands. "I should have thought this could happen. I should have prepared more thoroughly."

"You can't blame yourself." Rebecca brought her hands to his arm, "There's no way you could have known what would happen to Mr. Reiner."

"I should have. I'm a lawyer. It's my job to prepare for contingencies." He berated himself.

"You will find a way. You always do. You have a sharp mind. I know you'll find a way for us," Rebecca said, soothing Eli, soothing herself.

* * *

Rumors circulated Munich. Silent glances spoke unspoken words. Whispers fluttered in the cold air. The autumn weather brought with it trees that shed their colorful leaves, preparing to become barren. Like the trees, the streets soon followed. People became a scarce commodity. Jews disappeared in the morning, in the evening, from their homes, from their place of business. People speculated they were being sent to a concentration camp for labor, taken away on any number of charges from consorting with German girls to imitating the Nazi salute. The rumors began in August and escalated every month.

On August twentieth, the American Jewish Congress declared a boycott against Nazi Germany. Coupled with the European boycott of the previous year, the world began to take notice of the conditions in Hitler's Germany and show its disapproval. But Hitler needed the world's approval and, like a wolf that played in the morning and stalked its prey at night, he hid the atrocities from public view whenever influential visitors came from other countries.

* * *

Eli's mind focused on retrieving the visas he needed to purchase his ticket for the next ship out of Hamburg. The immigration office had no word about his application yet. With Mr. Reiner still missing, he knew no other Jewish man who could obtain counterfeit documents. He also knew he had to keep himself inconspicuous, because the Gestapo tracked him once before.

They had kept a careful watch on the Levin home until they departed Hamburg, leaving the Gestapo with the certainty Eli had escaped. Though Germany encouraged the emigration of Jews in a sure attempt to rid themselves of the Jewish problem, the Nazis needed few reasons to betray this encouragement and even less reasons to cause harm.

Eli met with Aaron at his old office where his father Ezekiel had bolted the doors and walked away. Aaron waited for Eli behind the building, remaining off the main street. Posters of discrimination and propaganda still plastered the walls. Many torn down over the course of Eli working there were replaced by the eager hands of young Germans initiated into Hitler's Youth.

Aaron held his passport and documents in a file inside a brown bag strapped around his shoulder. He wiped the sweat from his forehead, not there as a result of humid weather, but from his nervousness at carrying illegal documents in a Nazi saturated city. Eli brushed up against Aaron's arm from behind. Aaron reacted in alarm and jerked around until he saw Eli's face and not the Gestapo.

"Eli, don't do that."

"Don't do what?" Eli asked in sincere ignorance.

"Surprise me from behind." Aaron wiped a drop of sweat from his nose.

"Nervous?"

"Is there ever a reason not to be these days?" Aaron retorted and Eli gripped the bag on his shoulder.

"Your papers are in here?" Eli inquired while Aaron lowered his shoulder, allowing the bag to fall into Eli's hands.

"You think this is going to work?" Aaron's brows twisted and the wrinkles around the corners of his mouth showed Eli he doubted it.

"It has to. What other option is there?"

"You could sneak aboard the ship. It has its risks, but no more than forging your own documents, and maybe less," Aaron reasoned.

"This can work," Eli protested, trying to persuade the disbelief in Aaron's expression. "If I can get an idea of what the visa documentation looks like, I can try to mimic it well enough to manage a ticket for myself."

"And once we dock in New York? How is a poor counterfeit going to fool the immigration offices?" Aaron demanded.

"And how is sneaking aboard going to solve that?" Eli concluded, winning the disagreement. "I have to try something. You know as well as I that the Embassy isn't going to process my application soon enough and, when they finally get around to it, it will likely be denied because of President Roosevelt's quota restraints."

Aaron sighed at Eli's truth and then Eli furthered the desperation, "Plus I need your papers to help duplicate my German police permit and records since I turned them into immigration months ago." Eli tugged on the bag to open it and searched the papers to ensure it was all there. "I've been flagged by Gestapo and there's no way the police will grant me a permit again."

"You're right, I'm sorry. I just wish there was something more I could do," Aaron conceded, seeing the frustration in his friend's eyes.

"You've done everything you can. We just have to hope this will be enough." Eli pulled the bag over his shoulder. "I'll return your documents at the end of the week." Aaron nodded at Eli's words. He patted Eli's shoulder before departing to his parent's house.

It took Eli five days and nights of work on his spurious passport visa to address each page appropriately. He didn't want to alarm Rebecca with his dilemma. He blamed himself for not realizing sooner the unreliability of receiving a visa through immigration and for not taking the necessary measures to procure fraudulent documentation through Mr. Reiner. He knew this worry would weigh heavily on her already fragile state of emotions. Therefore he concentrated on its conception when she was out of the apartment or sleeping.

He went to the closet in the bedroom and pulled out the cardboard box he had packed away with the variety of office supplies he had gathered from his father's firm before it closed. The box held a variation of stamps with black and red ink, some placing a date mark and some marking solid lines. He took out his passport, the one he never had approved at the immigration office, and turned to the first page. J for Juden. The second page had a photo of himself.

The third page involved an artificial visa for entry into America from immigration. This page used the typewriter and various inks. Using Aaron's passport booklet, Eli mimicked what he saw.

The fourth page was a forged German police-approved permit for departure. Eli carefully constructed its form with the typewriter and stamp inks.

After the pages dried, he had to finalize them with German immigration stamps and German signatures. He scrutinized Aaron's passport meticulously to mirror the eagle like German stamp in black ink, sketching it and then creating a stencil of it to brush the black ink over his own passport. He practiced the signatures and, when he felt confident enough to forge his own, he used the black ink again with the tip of a bird feather for signing.

When Rebecca and Eli sat for dinner at their home that evening, he faked a smile so wide, even his own mutti might have believed its sincerity.

"What is it?" Rebecca asked.

"I got the visa from immigration today."

"You mean they...you were approved?" she asked, half elated and half in disbelief.

"I have it." He grinned and opened his passport with all its forged documentation. "We're on our way to a new life." As he spoke, Rebecca sighed with relief and a tear streamed down her left eye and over her cheek. She stood and hugged Eli.

"We're on our way." She nestled her face into his chest.

* * *

On the twenty sixth, he and Aaron arrived at the ship dock in Hamburg to purchase their tickets. As Eli handed Rebecca's passport and his passport to the ticket attendant, he also handed him his sponsorship letter from Rebecca's Aunt Martha, the German police permit which he forged, and his marriage contract to Rebecca. A rush of adrenaline and anxiety surged throughout his body which he tried to conceal by rubbing his hands. The attendant glanced at Eli with his hazel eyes, whisked his fingers though his hair, glanced at the picture in his passport and then disappeared behind the counter.

The minutes felt like hours in Eli's mind, afraid he'd be recognized as a man wanted by the Gestapo. The attendant returned with a cup of tea and set it on the counter before handing Eli his two tickets. Eli sighed with relief. Aaron followed, purchasing two for his parents and another for himself. The tickets were contracted for the second of September.

FRIDAY, SEPTEMBER 1, 1933

Rebecca was relieved to find out the tickets had been contracted and that she and Eli would both be on the ship soon. She packed four designer suitcases which her father had bought her before leaving for University. Eli managed to fit most everything he cared to bring into two smaller pieces of black luggage.

Clothes could be replaced easily, he thought to himself while packing the majority of his books in one of Rebecca's suitcases. The ten day journey would be comfortable, Eli explained, showing her brochures of the liner. All the necessary amenities would be aboard, along with a few extra-curricular opportunities such as lying on deck in one of the many reclining chairs provided, playing cards, and even deck tennis.

On September second, Eli dressed in his custard colored top with the top button undone and a pair of beige slacks and matching suit jacket.

Rebecca wore a long crème skirt that swayed below her knees and a matching blouse whose ruffles enveloped around her neck and folded over her breasts. She tightened the large black belt around her waist, drawing in her stomach and accenting her womanly figure.

Eli drove Rebecca early in the morning to the ship docks in Hamburg in her vehicle, knowing Robert had agreed to buy his old car during a phone call between the two of them after he had purchased the tickets. Eli left his car in the parking lot at the apartment and told them he would bring the keys to the dock.

As Eli drove up to the large building, trolley cars moved along the roads and tall street lights governed its borders. Thick clouds hung over the building longer then the apartment building Eli and Rebecca shared and almost as tall. People scattered over the paved floors leading to the doors, rushing to and fro, carrying luggage which held their lives. Eli pulled into the parking lot and the two of them began to take their suitcases out. From the corner of her eye, Rebecca saw Robert and Rosalyn approach from the right.

"Need some help with that?" Robert inquired from a block away in casual garb and a loud voice. Eli turned his head in Robert's direction.

"That would be most appreciated," Eli spoke loudly until Robert drew close. "We have six pieces of luggage to bring aboard."

Robert reached his hand into the backseat and pulled out two suitcases.

"Did you remember the keys?" Robert laid the luggage on the floor. "Here's the cash I promised for it. I hope it helps." Robert handed Eli a wad of money, not the price the vehicle had been originally sold for, but enough to help Eli start a new life in America. Eli took out the keys to his car, the car that had seen him through University, work at his father's firm, and a protest rally which ended in a broken windshield, and handed them to Robert. "I'll take good care of it." Robert finished and put his hands over the luggage to help carry the bags to the ship.

Rosalyn stood a few feet away in a pastel summer dress and a white hat that wrapped around her face, her head tilted and her eyes welled with tears, making her vision cloudy. Rebecca walked over and pulled Rosalyn into her arms for a long embrace.

"I can't believe you two are leaving." Rosalyn wiped her tears, "I mean you should, it's best for the two of you. It's just I am going to miss you both so much."

"Me too." Rebecca wiped her own tears beginning to fall at the sight of Rosalyn. "But I will write you and we can keep in touch." Rosalyn swung her arms around Rebecca and they hugged for a second time before the two of them joined Eli and Robert and helped carry the luggage to the ship. The walk through the calm building contrasted to the outside where everyone seemed to be in a frantic frenzy. Inside, an air of structure and certainty prevailed, as if once inside, the dread of missing the ship vanished.

The four of them waited on a long bench for the announcement to board. Aaron and his parents approached from the other door and, as they walked into the building, Eli and Rebecca stood at the sight of them in the distance. Aaron and his father preferred dark suits to Eli's beige colors and Aaron's mother clad herself in a sky blue chiffon dress. The delicate sleeves of the dress covered her thick arms and her lioness grey blond curls fell around her face, pinned up only over her forehead. Her sea grey eyes became apparent as Aaron and his parents approached. Eli outstretched his hand in a proper handshake with Aaron's father before sitting back down.

Rebecca greeted Aaron's mother with a warm smile and kiss on each of her cheeks and then made room for her to sit before finding another seat opposite Eli. Aaron introduced his parents to Rosalyn and Robert, the only two who had not met them yet. Eli and Rebecca had shared conversation with them on occasion at the synagogue in Munich and out of social decorum, Rebecca felt the weight of keeping the dialogue lively between Aaron's parents and her friends.

"This is my mama, Rachael, and my papa, Elijah," Aaron said and Rosalyn smiled while Robert shook their hands.

"Now that everyone is here, I should load Rebecca's car onto the ship," Eli said and departed in dutiful hurry. He made his way back to the parked car and drove it to the ship where deckhands secured the car behind a few others. Upon his return, Rebecca, Elijah and Rosalyn were laughing wildly at something Elijah said.

Rebecca whisked her eyes up at Eli and in a flirtatious gesture of her outstretched hand, wrapping itself around his and pulling him to her, Eli imagined the conversation was about him. Before he could ask Rebecca about it, the announcement for the boarding of the Hamburg American Liner echoed through the hall. The group made its way from inside the building to the ship.

Rosalyn grabbed Rebecca in an embrace again and tears welled in her eyes. "I keep telling myself to not cry, but I can't help it."

Rebecca wiped one of the tears rolling off Rosalyn's cheek onto her own. "I love you. You are like my sister. I will miss you so much." Rebecca started crying more.

Robert threw his arms around Eli and, in masculine expression, refrained from tears, but the genuine pull on his emotions could be seen in his sudden somber disposition. "Take care of yourself. Take care of Rebecca."

"I will," Eli promised and they released from their hold. Rebecca and Rosalyn soon let go of each other and Eli grabbed Rebecca's hand to walk up the gangplank to the ship that held their future. Aaron hugged each of them, the only two friends from his firm who remained true to him after he was fired, and then he boarded with his parents.

Eli, Rebecca and Aaron waved goodbye from the deck. The ship horn sounded and the vessel drew away from Hamburg on the Elbe River and toward the North Sea, then onto the Atlantic. As Eli and Rebecca left Germany, they wondered if their fatherland would ever become new again like freshly grown spring flowers, untouched and full of promise.

They found the ten day journey comfortable between dining, deck tennis, strolling along the decks and an occasional game of cards. There were a few other Jews like themselves fleeing Germany in the hopes of reaching a country with a better promise for a future. Some still considered German citizens did not agree with the new politics and laws of the country.

Beside a tussle that broke out at one of the card tables, the journey was for the most part uneventful. Rebecca enjoyed tea in the dining hall with Rachael while Eli, Aaron, and Elijah preferred to play cards with the other men. Some days the rains from a storm pelted against the ship's sides. Other days provided a canopy of warmth from the sun.

Somewhere in the middle of the journey, Eli found Rebecca gazing over the railing into the sea. Her crème skirt with all its heavy ruffles blew up from a passing breeze. He caressed her shoulders and drew his mouth to the lace of her blouse just over the nape of her neck. He rested for several minutes still and quiet in her essence. Rebecca could feel the light discharge of air from his nostrils over her blouse. She slipped her hand into his and passed him a small box with a white lace ribbon.

"Happy Early Birthday," she whispered. "I couldn't wait." Her smile widened, "And on this boat, viewing the ocean is the perfect place." Eli glanced down at the ship's wooden decks as he opened the box and found inside a pin plated in silver with a red rose and green petals. It shimmered under the sun and Rebecca helped him attach it to his shirt.

"I'll always wear it," he said and kissed her cheek.

"Are you going to read to me tonight?" Rebecca asked in a loud whisper and he lifted his head to see her eyes.

"Tonight and every night, my dearest." As Eli said those words, a tear fell from his left eye and he discreetly hid it from Rebecca with a tuck of his head returning to her chest. Rebecca raked her fingers through Eli's hair as his head gently rested on her breasts. She smiled, gazing into the wide ocean, and thought about her life in America.

"I can take up nursing when we arrive. American must need nurses." She grinned and her left brow quirked. "Will you find work as a lawyer?" she asked and Eli's eyes met hers with his tear dried against the fabric of her dress. A wrinkle furrowed between his brows and his chin lowered.

"I'll try," he said. Taking her hand into his, he guided her over the wooden deck. Other couples relaxed in lounging chairs, soaking up the light when it peeked out from behind thick clouds. Women flipped pages in magazines and chatted about the exquisite dining aboard the ship. A few women wore large hats, keeping their delicate pale complexions from the rays of the sun. Men closed their eyes on the lounge chairs or smoked cigars.

That evening, Eli and Rebecca lay on the bed in their private room. Rebecca's hand dangled over Eli's chest in playful strokes before he drew her fingers to his lips and kissed them several times as he contemplated names for the baby.

"If it's a girl, we can call her Sarah. I've always adored that name," Eli stated.

"We should name her after your mother. It would be an honor to her," Rebecca corrected.

"Deborah? I don't know. It sounds too old fashioned for our daughter. She would need a modern name, a strong American name," Eli debated.

Rebecca mulled over the suggestion. "Maybe you're right." She hesitantly agreed. "We could name her..."

"Bernard," Eli said.

"Bernard?" Rebecca's eyes darted to his and her brows furrowed.

"I mean if it is a boy."

"Oh." The name echoed in her mind and returned unpleasant memories. She shook her head. "I detest that name. I cannot and will not call my son Bernard."

"Ok, ok." Eli stroked her arm. "We won't call him Bernard." As Eli finished his counsel, Rebecca's eyes widen.

"If it's a boy, I know exactly what I'll name him." The name sat frozen on her lips and she did not divulge it, but let it reside in secret, untainted, and unused.

"You aren't going to tell me?" Eli pouted.

"I don't want to spoil the surprise in you eyes. He will be a boy. I just know it."

Eli grinned at Rebecca's thought. "We'll have a big two story house with a white picket fence, two boys and one girl to keep us occupied," Eli dreamed.

"Yes, that would be lovely, just lovely." Rebecca rested in Eli's words and on his chest. Eli wrapped his arms around her, feeling that, if he let go, she might just float away.

* * *

As the ship drew near the shores of New York harbor, spectators filled the dock to watch its arrival. Floods of people awaiting their friends or relatives pushed forward to greet the passengers disembarking the ship. The passengers queued and took out their passports and immigration papers to await approval at the immigration office before passing on to American soil. Sounds of the crowds on the shore grew loud in anticipation and excitement.

Aaron and his parents stood in front of Rebecca and Eli and when it was his turn, Aaron handed his documentation to the elderly immigration officer. After a couple of minutes of page turning and eye scrutiny, the officer waved him and his parents through. Aaron let out a breath which he had been holding during the inspection, and his parents grabbed hold of their son in gratitude and relief.

Rebecca handed the officer her passport and, upon glancing over her American citizenship and facial features, the officer took no more concern of her and waved her through. Eli braced himself as he supplied his passport and documents. The officer glanced over his papers once, looked away and then looked over them again. He inspected the black eagle German stamp and then the signatures created by Eli's own hand.

Rebecca stood in anxious desire to see her Eli cross the immigration line, a line separating them, and into her arms on America soil. She stood for five minutes until the officer waved a guard over to his booth to pull Eli away. Rebecca couldn't understand, readjusting her eyes in disbelief. Then the weight of it hit her and she fell to the floor at the sight of two guards forcing Eli away from the immigration booth, away from her, away from America.

"No!" Her words caught up with her heart. "No!" She grappled for what to say. "He is my husband! He is an American citizen through me!"

She screamed onto deaf ears. She ran back to the booth and threw her hands over the table. "Don't do this! Please, don't do this," she begged in angered sincerity.

The sound of Eli's voice broke the frenzy inside her mind, "I love you, Rebecca! Never forget that. Everything I did, I did so you could have a future; so our child could have a future." He kept shouting as they dragged him towards the ship.

"I'm sorry, madam, but his documents are fraudulent," the officer reasoned.

"No…no…no." Rebecca's voice began to fade and all she could muster to say was no. Watching Eli being pulled further away in the firm grip of immigration patrol, she saw his dark brown eyes, wide and pleading, focused on her, his cheeks wet with tears. The sound of his feet scrapping against the hard floors in defiance echoed in her shattering mind.

"God in heaven, I'm begging you!" She fell to her knees in front of the officer, who remained steadfast and immovable. Her body crumbled, wracked with sobs, gut wrenching and heartbreaking.

"Rebecca? Rebecca, please." Aaron had to help her back to her feet. Aaron's mother held her while Aaron shouted to Eli over the immigration booth, a table dividing freedom and the persecution of Germany.

"Where will you stay?"

"With Robert," Eli yelled, jerking his head around. "You knew this could happen, but we had to try. Take care of Rebecca for me."

"I promise," Aaron declared and then like a cloud that fades, Eli disappeared.

Aaron helped escort Rebecca out of the immigration area and onto American soil. She lay fragile in his hands, limp. The breathlessness she had gone to the hospital for in July returned. She placed her shaky feet on the soil and sobbed on Aaron's shoulder. Her Grandma Adel and Aunt Martha waited for her there, but she hardly recognized them in her state. When she finally broke her face away from Aaron's shoulder and glanced up, she saw Eli's family approaching through the crowd.

She couldn't speak to them. She couldn't tell them they had lost their only son. Her lips became heavy, unable to open. Her face lost its alabaster color and became pale. She fainted, almost hitting the ground if it had not been for Aaron's catch.

Rebecca awoke lying across an elegant sofa most certainly in her Grandma Adel's house. The Levin family was not seen nor heard. Aaron was also absent. Her Aunt Martha sat in a chair across from her, kitting a sweater and when Rebecca's eyes opened, Martha rushed to her side. She wiped a wet washrag over Rebecca's face and then sat her up to drink a cup of ginger tea.

"How are you feeling?" Martha asked.

"Where's Aaron? Where's Ezekiel?" Rebecca asked, concerned their presence had been all a dream.

"They've taken residence up some blocks away at a house for rent. I know the owner and drove them there."

"Where's Eli?" Rebecca asked, knowing the answer, but needing the answer to be different.

"I imagine he's on his way back to Germany." Martha's tender blue eyes and warm smile tried to comfort Rebecca.

"I'm cold." Rebecca shivered under a thick quilt and Martha brought her another blanket.

Placing a hand on her forehead, she drew back. "You've got a fever. We're putting you to bed." They moved her to a bedroom upstairs, where she tossed and turned in her sleep, tormented at the notion of never seeing Eli again or worse, Eli's death.

After seven days of ill health, she managed to pull herself out of bed and join her aunt and grandmother downstairs. Aaron sat at the breakfast table, eating with Martha when Rebecca walked into the dining room. She raced to Aaron's side and pulled him close as if it would somehow make Eli closer to her.

Aaron handed her a note. "Eli wanted me to give you this in case he didn't make it." He slipped the note into Rebecca's fragile hands and she brought it to her nose to smell Eli's scent before opening it. Packaged underneath the letter Rebecca felt a photograph and lifted it to the forefront to view. A black and white shot of Eli stretching backward over her banister reminded her of the time he brought his new camera home and they played with it while taking photos of themselves.

She remembered taking this photograph of him. His brown scarf danced in the wind and his smile was crooked. His soft eyes and laughter transcended the picture and Rebecca found her fingers caressing his image, needing him to be there with her. A tear rolled down her left cheek into the pink hues of her skin and she lifted his letter to read.

My Dearest Rebecca,

I know you are in the gravest of states with my departure, and I am sorry I could not divulge the truth to you in Munich, but I knew you would never leave without the reassurance that I would be able to join you in America. I love you too much to make that kind of sacrifice for me. I love our baby too much. It is enough for me to know you and our unborn child will be safe and happy. I can endure any suffering my fatherland has to offer me, knowing the two people I love more than my own life are finally free.

I will stay with Robert while in Munich, until I find another way to you. Don't fret for me, but spend your time taking care of yourself and our baby. Please do not be angry with me or waste time in idle depression. When things have changed and it is safe to travel, I will come to you, my love, and begin the family we promised, you, me, and our little one.

Love,
Eli

* * *

Rebecca spent the next five years waiting for the man she loved, for the man who would never return to her. But as the slow years progressed, the pain lessened and, as she watched her son whom she named Eli grow from a baby to a toddler and then to a child about to enter Kindergarten, she could see in his expressions a hint of his father in the nose, the lips, the eyes, and one day she finally let Eli go. She let him return to Germany without her. Everything about her son reminded her of the man she loved, the only man she could ever love like this, and though Eli was no longer there, he was her forever, and in her son she knew he would always be with her.

THE END

The Day the Flowers Died

Ami Blackwelder is a teacher and a writer. She has written three religious books and two anthologies and a few children stories.

She is currently involved in finishing her Guardians of the Gate saga and promoting her first historical fiction: *The Day the Flowers Died.*

Order this book on Kindle, Nook, iPad, or order from your local bookstore. You may also order prints online. Find out more at her website.

All her work is available at her website :

http://amiblackwelder.blogspot.com

http://historicalromancereaders.blogspot.com

Author's note:

Thank you to all my supporters, family, friends and fans for keeping me encouraged and look for my new SciFi Paranormal Romance saga: Shifter Evolutions.

Meeting the Challenge of Genocide

http://ushmm.org

Learn about Holocaust history
Prevent Genocide
Confront Anti-Semitism

All over the world Genocide
has destroyed families.
From Rwanda to Cambodia.
From Europe to Tibet.

Don't let ignorance and hate prevail.